STOLEN PROMISES

Marc and Melanie's Story

Traci Wooden-Carlisle

D1707051

STOLEN PROMISES
(Promises to Zion Series)

Cover Design: Designs By Dana

Editor: Paula – paulaproofreader.wixsite.com

But as for you, ye thought evil against me; but God meant it unto good, to bring to pass, as it is this day, to save much people alive.

Genesis 50:20

Dedication

Thank you, God for pouring out in me and trusting me to share what you've given me as best I can.

Thank you, Daddy for your continued love and support.

This book is dedicated to each and every person who realized in the midst of their struggle that what the enemy meant for their demise, God used for their good and the good of those around them.

Prologue

The momentary reprieve from pain was almost euphoric. It didn't take drugs, alcohol or any substance to bring her to that state. All it took was the absence of pain. Melanie was so tired. Almost too tired to be afraid. Almost. She took a deep breath which caused a twinge of pain in her side. She stopped and took more shallow breaths.

The bright lights of the delivery room made her squint, so she kept her eyes shut and just listened to what was going on around her. She kept her focus on the room. It was a trick her mother taught her—not that Mel would ever thank her for the skill or anything else her mother had plotted or planned for her over the last year and a half.

Her childhood was over, her innocence gone. Her eyes and mind were open to the pain of heartache, betrayal, and now childbirth, and she had her entire teenage and adult life ahead of her.

"You did very good." Mel opened her eyes to see a nurse with a sympathetic face smiling down at her.

Melanie offered back a shadow of a smile before closing her eyes again. She wanted to preserve her energy. She was only halfway done.

"Do you want to hold him?" The question came from her other side along with a cry that penetrated the quiet of the room. She gathered her strength, opened her eyes and watched as the squirming bundle was placed on her chest.

There he was in her small arms, lying on her equally small chest: warm, moving and alive. He was breathing, wailing and waving his small fists. He was the color of warm cream, his hair looked like black silk, and when he stopped protesting and opened his eyes his pink lips pursed into a beautiful pout. He was perfect and she was in love. Well, maybe she had something to thank her mother for, after all.

Melanie brought him closer so she could rub her cheek against his head and take in his scent. She didn't care about the twinge in her side or the pressure starting in her lower back. She stared at her baby boy trying to memorize his features and imagine what he would look like as a toddler, then a child. She stared at him even as the pressure turned into pain, and the pain went from tolerable to agonizing because as soon as he left her arms it would be a while before she saw him again.

Melanie finally let out a small growl against the pain. She had tried to hide the grimace as long as possible but when she felt the urge to bear down again and when the stupid monitor started beeping out of rhythm she handed over her son.

An hour later she was almost delusional with pain. It was supposed to be smooth sailing after delivering the first twin. Almost every nurse in the room had said it. So why was she in more pain and still in labor? Why was it taking so long? The fear came back in waves almost overriding the pain. This was taking too long.

She glanced at the clock and blew out a breath. It wasn't as late as she thought. It only seemed like each minute lasted an hour. Still, something was wrong. She heard the nurses whispering to each other almost frantically at times. If she didn't know better, she'd think with each push she was losing blood.

"I just can't do this," she finally said after digging deep as the nurse had suggested and finding her well of energy empty.

"Honey. It looks like we will have to do a cesarean. You are losing too much blood, and we don't want this baby to go into duress."

Melanie nodded, making up her mind. "I need Brian. Bring me Brian."

"Who's Brian?" She heard one of the nurses ask.

"The father." she breathed out while saying. "Waiting room."

"You can't give up," the nurse said.

"Not giving up. I need Brian," she said just loud enough to be heard.

"He shouldn't be in here."

Melanie took a breath and used the pain of the next contraction to scream as loud as possible. "Brian!"

Her next scream wasn't quite as loud but it did the job.

"Brian!"

"Go get the boy and his grandfather. The girl may do better after they talk."

As the contraction ebbed, so did Mel's energy. They would have to take this baby, but if she didn't survive, she wanted to make sure her little girl didn't go to her mom. She would have to convince Brian to take both of her twins.

She drifted off for a moment but opened her eyes when she heard her name. "Grace Melanie?"

"Hey," she whispered looking into Brian's gentle brown eyes. She swallowed the fear and lifted her lips into a smile. She glanced beyond him briefly to see his grandfather stride to the window, his back ramrod straight and hands folded behind him.

Brian leaned in close and she stared at him for a few seconds.

"Did you see him? Isn't he beautiful?" Melanie said through shallow breaths.

Brian nodded. "Yes. He's kinda loud. They say he's got good lungs."

Melanie nodded then set her mind on her task.

"This one's making it rough," Melanie said through pants. "Stubborn thing…wants to…come out feet first and is bigger than her brother."

Brian's face blurred when he moved in to kiss her forehead. "You'll do fine. We have a plan."

She tried to smile at his remark. They had a few plans, which was why she needed to talk to him. "They have to go in to take her out. I think Plan A is off the table. I might not make it."

He paused to look at her. She saw the anguish roll across his face when he realized what she was saying.

"No. You not making it is not an option." His voice quivered slightly.

She saw the façade slip, revealing the scared little boy beneath. He was only a year older than she was, and that still made him too young to be in this situation. Thank goodness for his grandfather. She knew if it were up to his parents, she would be on her own.

Maybe it was the continual pain, but Melanie no longer thought the adoption of her daughter to an anonymous family, in the event of her death, would work. The only guarantee was for Brian and his grandfather to take both babies if she died.

"We know my mom...Mom can't have her. Not...not without...me. You have to take her too." Breathing was so hard, but she had to convince him to take both babies in the event of her death. It would be less likely for her mother to believe that neither child survived. She would search the ends of the earth, and if the children were with Brian's grandfather they would have a decent chance of staying out of her grip.

"I need you to..." he began, but Melanie touched his cheek to interrupt him.

"Promise me," she said through her teeth.

"Live," Brian replied.

"Promise me," she said again.

Brian stared at her. His eyes filled with tears which spilled over and down his cheeks. "I promise."

She sighed and was ready to relax, but Brian spoke up. "I need you to do everything you can to stay alive. Please, I love you."

She opened her eyes again and could feel his energy through his stare. He stage-whispered, "After everything she's done, you can't let her win. You have to live, even if we can't be together for a long time."

She thought it sounded like something someone older and more mature would say, but maturity didn't always come with a number. It came with experience and the ability to accept what life delivered.

Brian gripped her hand, a determined look replacing the terror in his eyes.

She took a few breaths against the oncoming contraction.

"I'll live," she said as firmly as she could.

Fatigue hit her heavy and her eyes closed.

"Grace Melanie?" Brian's voice held panic. She was so tired.

"Her pulse is dropping," a nurse said, which sounded far away.

She's hemorrhaging," announced a voice even more in the distance.

He shook her hand, and she used the last of her strength to open her eyes. "Fight, Grace Melanie. I need you to fight. For Brian and Briar Rose.

"Kay," Melanie spoke while she breathed out then was enveloped into the sweet arms of darkness.

Chapter 1

One year later

Reaching over the railing, Melanie rubbed her daughter's back. If she were honest, the motion soothed her as much as it did Paige. Her child sighed in her sleep, her lips lifting slightly at the edges. Paige was so beautiful. She was Melanie's gift for fighting and getting through the whole ordeal of the last two and a half years. It made her proud for not giving up.

Melanie picked up the baby monitor and carried it to her room. With her mother and father at work she used the time when she wasn't studying or taking care of Paige to write in her journal. Today, though, she was going to try something new. Writing to herself or just putting her thoughts down on paper was no longer helping with the heartache. She needed to talk to Brian, even if it were only in her mind.

She sat at the white-and-yellow desk that matched the other bedroom furniture her mother bought her when she came home from the hospital. Her lips curved into a sardonic smirk. She wondered what she would have been given if she'd stayed sleeping for a week after having Paige. Maybe a television to go with her stereo? Probably not. A television in her room would be too hard to monitor.

It wouldn't have mattered. She was too depressed and afraid to watch television. She'd stayed up for thirty-six hours once she got home, she was so afraid of her mom taking Paige away if she fell asleep.

The following month she remained in constant panic that her mom would find a reason for her to give up her baby even though she and Melanie's dad had placed their names on the amended birth certificate after adopting Paige as their own. Her blood pressure stayed elevated until her father came home.

That, plus the realization that she wouldn't be able to be with Brian and her son sometimes kept her from breathing deeply. Those were dark days. The tears came too easily, and they were way too hard to shut off. It felt as if half of her was missing. In the back of her mind she felt bad for not just being happy with Paige. After all, she was part of Brian.

Sometimes she would stare at Paige and try to discern who their child favored more. She studied her baby girl's features, looking for pieces of Brian she could keep close. Paige had both the color and shape of her eyes along with the pointy chin. Her nose and mouth could go either way, but her baby's ears were definitely Brian's. They had the same small point at the top and when Paige was born the skin was almost translucent. They also turned bright red when Paige became upset which wasn't too often. It seemed like after all of the drama Paige caused during labor and delivery she was happy just to be alive. Melanie was grateful for her baby's happy demeanor. The less Grace had to complain about, the better it was for the household.

Though his presence brought some comfort, her once close relationship with her father was strained. Melanie had tried to cross the great divide between them since he came back from deployment with no great success. She could understand his disappointment. Her mother told her to expect it, but no one could have prepared her for his anger. He didn't yell or rant. In fact, he hardly spoke to her. They used to talk about anything and everything. She never thought she would doubt his love for her, but for the first few months he was home she wasn't sure if he even liked her.

He didn't check her homework as he used to when he came home. He barely acknowledged her across the dinner table, and worse of all, her birthday came and went without a whisper of celebration. It made her feel even more alone, if that was possible.

Melanie took a sheet of paper from the small shelf on her desk and picked up her favorite pen. She stared at the paper for a moment not sure where to start. She took a deep breath and just started writing.

Dear Brian,

She quelled the temptation to write it over and over until the shaky letters were as smooth and beautiful as his memory. Her penmanship had improved with all of her journal writing, but this was precious. Melanie squeezed the pen until the urge passed. She only had so long to write this letter. She blew out another breath and place the pen to paper again.

I read that writing to you might help make me feel less alone. I thought if I wrote this letter like you were going to see it, I might feel like I was talking to you. I'm not sure it's working because I just want to cry.

I see you everywhere. I thought I saw you in the mall when my mom and I went school-clothes shopping last week. I did a double take even though I knew it couldn't be you. It's only my mind playing tricks on me because I miss you so much.

I think about you and Brian Jr. all the time. I wonder where you are and what you're doing. I wonder if B.J. still cries loudly, if he remembers me. Probably not. I don't remember anything from when I was a baby. Sometimes I wonder if the pain I feel now in my heart is worse than the pain when I had Brian. It's not the same feeling, but it still feels like I'm being split in half.

A tear dropped on the paper, and Melanie chastised herself for making a mess. She got a tissue and pressed it on the paper to absorb the wetness. She lifted it to see the damage and was happy that only a couple of letters were smeared.

The day Mom came in and told me you'd died I cried until I was sick. I would have stayed in bed for a week if I didn't have Briar Rose. Even though Mom moved us off the base, I found a copy of your obituary at the library here. Two city papers reported on your death. One paper said everyone they interviewed said you were really nice, a good student and classmate. Your parents declined to comment.

Brian, you were more than what they said. You were more than just a nice boy with good grades. If the news reporters found me, Mom would have had a fit, but I would have told them how protective you were, how smart and sweet you were, and that there was never a better friend. You were kind and always made me feel special. You had the best eyes, but most of all, you were mine, and I was yours.

Feeling the tears welling up, she shoved the paper forward. Brian's smiling eyes flashed in her mind, and Melanie's stomach clenched. She balled her small hands into fists and pounded them on the desk before remembering the sound might be loud enough to wake Paige in the other room. Melanie wiped her eyes in frustration. She couldn't keep crying if she were going to finish her thoughts. She let her thoughts of Paige calm her and continued writing.

Paige—that's what Mom wants us to call her—is beautiful. She's chubby. It's funny to see her walk. She isn't too steady, but she can get from the couch to the chair on the other side of the living room without falling now. She laughs a lot. She's a happy baby. I think it's because I cuddle and play with her as much as possible. I think she knows she is loved.

Things were hard when Daddy got back. He looked at me differently for a while. I could tell he was disappointed in me. He didn't take me out on Saturday afternoons like he used to, and we barely spoke. I tried to avoid him when I could because he asked questions I couldn't answer without getting into trouble with Mom, but after a few months he started treating Paige like a daughter. Sometimes I think he wishes she was his instead of me.

Seeing the words on paper somehow made it more real. It was so unfair. She did everything her mom told her to do. Everything until she learned what her mom was planning. Melanie shook her head to bring her back to her task.

I start school this fall. I am not looking forward to being the new kid all over again. I wish you could be on the bus like you were before. It will be a nightmare if no one lets me sit next to them. What do I talk about? My mom has already been coaching me on what to say about last year or the year before if anyone finds out. I hate lying, but she says it will keep people from looking at me crazy.

The anger that sparked in her made her want to bang her fists on the table again, but she stopped herself. It was so unfair that she had to pay for all the things her mom had her do. The only thing that made Melanie feel better was knowing that her mother didn't get her and Brian's son.

Life is so unfair. I don't even know what kids my age do anymore. I feel like I'm forty years old, but I'm not. If it weren't for our daughter I wouldn't do it. I know you told me not to talk like that, but at least your grandfather loves you. I'm sorry for what my mom did. I'm sorry for not stopping her before you got hurt.

I miss you. I love you, no matter what.

Sincerely,

Grace Melanie

Melanie kissed the paper softly then held it to her heart for a few moments. She wasn't sure if being away from the one you loved was easier if you were old like thirty. Maybe it slowly got easier as you aged each year. She hoped so. She couldn't imagine feeling like this twenty, or even ten years from now. A day was too long.

She folded the piece of paper up and opened her desk drawer for a small envelope. She placed the paper inside then licked and sealed the envelope.

She got up and walked to the bathroom taking the baby monitor with her. She sat on the edge of the tub staring at the envelope for a few minutes. She knew what she had to do, but she really didn't want to. She forced herself to think of what would happen if her parents got the letter, and it gave her the strength to go to the drawer where her mom kept the lighter for the candles she liked to use when she took a bath.

Melanie held the envelope to the lighter's flame and burst into tears as the envelope caught fire.

Writing a letter was stupid. It only made her feel worse.

Chapter 2

Three years later

Melanie held her books close to her chest. She'd read in her dad's old psychology book that this action screamed insecurity and fear which would draw every predator in the school to her, but she was cold. Not goosebumps on the skin cold, but bone-deep, gray clouds and ice in your shoes cold. She felt the shivers in her soul after spotting him again. It couldn't be a coincidence. He had been in the exact same place at the same time the day before.

There wasn't any particular thing that screamed out about him. He was actually decent looking with his hazelnut-colored skin and slightly darker eyes, dark brown hair, cut close to his scalp, and goatee. He wasn't old, but he definitely wasn't in high school. Melanie didn't look at men more than the few seconds it took to surmise that they weren't a threat. Melanie didn't look at boys either, no matter how many had tried to talk to her in school. If it were subject related or they were inside of the classroom she was easygoing and more than happy to lend a pen, paper or help answer questions. Once the bell rang, though, she moved on to the next class, the library or her hiding place under the stairs in the old Economic building during lunch, or straight home.

She could have had friends. She could have been popular instead of owning her nickname, "Black Ice," but she couldn't chance anyone getting close. She was still dealing with the emotional affects of the last time she got close to someone outside of her immediate family. She couldn't risk anyone wanting to

14

come over, getting on her mother's radar or overhearing Paige calling her Mommy as she sometimes mistakenly did. Melanie didn't blame the child. She was more of a mom to Paige than Grace was, but she didn't mind. In many ways Paige saved her life and the guilt of being used to hurt someone else could kill her.

Melanie glanced across the street one more time at the group of men clad in construction gear circling a table. At that moment the man looked up from the table meeting her eyes. She couldn't tell if the shiver that ran through her signaled foreboding or awareness, but both had her hastily looking away and picking up her pace through the school doors.

She might be sixteen, but for all intents and purposes she was a junior high student and fourteen-year-old. No matter how well developed fourteen-year-olds were physically, they didn't stare at construction workers. At least she didn't think they did.

Melanie tried to shrug off the unease she felt. Maybe she could befriend some girls for the week so that she had someone to walk from the bus with in the morning. Melanie shook her head at herself. That would be too much work just to hide.

There could be another reason why she kept catching his eye. She dashed the hope that bloomed in her heart just as it broke through the hardpacked dirt she'd buried her dreams in. Why would Brian use anyone else to get in touch with her. He'd told her he wouldn't contact her or reach out to her for their son's sake. He'd left her a few words on a piece of paper that wouldn't mean anything to anyone else who came across it. A piece of paper with the power to bring them face-to-face again in the event of an

15

emergency. An emergency that would put both Brian and their son in danger.

After four years of radio silence with no change in her life to warrant contact, any fantasies Melanie had of seeing or hearing from Brian were just that. A fantasy.

It was more likely that he was an investigator for one of the many families her mother betrayed when she gave over their financial records to the FBI. The same FBI that stopped protecting them when they were told that she hired someone to kill Brian.

Melanie wasn't supposed to know any of this, but her mother's penchant for newspaper clippings gave Melanie a number of answers as to why they moved even more frequently than her father's job could explain, and why unmarked cars sometimes followed her home. After reading some of the articles at the library and researching the names of the families her mother ratted on, she became paranoid. She started paying attention to her surroundings more keenly and was aware of every unfamiliar car near her home or school. When there were no attempts on her life or safety after a few months she relaxed a little but kept an eye out nonetheless.

Too many secrets. So many lies. She would be the good girl and do what was expected of her until she could gain some freedom and make sure her child stayed safe.

Throughout the day Melanie's thoughts drifted back to goatee man, and she constantly chastised herself on her lack of focus. There was just something about his eyes though. At first glance they were intense like he was trying to see through her, but at that last glance she thought she caught the beginnings of a smile before she turned away and ran into the school. She had to be wrong. Why would a stranger smile at a young girl?

Maybe because he is a nice person, you dolt. Boy, you have let your mom turn you into a paranoid freak.

Melanie shook her head again and stopped. If she kept this up she would be more of a social outcast, but instead of seeming aloof and untouchable people would start to think she was crazy, and she just didn't need that kind of attention.

***

Melanie decided to take the long way to the buses that day by leaving the school through the side door closest to the field. It was just as popular as the front but a little smaller, so she hoped to get lost in the crowd of kids bottlenecked in the narrower corridor.

She took a quick look around the area but saw nothing to bring her alarm. She walked a little faster toward her bus making sure to keep her head low in the crowd and stepped onto it with a sigh of relief and a warm smile for the bus driver.

"How was school?" the bus driver asked as part of their daily ritual.

Melanie paused and looked her in the eye. "It was a good day. I learned stuff. I had peanut butter and jelly for lunch, and you know how much I love peanut butter and jelly." Melanie leaned in conspiratorially.

The bus driver started shaking her head. "Peanut butter and jelly again?"

"It works. Why ruin a good thing?" Melanie said, finishing their daily repartee and walking to a seat a couple of rows back.

Melanie smiled to herself as she adjusted her backpack for the ride home. She took out her latest novel, a new adult romantic fantasy about a princess who had received almost everything she'd wanted in life from her father. She had been mostly happy with her life until she learned that on her eighteenth birthday she was to start meeting suitors. The princess wasn't really interested in marriage, but also learned that if she didn't marry by her twenty-first birthday she would turn into a statue. The catch was that the princess was the last swan and would remain an ugly duckling until she fell in love.

Melanie considered the book a guilty pleasure, but the bus ride to and from school was the only time she allowed herself to venture into other worlds via books. The thirty-minute ride was her time to herself. She wasn't being told what to study, or read, or finishing homework, making dinner, taking care of a four-year-old, or trying to live up to unreachable standards.

She looked up from her book as she always did when the bus's engine turned over. She hadn't gotten the five extra minutes while waiting for all of the other students to board since she'd taken the long way. She scanned the street out of habit and her heartbeat kicked into high gear when she spotted a familiar figure walking to the coffee shop across the street. It was down a ways, but when he reached the door and glanced behind him before entering, she saw his face clearly. Though he looked in her general direction she didn't think he saw her on the bus. It didn't matter to her heart though. That organ set up a racket in her chest, not settling down until she was halfway home. Melanie's thoughts followed suit, and she lost a good fifteen minutes to her vivid imagination and curiosity over a man she had no business even noticing.

***

Melanie was greeted with squeals of delight when she opened the door to the modest two-story home with three bedrooms and converted den. She hadn't even finished locking the door before she was accosted by toddler-sized arms around her knees. Melanie turned to look down at Paige's smiling face. The girl giggled up at her in mischief while tightening her hold.

"Mom," Melanie stage whispered, pretending to call out. "I can't move. There's something wrong with my legs." She tried to move away from the door, but her child's surprisingly long, strong grip only allowed her to gain an inch or two away from the door.

Melanie pretended to cry knowing the action would help free her from her bonds. She put her backpack down and brought her fists up to her eyes and heaved a sigh. She opened her eyes to small slits so Paige wouldn't see her looking.

"Boo hoo hoo," she wailed and felt the small arms shift as Paige tried to see if she were indeed crying.

"Boo hoo hoo. I'm stuck and cannot move. What am I to do. I will have to stay here all night." Melanie felt Paige's arms loosen a fraction more.

"Boo hoo hoo. I won't be able to make dinner or dessert, and I am so hungry," Melanie said behind the false tears and felt the arms slip away. She kept the position for a few more seconds and felt the small pat of a hand on her thigh.

"Menanee. Menanee, you don't have to cry. You're free." The small palm patting her thigh was joined by another, and Melanie decided to end the game.

19

"Gotcha!" she yelled, removing her hands from her eyes and bending down in one move to scoop up the now screaming and laughing toddler. She hugged the warm and wiggling child to her, inhaling her unique smell. Melanie turned her face and blew raspberries into Paige's neck making her daughter laugh louder.

"If she has an accident it will be your own fault," her mother said as she came down the stairs.

Their antics stopped on cue because her mother's voice had a way of stifling laughter.

"Hi, Mom," she said, settling Paige on her hip.

"Hi, Mom," mimicked Paige, and Melanie's heart squeezed at her child's hopeful expression.

When Grace reached the bottom of the stairs she adjusted her shirt and looked at the two of them. She reached out and rubbed her thumb along the back of Paige's chubby hand. Melanie released the breath she didn't know she was holding, relieved for the small amount of attention her mother paid to Paige.

"I took the lamb chops out of the freezer this morning since you didn't do it before you left," Grace said as she rounded the banister to walk down the hall to the kitchen.

The small sting in Grace's lack of acknowledgment was quickly extinguished by Paige's lips on Mel's cheek. She looked at her daughter and was surprised by her pouting.

"What's wrong?" she asked quietly, hoping that by whispering Paige would do the same.

"I think Mommy's upset. She yelled at Daddy before he left this morning." Melanie was surprised at Paige's revelation. She didn't know of anything going on between her parents.

"Really," Melanie said, hoping Paige would elaborate.

Paige nodded somberly. "Daddy was so angry he forgot to give me a goodbye hug and kiss," Paige said, referring to the small ritual her dad and Paige went through every morning. Melanie missed the interaction most mornings since she had to leave to meet the bus before her dad left for work.

"You know he wasn't angry with *you*, though, right?" Melanie said while rubbing Paige's back.

Paige's bottom lip trembled slightly but she nodded. Melanie kissed Paige's cheek and blew one more raspberry eliciting a giggle before setting her down and picking up her backpack.

Melanie followed Paige and made a left toward the kitchen after entering the room at the end of the hall. Paige turned right toward the couch at the other end of the space and sat in front of the television.

Melanie walked past the breakfast bar to the small round kitchen table nestled in the corner of the kitchen space. She hung her backpack on the back of a chair and went to the kitchen sink to wash her hands.

"I left the recipe for dinner on the counter," her mom said from the pantry. "We have a meeting before my shift starts today so I will have to go in early. Paige has had her snack, and your father will be home at the regular time." Grace came away from the pantry with a bag of small potatoes. Melanie stood at the edge

21

of the counter, watching her mother's agitated movements She wanted to ask her mother what was wrong but was afraid of becoming the center of her ire.

She'd learned to stay out of Grace's way when she was upset. No one was safe. She glanced over to where Paige was sitting on the couch watching an age-appropriate video. It was part of the daily ritual. Melanie would sit at the kitchen table and divide her time between her homework and cooking dinner. Meanwhile, Paige would sit and watch television until dinner was served. The family would eat dinner at six o'clock, and Grace would leave for work at seven thirty.

Once her mom left the house it seemed as if the house itself sighed and everyone relaxed. Melanie would play on the floor with Paige after dinner then take her up for her bath. Her father would tuck Paige in and read her a story before either coming back down to watch television in the living room or her parent's bedroom depending on how tired he was.

Tonight, they would be able to heave that sigh of relief sooner. She wondered if her father would be up for a game of Chutes and Ladders with Paige if Melanie could get dinner on the table sooner.

"I need you to start the wash tonight. I will finish it in the morning before I take Paige to daycare," Grace said glancing at Melanie. *Maybe they could play Chutes and Ladders tomorrow.*

"We all have to do our part, Mel. I don't think it's too much to ask for you to make dinner occasionally and start the clothes washing. It's not like you have to come home from school and then go to work." Grace obviously took Mel's sour look as a response to being asked to wash clothes. Mel had long since learned that trying to correct Grace was futile. She would get herself in more trouble trying to defend herself.

"I understand," she said in response to her mother's small rant, looking her in the eye. At her mother's nod, Melanie relaxed and walked around the counter to pick up the recipe.

***

Dinner was quiet. After Paige finished sharing her day with Melanie and her dad, there wasn't much to say. Since most of Melanie's thoughts outside of school and home surrounded the man at the construction site, she chose to keep quiet after talking about her interest in taking photography classes the next year. Her father's unaccustomed silence made a conversation almost impossible, and after a while she stopped trying.

Melanie played with Paige for half an hour then took her up for her bath. As usual when she had Paige all tucked in her father appeared in the doorway with a book in hand. She gave Paige a longer than normal kiss and hug and wished her a good night.

While her dad read to Paige, Mel collected, sorted and started the wash. By the time she was done with her homework it was after ten and she was exhausted, but she wanted to see if her dad was okay.

She walked to the door of his office and watched as he read over documents in his hand, at his desk. Her dad was a handsome man. He was tall and lean. There was a wiriness about his physique that intimidated people. She's seen it many times. He kept his hair cut close to his scalp but she was able to see graying at his temples. She remembered when his medium brown eyes were kind and soft,

23

but their hardness now didn't take away from his looks, it just made him unapproachable.

"Are you just going to stand there staring at me, or are you going to ask your question?" her father asked without looking up from the paper in his hand.

Melanie had gotten to know this side of her dad well over the last four years. It was one of the reasons for her hesitation. Her heart sank at his tone because there was little chance that he would give her a satisfactory answer, but she needed to ask and tell him what had been on her mind for a while.

She slid inside the room and stood in front of his desk. She waited silently until he finished reading whatever was in his hand and looked up at her: impatience stamped across his features.

She took a deep breath forcing her hands that wanted to wring themselves together to stay apart. "How are you doing?"

The surprise that glinted in his eyes for a second helped her relax. Maybe he thought she was going to ask him *for* something. He put the papers down and watched her before answering.

"It's been a rough day, but I'm doing pretty good. Why?"

"You seemed really preoccupied at dinner, and Paige said you and Mom were arguing really loud earlier. I just wanted to see if there was anything I could do for you." She shrugged then stood there hoping he would take her words as the peace offering they were. She'd tried many times over the years to bridge the gap in their relationship. Even though he never threw her offering in her face, she saw the wariness in his eyes and mourned what she'd lost. She wanted him to come from around the desk and hug her and tell her everything would be all right, that she didn't need to worry; he still loved her and always would.

He leaned back in his chair and studied her. "It's not your job to make things right, Melly," he said using the nickname she thought he'd abandoned.

She swallowed hard at the lump forming in her throat. She watched as he fiddled with the pen in his hand. He opened his mouth as if to speak then closed it.

She couldn't take the not knowing anymore. She blurted out, "Are you divorcing Mom?

The surprise that flitted across his features was not accompanied with a fast enough denial, and Mel's chest constricted in fear. "I promise I'll be good. I've been good since…" Her words faded when her thoughts shied away from where she was about to go.

"I won't get into any more trouble. I'll take care of Paige more." She desperately tried to think of something that would keep him with them. She couldn't fathom the nightmare her life would become if he left them. Grace's full attention would be on her.

She went on blabbering, trying hard not to cry. "I'm sorry for not being your little girl anymore. I'm sorry that what I did made you not want to be around me…" She tried to go on, but the stupid tears clouded her vision. She wiped at her eyes furiously.

Her dad got up and came around the desk. He placed his hand on her shoulders. "Stop, Mel. You are not to blame for how this family is. You are a casualty."

She tried to compose herself so she could comprehend what he was saying, but he wasn't making sense to her. She tried again to say something that would change his mind or convince him things could be different, even if she weren't sure of it herself.

"I'm really sorry. I can do better," she began and was angry at the tears that clogged her throat.

The hug she was enveloped in startled her into silence. She wrapped her arms around him, holding on to him as if he were her lifeline. She'd missed his comfort. She missed her dad.

Just as quickly as he hugged her, he set her aside. It took her a moment to put her arms down; the loss was staggering.

"You are not to blame, Grace Melanie." She looked up into his eyes. The use of her full name caught her attention.

"But things can't be as they were." Her heart felt like it was breaking. What was she going to do? Her mind went in so many different directions it took a moment for her to realize he was speaking again.

"I love you. I do. Never doubt that. We all make mistakes. It is a part of life. But you must also learn to forgive yourself, or you will spend your life trying to make up for something you had no control of." He bent down so their eyes were on the same level. His fingers squeezed her arms briefly.

"Do you understand what I'm trying to say?" he asked.

She shook her head to the negative because he was speaking in riddles.

I wish I could tell you it will get better, but it won't. Your mother... Your mother is very angry."

"At you?" she asked, leaning back to see his face.

He shook his head.

"At me?" She had tried to stay on her mother's good side as much as she could.

"No, hon. At life," he said with a sincerity that gave her the chills.

"But you. You have a resilience and beautiful strength that is rare. It could have been extinguished by all that happened, but you've not only persevered, you've done it without letting the anger and unfairness of what you went through make you bitter." He stepped back and leaned against the desk.

"In some ways you are stronger than your mother because you choose to love instead of letting anger consume you." He looked at her with a pride she'd been longing to see in his eyes for a long time. It warmed her more than the sun and she basked in it.

She'd noticed he hadn't answered her question regarding whether or not he was going to divorce her mother, but she had him right now.

"May I just stay in here for a little bit? I won't make any noise. I just want to be near you for a little longer." She watched him swallow and hoped he would say yes.

"Have you finished your homework?"

She shook her head to the negative.

"Go get it and bring it in here."

She felt like she had been pardoned. She leaned in, gave him a quick hug and ran out of the room so she could get her books.

27

***

After spending a couple of hours in companionable silence in her dad's study she began to doze off. He ushered her to bed, and Mel slept deeper than she had in months. Though Mel hoped the night before would be a new beginning she wouldn't kid herself. There was still a lot they needed to talk about, but she wouldn't push it. It was a start, and it made getting up that morning easier.

Mel didn't even mind Paige's early morning grumpiness. The child was so full of joy and happiness any other part of the day but waking her up was like waking a bear in the middle of winter. Nothing could bribe her, not even the promise of pancakes. The child was not a morning person which made getting her ready for preschool a chore.

This morning, however, Mel's mood could not be altered. She worked to keep the smile off her face as she dressed Paige and made breakfast. She didn't want to draw attention to herself and ruin the fragile truce cultivated between her and her father.

Instead of reading on the bus she watched the traffic and different people in their cars doing everything from applying makeup to… Was that person reading their e-reader? She watched the person until the bus moved them out of her sight.

For the rest of the bus ride Mel reminisced about her conversation with her dad. She ignored the trepidation she felt regarding his lack of response to her question about the future of her parents' marriage. She chose instead to continue to hug the feeling from the night before close to her.

The bus turned the corner, and her eyes automatically went to the corner where she'd seen the construction workers the day before. There was a group of men working around the same table. She scanned each of their faces until she saw him. The man with the goatee and the kind brown eyes. She gave herself permission to watch him until the bus pulled into its parking space. He seemed like a large man on his own, but next to the other men he looked average. She could tell that his shoulders were broad under his jacket, but she couldn't make out the rest of his physique. He had on work gloves, so she couldn't tell if he were married, and the hard hat was hiding his eyes, but as soon as she stepped off the bus she felt his eyes on her.

As she walked up the steps she chanced a glance back his way and caught him staring at her. This time she watched him long enough to see a smile form on his lips. It was a nice smile, just like his eyes.

Once again he monopolized her thoughts throughout the day and again she considered what she was doing and took the long way to the bus. She hid among the crowd of students and slipped on the bus. This time she refused to look anywhere near the construction site and patted herself on the back for her discipline.

Melanie's mother was up again when she got home. Her mom looked tired, but there was energy buzzing around her that made Mel feel anxious. She wanted to ask her mother what was going on but figured it was better for her mother to tell her in her own time. When her mom let her know her father wouldn't be home until close to midnight she was disappointed she wouldn't get to spend time with him, but she was sure she would get another chance.

The next morning Mel went through the same routine of getting Paige up and ready for preschool and catching the bus. She

29

finished her book on the bus and purposefully kept her eyes averted when the bus rounded the corner. She wouldn't do anything that might jeopardize her relationship with her dad. Continuing to play eye tag with a man working construction across the street from her school wasn't smart.

She didn't know how she would handle things if he ever decided to do more than just smile at her but it was Friday. She had a whole weekend to put up a thicker guard.

Chapter 3

Marc checked the address on the slip of paper against the number on the home in front of him. He couldn't believe he'd agreed to come to this location without backup, but the note he found in his personal car two days before made it very clear that he was to come alone and not to tell anyone.

He wasn't a stupid man. He hadn't gotten where he was in the bureau for being stupid or careless. Well, not stupid, anyway. This was a careless move, but he couldn't help being curious about the note and who would have the audacity to put it in his car while it was in the parking lot of the bureau. Marc made sure that if this meeting resulted in foul play his office would have big bread crumbs.

He'd done his due diligence and researched the address so he knew who owned the home. He just wasn't sure what the man wanted with him. Usually men of the owner's stature went out of their way to avoid members of the FBI. They may not be doing anything illegal, but they wanted to stay under the radar nonetheless.

Marc didn't have to do too much research to find out that his new assignment may have something to do with this odd "request," but still, he was sure he wasn't the first to have been given the "honor" of watching the Morgansons. The assignment essentially made him a glorified babysitter. He knew that being new to the bureau meant he had to prove himself and pay his dues, but disguising himself as a construction worker to spy on the child of a woman that villains in fairy tales were based on, seemed like overkill. Grace Morganson's machinations hadn't landed her in jail but had booted her out of witness protection. If rumors were correct, Grace's betrayal reverberated throughout wealthy Italian families with enough power to rival certain mobs. There were no illegal dealings that could be traced to the family, but most people who even thought about doing what she actually attempted would have disappeared, only to have pieces of themselves surface decades later.

The woman either had something very incriminating that she was holding over the family or she'd made a pact with the devil.

The daughter didn't seem to share any of her mother's notorious habits. Instead she kept to herself but walked with quiet confidence and presence that drew the eyes of the other children. As he watched he could tell that the other kids didn't really know what to make of her but instead of making fun of or teasing her as most kids do at that age, they seemed to revere her.

He'd been watching her for three days from across the street when she glanced at him and paused as if stunned for a moment before moving quickly toward the school building. In that one glance he saw what the other children did. He knew from what he'd read in the records that she was two years older than what her school records stated. He couldn't understand what would cause a parent to keep their child back for two years. Was the woman punishing the child, or was there more to it?

He knew Grace Melanie was five feet, five inches. She had her mother's deep brown coloring and hazel eyes. But he wasn't prepared for the combination of those descriptions. When she turned that somber hazel gaze on him, he was powerless to move. A feeling of protectiveness rose up in him so strong he had to check his impulsiveness to march across the street and carry her away. Her golden stare only lasted for a second or two, but it was long enough to convey a lifetime of pain, and though she was only sixteen he saw hints of the beautiful woman she would become, and he mourned the fact that she would take that pain into her adulthood.

Marc placed the car in park and took a breath before checking his rearview and side-view mirrors before opening his door. The street seemed unusually quiet for midmorning. School was still in, but he had a feeling that even if it were summer the beautiful tree-lined street, with the big older brick houses that sat back on their property, would be just as quiet.

Marc scanned the houses again to see if anyone was peeking from the windows. The hairs on the back of his neck were standing up firmly, letting him know that he was being watched. He walked around his car and up the long walkway to the house. He slowly alighted the steps to the front door, and not seeing a doorbell he used the bronze knocker with an eagle's head. He took one more look behind him then up and down the street just before the locks turned in the door.

The man on the other side was tall and lean with a steely look of intelligence in his eyes. He surveyed Marc for a few seconds, but before Marc could speak the man stepped back and opened the door enough for Marc to enter.

"Mr. Marcus Miller?"

Marc nodded, hating to be at a disadvantage. "And you are?"

33

"The help," the man responded as he gestured for Marc to enter.

Marc knew walking in the house would take more control away from him, but he wasn't completely without secrets of his own. The shoulder and ankle holsters gave him a modicum of security, but if it came to that he probably wouldn't leave under his own power.

Marc hesitated for a second more before crossing the threshold knowing bone-deep that his life was about to change. He was led through the house and tried not to gawk at the double stairway leading to the second floor. Each staircase began at opposite sides of the entryway and curved as they rose to meet at the top on either side of an elegantly enclosed landing.

The rose-colored, quartz-and-granite marble flooring, small and life-sized sculptures and impressionistic paintings that lined the walls made him want to put his hand in his pockets to keep from accidentally bumping anything and becoming an indentured servant for life. Marc was ushered into his dream study. The spacious room was decorated in earth tones from gleaming cherry-wood flooring to the presidential-style desk made in... *Was that rosewood?* The maple shelf-lined walls were full of books, and he'd bet the Persian rug which covered a third of the room was silk and wool. He could thank his mother for her love of home decorating shows and her interior design hobby turned business for his ability to discern one wood from another.

"Special Agent Miller." Marc turned around at the sound of his name spoken with a pronounced Italian accent. He was surprised to see that his original host had disappeared, and in his place was a distinguished Italian gentleman with intelligent, dark brown eyes and almost jet-black hair starting to gray at the temples. His height mirrored Marc's own six feet, but where Marc was wide at the chest this man was lean. He wasn't thin by any means. He emitted a lethal grace that instantly intrigued Marc.

"I'm Luca Sable." The man offered his hand, and Marc accepted it making sure to keep eye contact with the man whose handshake was as strong as his presence was in the room. Marc took in the Hugo Boss casual business attire and gave a silent nod of approval even if it were done so begrudgingly. He wasn't a man made by his attire.

"Mr. Sable," Marc mimicked and followed the man to his desk.

The curtains had been opened, but the sunshades prevented the warmth of the uncommonly, sunny spring day from entering the room.

Luca Sable sat behind his desk and gestured for Marc to sit at one of the leather chairs facing him. Marc accepted the seat and waited for the man to begin. Luca's shrewd gaze never left Marc, but he said nothing for a few seconds. Marc stared back at him, curious, but not allowing himself to get caught up in whatever mind game this man was playing.

Marc knew who he was. He didn't doubt his place in life. He had a wonderful family with loving parents and siblings. He was working in his dream job and wanted for nothing. He wasn't seeing anyone because he'd spent the last year proving himself by taking all of the unsavory assignments that would keep him up all hours of the night, working weekends and some holidays. He figured love would present itself when he gave it an opportunity to do so.

"Do you know who I am, Special Agent Miller?" Mr. Sable asked still not looking away from him.

"I know *of* you. I know what your company does and I know pieces of your history, all of which I've read from documents supplied by my work." Marc added the last part to remind Mr. Sable to whom he was talking.

Mr. Sable's lips twitched, but just when Marc thought he might smile his lips thinned. "Special Agent Miller, there is no need to be concerned about your safety. And even though you might not be able to reach either one of your guns before you become incapacitated, if I felt threatened by you in any way I would not have invited you into my home, let alone allow you to carry your weapons past my front door."

Marc allowed his words to sink in then went over them again before responding. "But this is not a social call because if it were you wouldn't have invaded my privacy by breaking into my car in order to leave me your invitation."

Mr. Sable did smile then. It was a slow shifting of his lips that sent his face through a metamorphosis that would make a lesser man shiver. Where most smiles drew people in, Luca Sable's was predatory and downright lethal looking.

"I wanted to make sure I had your attention," Mr. Sable replied nonchalantly.

Marc took in the man's posture, arm placement and the pulse in his neck. Sable's relaxed attitude was a pretense, and Marc was even more alert than he'd been when he'd first stepped in the office.

Mr. Sable leaned forward and clasped his hands on his desk. "I want to offer you a job."

Marc stared at him for a moment. "I already have a job."

"That wouldn't have to change. It is one of the reasons that make you perfect."

Marc swallowed down the offense that rose up in him at his assumption of what Mr. Sable was asking. He masked any expression that would have given his feelings away.

"I'm more than sure that you have made the connection between me and Grace Morganson," Luca stated.

"Some of it," Marc replied and Luca nodded.

"What you know is sufficient for the conversation we are having now, but if you choose to take me up on my offer, I will need you to sign a nondisclosure form before I reveal anything else."

Marc didn't want to be curious, but he was. He hated the feeling that he was being manipulated. If the man wanted something from him why didn't he just ask it already?

"I find myself in a difficult situation, Mr. Sable. And I don't think I need to tell you how uncommon that is for me." Marc watched Mr. Sable shift in his seat. He actually seemed uncomfortable. This was getting interesting. Marc sat as still as a statue and continued to openly observe the man who, only fifteen seconds ago, seemed unshakable.

"I'm looking at a man with integrity, good work ethics, a strong family core, and I am trying to convince him to take a chance." Marc stiffened, and Mr. Sable held up a finger as if he could stop Marc from continuing his thought.

"I said chance not risk. I know better than to ask you do something that would jeopardize what you've worked so hard for. I need you to listen to your gut, take a chance, and listen to my proposal with an open mind," the man finished and waited for his response.

Marc watched him, a little perturbed. Did the man think a few platitudes would cause Marc to change his mind about working for him?

"You are at a loss because there is nothing in your world that I want."

Mr. Sable tilted his head to the side, his lips lifting in a crooked grin. "Yes. I admit I usually have something to bargain with when I ask for a favor, but the same reason I can't buy your help is what makes you perfect." Mr. Sable looked a little sheepish.

"What do you want, Mr. Sable?" Marc asked, angry at himself for letting the man's words get to him.

"I want you to ask that your surveillance of Grace Melanie Morganson become one of your permanent assignments."

At first, Marc thought he'd heard wrong. If anything, he'd expected the man to warn him away from the girl.

"Why?" Marc couldn't stop the word from leaving his lips.

38

"Because her life is in constant danger and she is about to disappear," the man said without changing the fluctuation of his voice.

"What do you mean she's about to disappear? The jolt the information sent to his heart was uncomfortable. The thought of the young girl in danger grabbed hold of every protective instinct he had and yanked on them violently.

"Grace Melanie's mother is something of a loose cannon." Marc watched Mr. Sable's eyes become unfocused as if he were picturing the woman. The brief flash of sorrow that crossed the man's face could have been his imagination, but he doubted it.

Marc was perplexed by the man's reaction. Why would a man care about the safety of the daughter of the woman who tried to have his grandson killed?

"She is about to run or…relocate. Whichever you wish to call it." Mr. Sable waved his hand in a dismissive gesture.

"She can't do that without letting us know," Marc blurted, then could have kicked himself.

"When Grace sets her mind to something, there is very little that can stop her."

"Yes. I misspoke. I know she can, but her husband is in the military. If he moves it only takes a phone call. How far did she think they would get?"

"She doesn't do things like this to evade you. She does it to see how long it takes for you to notice. Since the bureau just used you to conduct its yearly surveillance and her husband recently received transfer orders she is, as you say, pushing the envelope."

The fact that Mr. Sable answered his question told him the man was truly concerned.

"How do you know she is about to move?"

Mr. Sable's demeanor changed, and Marc realized he'd gotten too comfortable.

"That is none of your concern at the moment," Mr. Sable said, his eyes losing whatever softness they'd gained with his thoughts of Grace and her daughter.

"Why me?" Marc asked approaching the problem from another angle.

"Like I said. Your characteristics make you her perfect guardian."

Marc raised his hands in surrender both regretful and relieved that he wouldn't be able to take the job. "If they are relocating, I certainly can't continue to watch her. I'm stationed here, and I haven't put in enough time to ask for a transfer; not that I would want to.

"I don't need you to move or change your life in any big way. In fact, I would rather you kept doing exactly what you're doing. I just want you to look in on Grace Melanie once a month. It would be a couple of days at the most. I would take care of your expenses, and all I would ask for is a short report on your observations."

Marc raised a hand again to halt the man's words. His mind was filled with words, and they were beginning to get all jumbled. It was something that hadn't happened to him since he'd learned to push down or set aside his emotions in the midst of a challenging situation that called for his keen observation. Mr. Sable had caught him off guard with his proposal.

"So you want me to go watch this girl for a couple of days once a month?" Marc rubbed his thumb along his fingertips and went over their conversation in his head again. He couldn't believe he was considering this.

"What would make you think I would say yes to something like this?" He hoped what Mr. Sable said would dissuade him from taking the man up on his offer.

Mr. Sable stared at him as if he could read his mind then rubbed his forehead and spoke. "I'm sure you've guessed by now that there is something special about Grace Melanie. She stands in the middle of a crowd of children wanting to hide, but she shines too brightly, and everyone sees it, even the kids. It's why they come to her defense if anyone dares to say a bad word about her and want to be her friend, but she keeps them all at a distance outside of the classroom. Inside of the classroom, though, she is a mother hen, showing no favoritism nor judging. It's a weird dichotomy, especially for junior high children, but I'm grateful. It makes my life easier."

Mr. Sable took a breath giving Marc the opportunity to ask him the question foremost on his mind. "Are you her father?"

He didn't know what he'd expected, but it wasn't the deep pain that flashed in the man's eyes before he blinked the mask back in place. "No. I am not, but she is special."

Marc didn't have any reason to doubt the man. As far as he knew, everything Mr. Sable had said was true. He didn't, however, think the man had given him the whole answer. He was considering which questions would give him his answers when Mr. Sable continued.

"I watched you. That third morning you were watching Grace Melanie; I saw her notice you." Marc observed the twinkle of pride in the man's eyes even as he checked his reaction so as not to give anything away.

Mr. Sable gave a small shrug. "You don't need to respond. I came back on the fourth and fifth day to watch you. I was... pleasantly surprised," Mr. Sable said, his eyes boring through Marc.

"Special Agent Miller, I can pay people I trust to protect Grace Melanie, and they will do a decent job because they want to stay in good standing with me. I need someone who wants to protect her because they don't want to fail *her*."

Marc swallowed. Mr. Sable had slowly reeled him in, feeding into his belief that he had nothing Marc wanted, until Mr. Sable showed him a part of him he had a hard time ignoring. He wasn't surprised that Mr. Sable guessed correctly. He had been fighting the temptation to rescue the girl from the moment he saw her. It didn't matter how much he talked to himself when he got home. He would leave the house with a renewed determination to stay objective and detached, but by the time his surveillance was over for the day he was right back wanting to protect the melancholy golden-eyed girl.

Marc leaned against the back of his chair and thought over his options. His heart beat heavy in his chest chanting an echo of what he wanted. Though the injustice of her life called for him to act he was pretty sure he could walk away. If he accepted Mr. Sable's offer he could personally make sure of Grace Melanie's well-being. He measured his feelings against both scenarios and knew what he had to do.

He leaned forward and extended his hand to Mr. Sable. "Thank you for your offer, Mr. Sable, but I will have to decline at this time."

He watched Mr. Sable's expression but the man gave nothing away. Marc didn't know if he were relieved or offended by his lack of reaction. His expression was stoic as he looked at Marc's hand. "May I ask you why you have decided to decline my offer?"

"I won't owe a debt I can't repay in this lifetime," he said, standing with no more explanation.

Mr. Sable quietly studied him for what seemed like minutes before he stood and shook his hand. He saw a hint of respect in the man's eyes. "I will respect your wishes, but I want you to know that I will keep this offer open for as long as I can."

Marc smiled at the man's last attempts at manipulation. "You are Luca Sable. There is little you can't do."

Mr. Sable smiled blandly at Marc's volley. "Son, even I have my limitations."

They were at the study door when Mr. Sable spoke again. "Would you consider the first part of my request and ask to make her yearly surveillance a permanent part of your job?"

Marc tried to set aside his heavy heart and make a logical decision, but his emotions won the battle. "I will put in the request. It doesn't mean I will get it, but I'll put it in."

Mr. Sable's features relaxed slightly. "Thank you."

Marc only nodded in return. He'd let his heart overrule his mind, and he was bothered by what that said about his carefully crafted skill of shutting off his emotions.

Mr. Sable placed his hand on the doorknob and turned back to Marc. "I know I don't really have to tell you that anything said in this room should stay in here, but it must be said." He gave Marc a partial shrug letting Marc know though he was apologetic for having to state it, he was serious.

"I understand," Marc replied before exiting the room. With each step he felt as if he were taking on weight. His heart grew heavy, and by the time he reached the front door to the mansion he felt as if he'd left something behind. Yeah, he'd made the right decision.

Chapter 4

Consciousness was forced upon her by the light shake of her shoulders. The room was dark with only the hall light for illumination.

"Come on, wake up," her mother whispered. "I need you to get up and dressed, and help Paige put on the clothes I've laid out for her."

Melanie blinked in the dark not only to clear her vision but help the fog in her head dissipate. She rubbed her face and gave into a jaw-cracking yawn before reluctantly pushing aside the warm covers. She slowly shuffled to the bathroom between her and Paige's room. She turned on the water and splashed some on her face while it was still cold to help wake her up.

After patting her face dry with a towel she looked down to see that almost all of her toiletries were gone. The normally slightly cluttered countertop was bare except for her toothbrush in its carrier, toothpaste, a travel-size bottle of body wash and a ponytail holder.

She glanced around the bathroom and took in what she was too groggy to see before. *Oh no!* She put down the towel and went in search of her mom.

The hall was dark since the early morning light was still a couple of hours away. She rounded the corner and nearly collided with her mom at the top of the stairs.

"Mom, what's going on?" Melanie asked, taking in her mom's anxious movements.

"I don't have time for any long, drawn-out conversations. I just need you to do what I asked," her mom said, making to step around her.

Melanie stepped in her path. "Where are we going? Where's Dad?"

Her movement seemed to take her mom by surprise. She stopped and looked at Melanie as if she'd not seen her before. There was a second of hesitation before she spoke, but from the frost that came over her eyes Melanie was no longer interested in hearing what she had to say.

"My job is to make sure you and your sister are taken care of. That the two of you are fed and have a roof over your head. Your job is to follow my directions, and right now I want you to get dressed and prepared for the day in a T-shirt and a pair of jeans. Then I want you to get your sister up and ready so that by the time your breakfast is ready you two are ready to eat it."

Melanie wanted to stare her mom down. She wanted to demand that her mom tell her where they were going and where her dad was. She wanted to stomp her feet and refuse to budge until she got answers, but she didn't. She didn't because she couldn't afford to be that type of daughter. She couldn't jeopardize everything she'd sacrificed. She had to be meek, obedient, and continuously contrite in front of her mother.

She dropped her head and turned back toward the bedrooms without saying another word, but it didn't mean her mind wasn't going a mile a minute. Where was her dad? Did he know what they were doing? He hadn't said anything the night before. Her heart dropped into her stomach. They were just starting to talk again. She couldn't lose him now.

Melanie opened her closet. She stilled, her hand raised. Quite a few pieces of her clothing were missing. This wasn't a short trip or vacation. They were leaving like thieves in the middle of the night or morning. When had her mom done all of the packing? She swallowed against the lump in her throat. She perused the items in her closet through a blur of tears. She let them fall while she pulled out a pair of jeans, a T-shirt and sweater.

She sobbed while she put on her clothes, not trying to smother the sound. Her heart squeezed at the thought of not being able to see him every day. Her movements slowed as she donned her socks and laced her shoes. She needed a moment before she had to try to wake up Paige. Maybe she would dress the child while she was still sleeping and save some time and drama. She just didn't want to deal with "the bear" this morning.

Twenty minutes later Melanie was putting the last barrette on the end of Paige's braids when her mom appeared at the door. Her mom took in her face and sucked her teeth in impatience. "What is wrong with you?"

Melanie wiped her eyes. She wasn't about to share the true reason for her pain. She sniffed and sat a still sleeping Paige up in bed. The child could sleep through a tornado.

"I hit my shin on the side of the bed, and I can't find my favorite red belt." Melanie put her cheek to Paige's to hide her face. She didn't really care about the red belt but she noticed it missing."

"It's packed with your other favorites. Breakfast is ready." Her mom stopped to stare at Paige.

"Is she still asleep?"

Melanie looked at her mom around Paige's head which rested on her shoulder. "Yes."

A thoughtful look crossed her mother's features. "Mmm. Good idea."

At any other time, the words of approval would have at least registered in Melanie's heart. At that moment she just didn't care.

She picked up Paige and took her into the bathroom to wash her face and wake her up.

An hour later she and Paige were snuggled in the back among Paige's stuffed animals in her mom's van. Breakfast had gone pretty smoothly until Paige asked for their daddy. Not knowing what to say Melanie deferred to her mom who looked uncomfortable for a moment before telling them that he would be following them in a few days.

Melanie's breath caught at her mother's answer. Melanie tried to check the hope that bloomed in her heart. She wanted to believe her mother so badly, but her father's lack of response to her question regarding the future of their marriage made her doubt the legitimacy of her mother's claim.

She hugged Paige as close as she could within the confinement of the seat belts. The girl was asleep before they were an hour into the drive. Melanie watched her features contort and smooth in sleep relaying vaguely what she was dreaming. Her features had matured even more over the last year. Melanie could make out the small indents above her nostrils that were similar to Brian's. The small thin earlobes were also much like his. She remembered rubbing them between her thumb and forefinger as she lay on his chest when she would get tired of watching the stars in her backyard. Her heart lurched at the memory, and she refocused on her child's sleeping face. She let herself dream, for a few seconds, of her son's face. Were they almost identical or was he a replica of his father? She never knew which one she would prefer when she considered her baby boy. She was sure either would be beautiful.

She looked out the window at everything and nothing, trying to get a bearing on her swirling emotions. There was so much grass. It was as if the road had been carved out of a sea of green. It wound around the occasional hill but for the most part everything was flat. It made it easy to daydream, and the first new thought was about the man with the goatee. She wished now that she'd taken the opportunity to purposefully memorize his features. It was something she could take with her that even her mom couldn't take away.

She wished she was an artist then she could recreate his portrait, but she did have her words so she took out the small notebook she kept in the bottom of her backpack. She turned the pages until she came to a blank lined sheet. She slipped the accompanying pencil from its sheath and started writing.

What color are your eyes? I can't quite place the brown. There are so many shades that make up that five-letter word. So many similarities. I've seen that color in expensive furniture, horses on television and a couple of pieces of old glass. She knew

49

no matter what her mind kept over the years, it would never come close to what he probably looked like close-up. She wondered if his lashes were as long as they looked far away or if the nicely lined hair on his face was soft or prickly like her dad's. She would never know. She would never know, not because she didn't have the nerve to find out, but because she was being taken away once again from everything she knew.

As the miles grew between their car and the home and school she'd finally found some comfort in, she heated with anger. She usually tried to consider where the emotion would take her. She watched her actions to make sure she didn't do or say something that would end up hurting her Paige, but at that moment the unfairness of it all was too much. Her mother couldn't wait the two months it would take for her to graduate with the rest of her class? She had an A average, and though she hadn't had to work as hard as some for those grades, she'd put in the time and effort. She wondered how long her mother had planned this trip, how long her father knew they were moving. She wanted to scream and throw a fit like Paige sometimes did. It wouldn't change anything, but she might be able to relieve some of the heat in her chest.

God, she wanted the freedom to get away from these people, she thought, then immediately felt contrite at the realization that she had placed Paige on the list. Shame filled her and close on its heels was the hopelessness of the situation. She couldn't even get up a good steam of anger before she started feeling guilty. She'd had many conversations with herself. What child in their right mind wanted to be a mother at twelve, let alone have her family separated by a deal someone else had made with the devil.

Melanie bit her tongue until she tasted the metallic essence of her blood to keep herself from making a sound. She avoided looking at her daughter. One look at the child would often remind her of the one time she'd been able to get the upper hand, and it would go a long way in calming her, but right now she wanted to indulge in the heat of the anger. It would remind her that she couldn't become complacent, comfortable or forget that anything she grew attached to could be snatched away from her in an instant.

Eleven hours, five bladder breaks and one long lunch later they pulled into a decent-sized, ranch-style home. From what she gathered from reading the signs on the highway they were in some place named Ogden, Utah. They were no longer in Colorado Springs, no longer in Colorado, and she truly no longer had hope that Brian would come back and get her.

Five days later, as her mother had proclaimed, her father walked in the door, setting a couple of large suitcases down in the foyer. She outran her daughter getting to him. She couldn't have stopped the tears if she'd tried, the relief was so great. She could breathe. She could breathe.

Chapter 5

Four years later

Marc slowly sifted through the file he'd requested from the Utah branch office. He'd purposely waited until after the two newbies put in their surveillance paperwork before looking up her file and finding it sorely lacking. What was going on? Though he'd requested the permanent assignment of surveilling Grace Melanie Morganson, he'd been denied. He didn't think it was smart to appeal it, so instead he allowed the newbies who received the assignment to give him the information he needed to pass on to Mr. Sable.

He understood that he was only keeping half of his word, but it seemed easiest for him if he could remain at a certain distance. It had taken more than a few weeks or months to stop thinking of the girl. He had gone as far as getting in his car to drive to Utah from Denver to see how she was doing firsthand before he talked himself out of making the trip. He told himself that she wasn't his responsibility. That all of the people he helped keep safe from and in the event of child abduction was his responsibility. He'd joined the Child Abduction Rapid Deployment or CARD Team his second year at the Atlanta office.

He'd put in for the transfer after his dad had an on-the-job injury and his mom needed a little extra help. He let his apartment and girlfriend go after she told him she had no intentions of moving to Atlanta and preferred not to have a long-distance relationship. He had to give it to her; she knew what she wanted. It was more than he could say for himself.

His relationship with Sheila was nice. She was a beautiful, intelligent and giving woman. He'd met her at the gym, and after a few months of running into each other they'd exchanged numbers and he'd asked her out. They had a lot in common and he was very attracted to her, but there was something holding him back, and when he hadn't figured it out after a year and a half, their relationship was on its way to dying a slow death. When he received word of the opening on the CARD team in the Atlanta office, he thought it could be a new start for them. It turned out to be just a new start for him.

He was upset at first that she could so easily decide not to follow him, but after giving it some thought and experiencing his first week on the job, he knew it was for the best and that it may have been more of a bruised ego he suffered from than a broken heart. Sure, he thought about her often in the beginning. They had spent a lot of time together, and they communicated well. He could tell her about his day, well, at least the parts he could share, and she would listen intently before responding and ask him thought-provoking questions that would, in some instances, help him look at certain situations another way.

He would try and do the same for her, but as one of her firm's top paralegals, he thought she did way too much work for the pay and would tell her that frequently. Her intellect was sometimes dizzying, and he thought passing the bar would be a piece of cake for her, but she was happy where she was. He actually thought that if she left him it would be for a smarter guy not because she wanted to remain at her job. His mother told him it was all for the best. She was a believer of the idea of there being one special person in each individual's life, and she didn't think from what he'd shared with her about Sheila that she was the one.

Marc didn't know if he believed in there being that one special person. He also wasn't terribly romantic. He considered himself to be more pragmatic about relationships. He was attracted to beautiful women, sure, but they also had to have a certain confidence and strength. He'd learned that it worked both for him and against him, because that confidence and strength usually made them ambitious. Their ambitions usually took them away from him. He wished them well and knew that to begrudge them their dream would be hypocritical, since he was living his.

His parents had been together since they were teenagers, and even now when he would come home to visit he still caught them in the occasional lip-lock. From what he'd experienced, and seen among his friends' parents, the relationship between his mother and father was the exception.

He'd had two girlfriends in his life. One was in high school, where they both expected college to separate them. The other was Sheila. Marc figured at twenty-eight he was a little young to be concerned about finding "the one." His oldest brother, Malcolm, was thirty-five and had gotten engaged only the year before. He wasn't in a hurry. Besides, he had a name to make for himself on the job, and a family would only get in the way.

His immediate family wasn't excited about his career choice, but no one had been able to talk him out of it from the time he started going on about it at fourteen, after watching a documentary.

He could hear his mother praying some nights that God would present him with an opportunity to serve in a less dangerous way, but it was in his heart, and he couldn't think of doing anything else.

Marc remembered when he told his pastor about the career path he'd chosen. He didn't know what he expected, but it sure wasn't for the man he'd known all of his life to set down his pen, have his secretary cancel his appointments for the rest of the afternoon, and be taken to a section of the expansive park where tables were set up for the purpose of playing chess.

Pastor Roan sat at a table in the corner with him for hours asking him question after question about his academic achievements, home life, his reason for making such a decision and what he thought he could gain by serving in such a capacity. His pastor also asked him what his mother thought of his decision. When Marc told him about her prayers, Pastor Roan chuckled.

Once Pastor Roan's curiosity was appeased, he let Marc know that he had a nephew who served in a similar capacity. His pastor had always thought of Marc as a servant, a lover of men's souls, and his quiet demeanor made him perfect for serving in a church. To say his pastor was concerned was an understatement at that point, but he knew that wherever Marc went he would serve in pretty much the same way: with diligence, integrity and love for souls.

He left Marc with one thought that reverberated through him and caught hold. From time to time, when Marc would get discouraged, his pastor's words would lift up in his spirit. Pastor

Roan told him that serving in certain departments of government opened men's eyes to the evils that most people were blind to. That evil was not new. It was not overwhelming, and ultimately it would not win. There were still those who chose to do right and be used by God and not give in to the flesh. The job that he was enlisting in was to protect all men. He could not pick and choose whom he protected, just what he protected them from.

A couple of years into Marc's career, he found himself staggering under the burden of knowledge he'd received. One night after a prayer filled with desperation, anger and frustration, he went quiet, as his mother had taught him. Pastor Roan's words came forth like a balm, relieving him of the burden of judgment and allowing him to see the effectualness of his work.

It comforted him even now when his dream job bordered on a nightmare because of greed, bureaucracy and politics.

He loved his work on the CARD team. In the beginning he told himself it was due to his passion for children and his need to keep them safe, but he knew deep down he was trying to make up for not fulfilling his promise. As he became more familiar with the position, the more the guilt faded, and his yearly updates on Grace Melanie were performed more out of a commitment to keep his word than an overwhelming desire to keep her safe. He purposely avoided any pictures of Grace Melanie. He considered it self-preservation. He didn't need the trouble that seeing her might evoke. He kept her categorized as a job. A job that need only be as inconvenient as he made it. Until now.

Marc read the last line in the report: Transferring to Atlanta Office. The date on the paperwork stated that Grace and her family had been residing in Atlanta for the last three months.

Marc's neck itched and that didn't bode well for him in any situation. This would surely bring him and Mr. Sable face-to-face again, and he would have to come clean about his duplicity. Maybe the man already knew and had written him off. Marc didn't think he would be so lucky.

"Miller." Marc looked up at the sound of his name and closed the file on his lap.

"I need you to go over these reports from Intel. I think we have a lead on the Bryant case."

Marc looked up at his co-worker Patrick Finn and reached for the file folder. Patrick had been with the FBI for over ten years but had only been part of the CARD team a few months more than Marc.

Marc put his thoughts of the Morganson family out of his head for the moment and concentrated on what he was reading. The Bryant case had been particularly heinous. Philip and Natalie Bryant had been taken from their beds in the middle of the night while staying with their paternal aunt for the weekend in Glendale, Missouri. Their mother, Myriad Bryant, was fighting an aggressive form of breast cancer and was spending the week in the hospital, receiving chemotherapy treatment. The mother and father were divorced, and she maintained primary custody.

The aunt, Beth Bryant, reported the children missing after coming in to wake them up. She led the police to believe that the father might be involved, but when it was discovered that the man had died a couple of months before due to a mugging gone terribly wrong, the focus of the investigation turned back to her. The father's body went unidentified until his prints were run through the national database.

A week after the FBI was brought on to the case, the aunt disappeared, and evidence was found that, although she was given the authority to take care of the children, she had a hand in their disappearance.

Marc scanned the report Finn handed him. His eyes caught on a name and his stomach dropped. He looked up at Finn's grim face. "Travenski?" Marc asked with the one word. Marc swallowed back the bile that had climbed up his throat in response to seeing the man's name.

Finn nodded once.

Avonoff Travenski was a Polish oligarch who popped up on the FBI's radar after a raid on a drug trafficking ring in Wisconsin six months previous. One of the men caught in the raid turned informant and mentioned Travenski as the head of the other leg of the organization's illegal dealings: child sex trafficking. He continued to read, and a fine sheen of sweat broke out on his upper lip.

"She sold them." Even as he said the words, the realization of what Beth Bryant had done hit him full force. He wasn't green. He had seen some things during his time in the bureau, but for an actual family member to take advantage of an already tragic situation in such a way turned his stomach.

"They followed the money trail from Robert Pierce, one of Travenski's men, whom the informant positively identified, to Beth

Bryant a couple of months before. Even though Pierce holds a lower position in the organization, the fact that he is connected to Travenski is a huge lead." Finn said.

"Do we know if their father tried to intervene, and they made his death look like a mugging?" Marc asked, not really looking for an answer. He and Finn usually bounced questions off each other in this way.

"I'm surprised the aunt is still alive. They had to know that she would have been investigated," Finn said in response as he sat across from Marc.

"Has she been questioned since these new findings?" Marc looked up at Finn, wondering if he had any information not in the file.

"Ross interrogated her two hours ago. We're waiting for a report," Finn said, leaning back in his chair.

"Any leads on the whereabouts of the children?" Marc asked, even as he wanted to close his ears to the answer.

"No," Finn said, his expression not giving away what he was thinking.

Marc passed the file back to Finn. "Has the mom had anything else to say?"

"Some more choice words for her sister-in-law but nothing else."

Marc couldn't imagine what she was going through. He knew his parents wouldn't stop searching if any of his siblings disappeared, and if anyone in their family brought harm to his immediate family, Marc was sure they would be visiting his dad in prison for assault. His father was the type to mortally wound an enemy and lead him to God before he bled out. Well maybe not mortally wound the person, but it would be a beating the person would never forget.

Marc glanced at his watch. He did a double take when he realized he was already off the clock.

He looked up at Finn who nodded at him.

"Murdock and Chessen want to go grab a beer at that new place off Sikes St. You want to join us?"

Marc's first instinct was to say no. He hated beer and crowds. If the place was new it would definitely draw a crowd, but he hadn't hung out with the guys in a few months, and sitting back listening to the interoffice gossip couldn't hurt.

"Sure. Why not. I only have a frozen pizza waiting for me at home."

Finn's elated expression turned to one of disgust. "I don't know why you do that to yourself."

"Because I like to eat," Marc said sarcastically.

"Why do you insist on putting that processed stuff in your body?"

Finn, who'd recently had a wake-up call in the form of a minor heart attack the year before, was trying to single-handedly save the rest of his co-workers one meal at a time. He'd not gone full vegetarian, but Marc couldn't remember the last time the man had indulged in a burger at one of the quarterly cookouts.

"I exercise regularly. See my doctor regularly. I don't drink or smoke, and I call my mother more than on her birthday and

Mother's Day," Marc said, straightening his desk. "I figure processed cheese, saturated-fat-filled salami, pepperoni, bacon, and sodium-injected olives will have to work extremely hard to take me out."

Finn just shook his head. "One day."

Marc lifted his forefinger more amused than irritated by his friend's healthy fanaticism. "If there ever comes a day when I need to make a drastic change in my diet, I will come to you first. I won't even talk to my doctor first. I will call you from the hospital."

Finn sucked his teeth. "I'm going to go get my stuff. I'll meet you outside?"

"Yep," Marc said, placing the file for the Morgansons in his lower drawer and locking it.

He and Finn had partnered on more than a few cases. He liked the ex-army sergeant. He was all business when it came to going after criminals. Marc had seen him put the fear of God into more than one offender, but Marc knew he was softer than a marshmallow when it came to children. In another life he was sure Finn would have been a great husband and father, but field bureau agents in their department rarely had "happy ever afters" when it came to relationships.

It didn't mean they didn't try. Lou Bailey, another agent, married his high school sweetheart during his second year with the bureau and was served with divorce papers three years later, after one child and thousands of fights over things he couldn't talk to his wife about.

Marc knew the woman he decided to marry would have to understand that there were just some things he would never be able to share with her. Yeah right. He would probably die a bachelor, much to his mother's chagrin.

Marc glanced around the parking structure as he normally did when exiting the elevator. He listened to check if anyone else was on his level. After a few beats of silence he continued to his car. He reached for the door and pulled back when he saw the folded note on his passenger seat.

He turned and scanned the area around his car and checked his internal alarm but felt no impending danger. The hairs on the back of his neck lay still, and his heartbeat had hardly quickened at all.

"Mr. Sable," Marc said to himself after exhaling slowly. He did a cursory sweep around the perimeter of his car just in case. After reassuring himself that the note was the only thing in his car, not there when he'd left it that morning, he slowly unlocked and opened his door.

Once he got in his car, he checked the dash and ignition to make sure there were no extra wires before picking up the note. Tuesday at 1:30 p.m. was scrawled on the cream-linen paper with the address typed across the bottom of the stationery. He knew he would receive one of these; it just happened sooner than he expected.

He couldn't help but wonder why Mr. Sable gave him so much time to consider his invitation. Tuesday was still five days away. Maybe the old man knew he would accept the invitation even if it were five months from now. He didn't owe the man anything, but he had a feeling Mr. Sable knew his curiosity would get the best of him. He still had no intention of working for the man or looking after the girl. He just wanted to know if that sad look was still her eyes. The pictures were impersonal and inadequate as far as he was concerned. They rarely caught more than her profile or bent head.

He sat back and rested his head on the padding of the driver's seat. He wasn't prone to praying outside of church or at the dinner table. It just didn't occur to him. He figured God had more than enough on his hands with people needing miracles for themselves or the ones they loved. He felt it was inconsiderate to constantly bombard Him with questions, mundane requests or idle chatter. At this moment though, he felt the need to whisper a few words on his own behalf. It wasn't a request per se. It was more a conversation to help ease his mind and make sure God was paying attention to the recent events in his life. If he threw in a comment or two about his concerns regarding whether he should get involved any further in Mr. Sable's business or Grace Melanie, it was just because he was feeling talkative.

After ten minutes, Marc started his car and pulled out of the parking structure to go meet his coworkers at the bar. He hoped by the morning he would receive a semblance of peace about the situation.

Chapter 6

He wasn't going.

Marc closed the folder on the Morganson family and picked up the one on the Bryant case. He wasn't satisfied with what he'd been able to find with the information revealed to him on Friday, or what came from the interrogation report that he read through on Saturday. He'd gone over the questions and answers a few times but wasn't satisfied with what he'd come up with, or more importantly, failed to come up with. He knew that if he'd been able to give the case his undivided attention, he might have discovered a solid lead or trail on the children beyond the aunt and whom she sold them to.

They'd been able to check out her story and trace the movement of the children until they reached the first handoff. He had to give it to Travenski. He ran a business built on distrust. One person on the ladder didn't know what the next was doing, and on up. The only reason they had his name was that their informant was higher on the ladder on the other side of the organization than the person Beth Bryant had contact with.

He was missing something, and the only reason he believed he hadn't found it yet was he couldn't get Mr. Sable or Grace Melanie out of his mind long enough to allow his mind to work through the different angles it usually did on a case. He considered it a talent. His mind worked through cases almost like a computer...or was it that computers worked through scenarios like his mind? He'd had instances where he'd looked over a case and worked through different angles consciously then went to sleep only to wake up with fresh scenarios from photos and files he'd looked over but didn't consciously select. Eight times out of ten, it helped to speed up the investigation.

He'd woken up Sunday morning with nothing. No new angle or prompting of where to go next, and he suspected it was due to his unnatural curiosity for Grace Melanie and her connection to Mr. Sable—or if he were to be completely honest—just about Grace Melanie.

He'd gone through all his feelings regarding her each time he'd seen her or read a report on her. There was no stirring of attraction, which he was relieved about each time he had the courage to seek within his heart. What he couldn't shake was the interest in her well-being. She was a girl the first time he'd seen her, and she'd pretty much stayed that age in his mind even though four years had passed. It made it that much harder to convince himself that she didn't need looking after, that she didn't need protecting, especially from her mother.

He'd done his digging. What self-respecting agent wouldn't? But outside of the obvious connection between Grace and Luca, which placed her in protective custody and got her kicked out, he didn't come up with anything. Why would a man be so insistent about protecting the child of the woman who tried to kill his grandson, unless she was family herself. Only, from the medical records he'd studied, the blood tests weren't a match. People had fudged things like that in the past, but then why involve him? Mr. Sable must have known he would do his research.

Marc was baffled, but the same deep curiosity and need to protect Grace was the reason for him distancing himself. He knew that if he got too close, it would suck him in, and he had children to save.

He wouldn't be taking Mr. Sable up on his invitation.

Monday mornings were slow for Marc since he usually came in on Saturdays to either catch up or get the first look at new information on cases, in the relative quietness of the office. He was feeling restless. They didn't have enough for the task force to move on, but he hoped they would soon. He was feeling a little rusty sitting at his desk this long. It had been almost three months since he'd gone out in the field, and he was edgy.

"Miller." He looked up startled to find Finn in front of his desk.

"Finn," he responded.

"Come on. I need a coffee, and the over roasted beans we have here just won't do it for me today." Finn put on the jacket he'd been holding, and Marc glanced down at the folder. It wasn't like the ideas were coming. Maybe he needed a small break.

"Okay." He got up from his desk and plucked his coat from the back of his chair. When he looked up again, Finn was standing there staring at him.

"What?" he asked, wondering if he had something on his face.

"That's two times in a row that you have taken me up on an invitation."

"What? Does this mean we're dating?"

66

"Whatever. Come on, if you're coming," Finn said then turned to leave the room.

Marc followed after him, smiling to himself. It was rare for Finn to let his sarcastic wit go unanswered.

They walked the two blocks to the Café on the Corner. He rarely came to the café, preferring his own coffee or tea in the early morning. He would continue to indulge Finn and get a sandwich or something.

"What's going on, Finn?"

"Why does anything have to be up?"

"Because it's not in your nature to just go out for coffee. You always have an ulterior motive."

"Not today," Finn responded, looking up at the uncommonly clear sky. "Today I just want to get a cup of really good coffee."

Marc waited a few seconds, counting down from ten to himself. He got to five when Finn spoke again.

"Well, that and Louise," Finn said with a lift of his eyebrow.

Marc thought about this for a moment but couldn't place the name. "Who's Louise?"

"She's the new barista," Finn answered with a lascivious grin.

Marc rolled his eyes. Finn was the biggest talker he knew, but for all of his bragging the man never made a move.

The café sold all types of coffee, pastries, sandwiches and soups. Marc considered it a treat when he could get to the café. Their chocolate éclairs were decadent. He tried to think back to the last time he'd set foot in the establishment and couldn't remember.

That was reason enough to indulge in the dark chocolatey and creamy goodness.

Finn opened the door, and the aroma of coffee and sugar hit Marc full force. The place was packed, and the low drone of conversation filled the rest of Marc's senses, making the usually calming atmosphere feel close. He was about to back out, but there were people behind him coming through the door. He squared his shoulders and followed Finn to the counter to order. He scanned the restaurant making sure all of the exits were still in the same place. He let his eyes roam over the occupants of the tables farthest from him as he usually did when walking into an establishment. He glanced at the faces and was about to bring his attention back to Finn, when his eyes caught a familiar face.

He did a double take and his breath caught. It was as if he had conjured her up. He squinted to double-check that his mind wasn't playing tricks on him. Well not quite this version of her. He wasn't sure if he had the imagination to conjure up this version of Grace Melanie. He actually felt his mouth go dry at the sight of her.

She was sitting at a booth with four other young ladies, facing him. Her eyes skimmed over him as she glanced around the room, and he caught his breath in expectation of her eyes coming back to him, but they didn't. She leaned across the table snatching up a doughnut hole and placing the entire glazed pastry in her mouth while her friend was turned. He watched memorized as she chewed quickly then stopped all movement when her friend turned back around. He watched as her friend looked at her plate then looked around the table until her gaze returned to Grace Melanie. The woman said something Marc couldn't make out, but Grace

Melanie gave her a sheepish smile and started chewing again. The woman said something to the table, and they all burst out laughing. The woman said one more thing, and Grace Melanie got up and headed his way.

She was dressed in a long-sleeve, gold-knit sweater that made her eyes shine even more than the humor in them. The sweater outlined her torso, proving it had indeed been four years since he last saw her in person. She wore a jean skirt that stopped a couple of inches above her knees, showing off her shapely smooth legs, and he forced himself not to stare. Her hair was in a ponytail at her crown with curls escaping around her face, making her look more angelic than human. With her hazel eyes tilted at the sides, her features had grown more exotic since he'd last seen her in person. If it weren't for the updated pictures in her file which did her no justice, the only way he would have recognized her was through the old stirring of protectiveness that accompanied the new attraction.

He couldn't take his eyes off her. She was...beautiful. He knew he should move, walk right out of the café before she really saw him. It would make it harder for him to stay incognito when he became head of her surveillance. Something he decided, right then, he needed to become. She glanced back at the table obviously overhearing something one of them had said, and the smile was still on her lips when she turned back around and came face-to-face with him. His breathing hitched, and his heart stalled then began beating double time.

At first he didn't think she recognized him, and disappointment ran alongside the relief in his chest. Her smile

69

slowly left her face making him desperate to think of something that would bring it back, but her eyes narrowed, and he watched a hint of recognition roll across her features. He wasn't sure if she remembered when and where she'd seen him, but he could tell she was making a note of his features. He warred against himself, wanting her to really see him and maintain his anonymity at the same time. Her full lips, colored with some type of pink sheen, opened, but the sound of his name echoing in the café didn't come from her.

"Miller." The moment felt surreal with his name coming from afar and Grace Melanie standing in front of him close enough to touch, her golden hazel eyes watching him with interest.

"Miller. What are you getting?" He tore his gaze from hers to see Finn eyeing him with both impatience and curiosity. He quickly called out his order and looked back to Grace Melanie, but she was continuing on to get to the back of the line.

Marc turned back to the counter. "An order of doughnut holes too."

Finn scrunched up his face but allowed it to be added to his tab. Marc stepped back from the counter to follow Grace Melanie, but stopped himself. What was he doing? He had lost parts of his mind. As far as she was concerned, he was supposed to be invisible, but he had just stood there staring at her daring her to remember him, and he wasn't completely sure she hadn't.

He forced his feet to stay in place until Finn was done speaking to the cashier, whom he guessed was Louise by the blush on her cheeks and shy smiles she kept giving Finn. Marc glanced

at some of the faces in line behind them and moved aside as a
second cashier arrived.

He stepped over to the pick-up side of the counter and glanced
Grace Melanie's way to make sure she was still in line. He
watched her out of the side of his eye. She fidgeted with her
fingers and glanced between him and her friends in the booth. He
was tempted to turn so he could see the silent conversation going
back and forth between them but settled on just watching her.

One of the servers called Finn's name, drawing Marc's
attention back to the counter. He picked up his coffee and the bag
of doughnut holes then tapped Finn on the arm as he passed him.
His throat went even drier as he covered the distance to her. He
tried to think of something clever that would make him stand out
or at least bring a smile to her lips, but his mind was so full of her,
nothing was coming. When he reached her, he held out the bag to
her.

"These are for you," he said when she made no move to take
the bag.

"Um, what?" she said, and he realized it was the first time
he'd heard her speak.

"Doughnut holes for you and your friends," he said, tipping
his head to her table of friends.

"Why?" she asked, still not reaching for the bag. He saw his
error right then. How could he tell her that he saw her take her
friend's doughnut hole and figured she'd been sent to buy some
more, without sounding creepy. He started to pull the bag back.
Then decided to be as truthful as he dared.

"I know this may sound strange, but when I walked in I thought I'd seen you before, and I was trying to figure it out when I saw you swipe your friend's doughnut. I thought maybe you got in line to get some more, so I bought them for you because the line is pretty long, and..." He thought over his next words for a couple of heartbeats. Once he went there, there was no going back.

"And I hoped you might give me your name as a thank you." He finished as he watched to see if she believed him.

She stared at him for a moment. Her golden eyes tried to read him. He put on the air of confidence he used when going over reports for a case with this team and held the bag back out to her.

She reached for it hesitantly. "Thank you." Her small smile made him forget where they were for a moment.

"Mel, um, Melanie."

He liked hearing her say the name he'd read so many times. Her voice was low and a little raspy. It brought to mind warmed brown sugar and cinnamon and seemed to wrap itself around him.

"Nice to meet you, Melanie. I'm Marc." He held out his other hand.

"Not Miller?" Melanie glanced at it then placed her small warm palm in his.

He was pleased to find out that she'd been paying attention when Finn called his name and was interested enough to remember it.

"That's my last name."

"Are you military? I know people in the air force. They only use last names or nicknames."

72

He shook his head in the negative then offered an answer before she guessed right. "I'm in law enforcement."

Her eyes pierced him before she nodded. "Nice to meet you too, Marc."

She graced him with a smile that touched her eyes, and the sight warmed him to his soul. He decided he would watch over her as Mr. Sable had asked so many years ago, but he would do it from much closer. Like right next to her.

Chapter 7

Melanie was free! Okay, well mostly free. Melanie nearly fainted when she received the letter stating that she'd been awarded a full scholarship to her dream college in Atlanta. At first she was afraid to hope that her mother would allow her to live so far away. It wasn't like Utah and Atlanta were next door to each other, and she had reservations about leaving Paige alone with Grace while their dad was on tour. Still, her mom found a way to surprise her by not only giving her permission to go to Atlanta, which legally she didn't need, but had to get for everyone's peace of mind. She informed Melanie that all of them would be moving to Atlanta at the end of Melanie's school year. It may have dimmed her elation a bit, but Melanie ended up with enough freedom to spread her proverbial wings even if she had no room to fly.

Melanie loved everything about college. She loved learning at a faster pace. She loved being able to choose subjects that interested her in addition to some of her general education courses. She loved being in an all-woman environment, but more than that, she loved being in charge of whom she hung out with for a few hours a day.

Melanie's class schedule was hectic. She was so worried Grace would change her mind at any moment about her higher education, she loaded up on credits her first and second semester, despite her counselor's discouragement. Most people balked when she told them she was carrying twenty units, but until she could secure funding of her own she was subject to her mother's whims. It wasn't rational. She knew her mother valued education, but she just didn't know how much her mother valued *her*.

She was thinking of biting the bullet and going for a student loan to pay for incidentals not covered by her scholarship so that she was completely out from under her mother's thumb, but knew that once she requested government aid she would have to disclose her real age. She didn't know what the big deal was now that she was out of high school, but she wouldn't jeopardize her college career by being reckless. She had too much to lose.

For the first time in eight years, Melanie had friends her age. She was befriended by Rickie on the first day of her creative writing class, and the two were almost inseparable. Rickie, a freshman from New York, was a five-foot-one-inch Puerto Rican dynamo. She had the energy of five toddlers souped up on sugar. She did everything fast. She talked fast, walked fast—and as Melanie would discover—took fast notes and made up her mind just as quickly about whom she wanted to hang out with, and that was Melanie. She was funny, sarcastic, extremely intelligent, and Melanie thought she was the greatest thing that could have happened to her in her first week in college.

Rickie introduced Melanie to Sophia later that week. She was a young woman Rickie started a conversation with in her statistics class. They had lunch together before Melanie's last class of the day. Like Melanie, Sophia was quiet but attentive and got a kick out of Rickie's larger-than-life attitude.

Sophia had skin the color of ebony and eyes a clear brown that sparkled against her skin. Her skin was so beautiful and smooth looking, she had a hard time not staring. Melanie thought she was gorgeous and was curious about her looks. She finally had to say something in case Sophia took her frequent glances the wrong way.

"I'm sorry for staring, but I've never seen someone with skin as beautiful as yours. And with your eyes, I just think you're gorgeous." Melanie closed her mouth afraid it would seem like she was gushing when she really just wanted to make sure the girl understood her. She was also going for comforting the girl, but her small rant may have just had the opposite effect.

Sophia gave her a brilliant smile, because why wouldn't she have one of those too. "Thank you," Sophia said graciously.

"You have the most striking eyes I've ever seen."

Not expecting the compliment, Melanie was momentarily at a loss for words. "Thank you."

"What about me?" Rickie chimed in dispelling some of the awkwardness that had crept in.

Sophia and Melanie turned to the spitfire and spoke in unison. "You're the shortest woman I've ever met."

They laughed at each other and then at Rickie's exaggerated frown and laughed harder.

A week later, Melanie shared her copy of the class syllabus with Katrina who had been delayed by a family trip to Europe: a trip she said she'd been trying to escape for a full month. She gave Melanie a running commentary by drawing picture after picture in cultural anatomy during the short film with photographed scenes of life and religion. By the time class was over, Melanie was looking forward to her next class with Katrina just to see what she would do. It turned out that she wouldn't have to wait since they shared Algebra II together.

Melanie introduced Rickie to Katrina and Sophia later that afternoon at the Café on the Corner. Rickie had brought Sophia and herself to the café a couple of days before since it was relatively close to the campus. Melanie had walked through the door of the coffee and bakery shop and knew she would go back every chance she got. The décor was something out of the fifties with its black-and-white-checkered tile floor and plush red leather booths: the glass display housing a variety of pastries, many of which she'd never seen before, was huge. Her mother was a stickler for keeping sweets out of the house, but it didn't stop her father, Paige and herself from going out for the occasional dessert, especially when there was something to celebrate—such as on their report cards.

Melanie scooted into what was quickly becoming their normal booth and gestured for Katrina to sit across from her. After making the introductions and telling Sophia and Rickie about Katrina's funny pictures accompanying the short film in their class, Rickie personally welcomed Katrina to their unofficial group with a handshake of comradery. Melanie should have known then that the two would try to outdo one another when it came to outrageous acts, but what did she really know. She hadn't allowed herself to have friends since Brian. Not that girls hadn't tried, especially when they moved to Utah, but after so many unaccepted invites they stopped and gave her a wide birth.

Atlanta was going to be different. In a lot of ways it already was, because she had decided it would be the moment she found out she was going. She deemed it the beginning of her life…well, at least this part of her life. There were too many people connecting her to her other life.

She looked around the booth at the new gifts she allowed herself to have and thought herself the most fortunate woman at that moment. She knew Rickie and Katrina could hold their own if her mother found out about them and had an issue with it. Sophia would have been someone Melanie avoided, not because they wouldn't have had anything in common with one another: on the contrary, Melanie thought they were more alike than the other two women in their group, and that was exactly the problem. She had no doubt that Rickie and Katrina would tell Grace exactly what was on their minds and wouldn't consider bowing to her whims. Sophia might be too polite or naïve to do the same. It was unfair for Melanie to make that assumption of Sophia, but if she went by what she saw in her new friend, she would make sure she never met her mother.

They talked and got to know each other better throughout their early dinner. Since neither she nor Katrina stayed in the dorms, when it was time for her to go, Katrina offered her a ride, but she refused, telling her that she would be picked up on the other side, a two-stop ride on the transit line. It was mostly true. She would get on the public transit rail, but the fifteen-minute walk from the station at her stop didn't warrant a ride to her home.

Melanie said goodbye to her friends at the door and walked down the street to the station as if she were floating.

***

She walked into the house as she had many times before. Paige had stopped racing to meet her when she started the first grade and Melanie picked her up on the way home from high school. With this new move, Melanie was once again the last one home, but the ritual had long since been put aside. Melanie wouldn't admit to anyone but herself that she missed the unadulterated show of love and affection. The awareness of who maintained the authority was beginning to overshadow where Paige automatically went for affection. The gap in their ages served to both solidify their roles and hinder the closeness of their relationship. There were so many times that Melanie wanted to reach out to Paige, to help her with more than her homework or play the occasional board game with her. She wanted to tell her that she was an extraordinary girl with the weight of one of the most powerful families in the United States behind her, but Melanie wasn't supposed to know that, so then Paige wouldn't until it was safe.

Melanie went to her room to get started on a couple of her assignments before going downstairs to start dinner. Grace had transferred jobs, again, and had chosen to work the night shift...again. Melanie had stopped wondering a long time ago why her mother was so averse to spending time with her family.

It was a quiet night. Their father had come back from tour number four a few months before and was even quieter than he'd been when he came back from the previous tour. It was a quietness that unnerved her. She couldn't put a name to it, but she would often hear him walking around the house in the early morning.

Though their relationship had healed over the last four years, there seemed to be less of him participating in it now. He just wasn't there.

She'd researched the psychological effects of war and learned some about post-traumatic stress disorder. She went against her instincts to wake him from bad dreams by touching him. Instead she would play classical music and turn it up until the violins woke him. Depending on how deep he was in the dream, it would take anywhere from a few seconds to a few minutes to bring him out. She found the most soothing and consistent-sounding music she could with as few highs and lows as possible. She definitely didn't want to startle him out of the dream but rather pull him out with sounds that she believed normally wouldn't be found in battle.

His first week home horrified her the most. She was only glad Paige was a heavy sleeper. She heard him from her bedroom down the hall. The scream chilled her to the bone. No one should ever revisit a place that made them scream like that. She knocked on the door of her parents' bedroom out of deference, but when her father didn't answer, she stepped inside, going straight for the stereo in the corner. She turned to a station she knew played soothing classical music after midnight and slowly turned it up until his flailing calmed then stopped altogether. The stereo had a remote control which she laid on the pillow where her mother usually slept and walked out of the room closing the door behind her. She figured he wouldn't be too happy to come face-to-face with any witnesses to his night terrors. She slowly walked back to her room but didn't go back to sleep until the music turned off.

She lost a lot of sleep that first month and was afraid she would have to start school with the handicap of little to no sleep, but unbeknownst to her, her father joined a support group, and the nightly terrors began to ease. It took her a while not to listen out for the sounds of his moans, but by the time two more months passed she was getting a great deal more sleep.

In all of that time, her father had only talked about it once to her. Two days after she'd begun leaving the stereo on for him he came to her room and asked if it was she or Paige who was leaving the music on. Melanie admitted to doing so and added that she'd done a little research.

"Thanks, but you shouldn't. You need your sleep," he said, seeming at a loss for words.

"I sleep better after," she said, referring to when the music went off.

He paused for a moment and she could see he was working out what she meant.

"Not when your mother's off though. Okay?" he said with a grim smile.

She nodded and waited for him to close her door before letting out the breath she'd been holding. She'd expected him to be angry, embarrassed or maybe in denial. She hadn't expected the quiet acceptance. She didn't know she was crying until a tear fell on a page in the book she was reading. She didn't even know why she was crying. She just knew she hated knowing her dad was in pain.

Melanie was taking the baked chicken out of the oven when her father walked into the kitchen. He had a curious look on his face, and she was immediately on the alert.

"You haven't told me about your classes or how you like school," he said, sitting at the kitchen table. She stared at him dumbfounded for a moment, confused by the attention he was paying her. When he raised an eyebrow she forced herself to think.

"It's been great. I really like my classes, especially creative writing. Anthropology isn't bad either." She started spooning broccoli from the pot to a serving dish.

"I saw from the schedule that you are carrying a heavy load this semester. Doesn't the school have counselors that discourage you from piling on too much at once?" he said, giving her his undivided attention.

She hesitated, wondering what he was getting at. "Yes. Most people tried to dissuade me"—she shrugged—"but I would rather do the heavy lifting now while I still have all of this support. I don't have a job, so I can put in a few more hours for research and assignments."

The intensity of her father's gaze unnerved her, and she had to look away.

"You got a full scholarship. There are very few things that are not covered. Why do you think that will change, or are you talking about losing other types of support?"

She was happy that she had turned to place the chicken on a platter. There was no way she could have hidden her expression. It was all she could do not to pause at his words.

"Melanie." The one word commanded her to turn and face him.

She did so but didn't meet his eyes.

"I know I've been gone, but I'm still your father. No matter how independent you've become I will still be your father. You can talk to me. I will listen and help where I can."

She looked at him, incredulous. "Even when you came home you weren't here. This is the first time you've talked to me about school since I called and told you I got the scholarship. With everything going on, I don't blame you, but please don't pretend you've been here when you haven't." She pinched her lips together to keep from voicing the less objective words pressing at the back of her throat.

Her father nodded. "Fair enough."

He went quiet for a moment, seeming to contemplate things.

"I want you to know that though we don't speak about...things much in this family, I know some of the sacrifices you've made and I'm sorry."

She tried to hide her response because it wasn't exactly honorable, or respectful for that matter. He was one to talk about sacrifices. He didn't know the half of it, and what half he should have known, he was too far away physically and mentally to be aware of.

"What?" her father asked.

She clucked her tongue at herself, frustrated by the fact that she wasn't able to keep her feelings in.

83

"I came straight home from school every day for six years so I could watch and play with my daughter who only knows me as her sister, do my homework, and cook dinner for the both of you. I rejected invitation after invitation to birthday parties, sleepovers, clubs and dates. I turned down overtures for friendships because I never wanted my mom to know about them." She breathed out in frustration.

"For eight years I have tiptoed around feeling like I was under house arrest, doing everything I could to work it off and make up for something I was manipulated into doing." She raised her hand in submission. "I take responsibility for it going as far as it did. There was no gun to my head, but you weren't there to help me get out of it, and you let me feel guilty for years about it before I came to you." She stopped, surprised at what she'd already said. She shrugged to herself. She might as well finish.

"I sacrificed a normal childhood, but that wasn't the hard part. The hard part was no longer being able to be your little girl. No longer getting to go out on Saturday trips and talk, no longer seeing the pride in your eyes or getting hugs from you. That was the true sacrifice." She set serving spoons in all of the dishes she'd placed on the table and straightened to her full height, feeling both drained and empowered. She had finally gotten it off her chest, but what good would it really do? She watched her father for a few seconds, and the look of guilt and pain stabbed her deeply. It wasn't fair that she cared so much. It wasn't fair that she was the only one willing to take responsibility. She was tired.

"I'm sorry. I'm no longer hungry. Can you see that Paige eats her broccoli? I'm just going to go up, finish my homework and go to bed." She waited to see what he said. When he nodded, she left the table, walked up the stairs and told Paige dinner was ready as she walked to her bedroom.

She spent the next two hours doing her homework, then she sat up to see if her father would come speak to her. When he didn't, she hardened her heart against him and turned toward what the next day would bring with her new friends.

Chapter 8

"I really, really need some coffee. Please come with me." Rickie pulled on Melanie's arm, pleading with her.

Melanie glanced at her watch. She didn't have another class for two hours. She was going to use the time to study for an anthropology quiz, but she was mostly sure of what she'd studied the night before. She could still get in an hour if they came right back.

"Okay, just a coffee and then we come back," Melanie said, trying to be stern about it. "I have a test to study for."

"Bring your book with you." Rickie raised her hands when Melanie opened her mouth to protest. "Just so you can go over the information while I get my caffeine."

As compromises went that sounded pretty good, so Melanie brought her messenger bag with her and followed Rickie down the hall. They hadn't taken more than a few steps when Katrina fell in step with them.

"We're going to the café," Rickie said, peeking around Melanie. "Would you like to come?"

Katrina looked at Melanie quizzically, but she nodded and held up her anthropology book. Katrina shrugged, and the two women began talking about different flavors they'd sampled over the last few months.

Melanie didn't drink coffee as a luxury. When she had caffeine, it was essential to keeping her up. She didn't experiment with flavors to see what she liked. It wasn't something she felt the need to spend her allowance on.

She gave her friends' conversation only half of her attention as she scanned the campus for Sophia. She wasn't familiar enough with her schedule to be able to guess where she was at the moment. She interrupted Rickie as they neared the edge of campus.

"Have you seen Sophia? Do you think she would like to come?" Melanie glanced at Rickie in between scanning the large lawn and the front doors, from what she could see of certain buildings.

"Uh, well, she's already there." Rickie looked at her sheepishly.

"She kind of gave me the idea. She's a walking anthropological dictionary with all of the places she's been with her parents. I thought it would also give you a little insight on what you were studying while I got some much-needed coffee." Rickie said the last part, pointing at herself with a smile.

Melanie slowed, then stopped walking and waited for the two women to notice. She had a mind to turn around and go back, but no need to add drama to something she wanted taken seriously.

Rickie and Katrina noticed her absence a few steps later and turned back. She saw Rickie take a deep breath and walk back to her slowly. Katrina was going to follow, but Melanie held up one finger requesting a moment with Rickie. She didn't need a witness to what she was going to say to Rickie. She didn't want her friend's defenses to go up any higher than they already were. She hated when her mother would give her a dressing down in front of people. It was humiliating, and she couldn't hear half of what her mom said because her blood was pumping so hard.

Melanie started talking once Rickie got within whispering range. "I don't know you well enough to tell if you deliberately left out the part about Sophia being at the café until we were across the street, or if it slipped your mind. Since you are my first friend in many years, I'm not altogether sure how to deal with things except head-on. I will only ever be straightforward with you, and I hope you will do the same." She leaned in just a little closer to share the more vulnerable piece of news.

I have lived with a person who gets a kick out of manipulating people. She enjoys giving vague pieces of information so she can shape situations to work in her favor. I always end up feeling used and belittled, and I am very sensitive to it." Melanie created some space between them by leaning back and raising her hands in a peaceful gesture.

"If you think I'm being oversensitive, just let me know, and we will squash this. If not, could we just make this something you just learned about me?"

Rickie leaned back a little more and stared at her. Melanie saw a number of emotions cross the Latina's features, including incredulity, respect and a little amusement which made Melanie's defenses rise.

"Girl. You weren't kidding about not having friends in a long time," Rickie said with a smirk.

Melanie couldn't believe this woman was making fun of her when she'd just gone out of her way to be respectful and shoulder the blame for her reaction to Rickie's antics.

"It is more than okay for you to say 'Rickie, don't do that again. I don't like it.' You don't need to add flowers or sugarcoat it," Rickie said, looking no worse for wear.

Wait. What was she saying? Melanie tried to push aside her rising anger and listen.

"I grew up with six siblings. If I didn't speak up, I wasn't going to be heard. If I do something you don't like. Say it straight. You don't need all the pretty words. They just blur things after a while." Rickie nodded at Melanie, and Melanie gave her speech a few seconds to sink in before nodding back.

"You don't like being manipulated. I think I can see how it looked from your side, but I didn't mean anything by it. We cool?" Once again Rickie nodded at Melanie, and Melanie waited for her brain to catch up with the words of the quickly spoken sentence.

"Um. Yeah," Melanie agreed a little hesitantly.

"What's wrong?" Rickie asked, looking up at her. "Don't you believe me?" The words held sincere curiosity and a little hurt.

"Yeah, Yes. You just talk so fast, and it doesn't help that I'm not familiar with your accent, even as light as it is. Sometimes you sound like one of those people who say the disclaimer at the end of a radio commercial," Melanie spurted, then hoped she hadn't been offensive.

Rickie looked at her, tipping her head to the side. "You know, my professor said the same thing…about the disclaimer thing. You think I could get a job at a radio station reading disclaimer scripts?"

89

Melanie wanted to burst out laughing, but she wasn't sure if Rickie was playing. "Uh. Maybe."

Rickie started laughing. "Girl, I was just playing. I don't want a job where people can't see me. It would be a waste."

Melanie did laugh at that. "Yes it would. No one would believe you were real if they didn't see it for themselves."

Rickie stopped laughing. "What you sayin'?"

"I'm saying you're a character and you know that," Melanie said, catching on to Rickie's joking.

"See. Now we're getting to know each other better," Rickie said while pulling her into a hug.

Melanie was startled by the movement, but after a couple of seconds she brought her arms up and returned the hug. She was ashamed to realize that it had been a very long time since she'd been hugged.

They turned back to Katrina, who tried to look like she hadn't overheard their conversation, and continued toward the café.

Just as Rickie had said, Sophia was already in the café saving their booth. Rickie and Katrina got in line, and Melanie went over to join Sophia. They talked about nothing of any importance until Katrina and Rickie joined them.

"A peace offering," Rickie said, setting a plate of doughnut holes in the middle of the table. Melanie reached for one as Sophia asked what the offering was for. Instead of answering, Melanie stuck a whole, round, glazed pastry in her mouth and looked pointedly at Rickie.

Rickie sighed and explained the misunderstanding while Melanie chewed and indulged in a little people watching.

"What do you think, Melanie?" Sophia asked once Rickie finished explaining.

"I think the doughnut holes were overkill, but I'm not going to look a gift horse in the mouth," Melanie said, just before popping another hole in her mouth. Instead of chewing, she squeezed the sweet dough between her tongue and the roof of her mouth and sighed as the oil released from the pastry.

"Well, then, you won't have a problem sharing," Rickie said, taking a doughnut from the pile and placing it on the side of her saucer. Katrina took Rickie's lead, and Sophia looked at Melanie for a few seconds before reaching forward and snatching one as well.

Melanie opened her book and notes, and she and Katrina quizzed each other for a half hour before she was satisfied with her knowledge of the subject. The doughnut holes on the plate had long since disappeared, but the one Rickie had set aside for herself was still on her saucer.

Melanie listened to the conversation as she went back to people watching and biding her time for when Rickie would turn away from her plate.

Katrina brought everyone's attention to one of the servers who'd recently come on shift. He seemed to hold Rickie's attention, and she watched him move throughout the café. Melanie watched Rickie, and when she turned, Melanie took the opportunity to snatch the doughnut hole and place it in her mouth.

When Rickie turned back to the table, her eyes were alight with excitement but dimmed when she caught everyone's looks.

"What?" she said, focusing on each woman until her eyes came back to Melanie. Her eyes narrowed at the slight bulge in Melanie's cheeks before she looked down to where her doughnut hole had been.

"I know you didn't just take my doughnut hole."

Melanie couldn't help but smile and gave up the ruse, chewing slowly.

"Ha ha ha. The joke's on you because you're about to buy this table another order of doughnut holes." The look Rickie gave Melanie let her know her friend wasn't playing. She understood that she may have just stepped over an invisible line.

She stood up without protesting but spoke just before heading to the line near the counter. "Maybe I can get that server you've been drooling over to get them for me." She moved away with an exaggerated swagger.

"I saw him first," Rickie said just loud enough for her to hear.

Melanie turned back around, walking backward a couple of steps. "No you didn't. Katrina did." She laughed at Rickie's glare and turned back around, almost running to someone. She looked up and opened her mouth to apologize, but she forgot the words when her eyes met the ones of the man she'd almost bumped into.

Her mouth went as dry as dust, and she got just a little lightheaded, which seemed odd to her at that moment because her heart was beating twice as fast. Didn't that send more blood and oxygen throughout the body? Her head was part of her body.

Goodness, he was fine. Like heart-racing, eye-dilating, air-stealing fine. How was it possible for a man to be that good looking?

Melanie let her gaze skim over his close-cropped, dark brown hair, or was it black? she mused. It was slightly longer on top with small waves that alluded to curls if it got long enough. His forehead was square and seemed like the perfect size. Melanie had no idea what the perfect size was for a forehead. She just knew his was neither too big nor small, and it was the perfect prelude to a spectacular pair of thick, dark eyebrows. Melanie hadn't looked at too many magazines with male models, so she wasn't too sure of her specific preferences, but she made up her mind right then that she loved thick eyebrows on men. Not wild, or heaven forbid, long enough to braid, but thick enough to fill in a precise space between the forehead and eyes without any hairs out of place.

They were only made more gorgeous by how they contrasted with his eyes which were just a couple of shades lighter than his skin. They were set wide on his face and seemed to read her. They were familiar somehow, but—she thought with a sigh—wouldn't she have remembered seeing someone this...this manly?

His full lips quirked up at the corner, drawing her eyes to his mouth. She glanced back at his eyes expecting to see amusement at the fool she was obviously making of herself, but they were quietly watching her as she assessed him. There was even a hint of recognition in them that pulled at her.

Melanie took in all of his features one more time so she could call them up and study them on her way home. The thought was so familiar it pulled her out of her stupor. Well that, and him looking

93

away from her to answer his friend's question, thus releasing her from whatever hold his beautiful gaze had held her with.

She took the opportunity to escape to the back of the line and take a few breaths, the actual thing that would have brought oxygen to her brain a few seconds ago. Was it really just seconds? She glanced at her table of friends and noted the curious look from Katrina, the openly amused look from Rickie who was fanning herself, and the slight frown on Sophia's face as she looked back and forth between her and the man at the counter. The attention suffused her cheeks with even more heat, and she couldn't help her embarrassed smile.

"He is fine!" Rickie mouthed the words in an overexaggerated fashion.

"I know!" Melanie responded silently but couldn't help the giggle which she stifled quickly. The woman in front of her turned slightly at the sound and she gave her a small smile.

"Who is he?" Rickie mouthed.

Melanie shrugged her shoulders then glanced around the line to see if the man was watching the exchange between Rickie and herself. He was collecting his coffee and a bag at the pick up counter. Her heartbeat that had finally calmed down picked up its pace when she realized that he would have to talk her way into leaving the café. Maybe he would talk to her. She hoped she didn't make a fool of herself if he did.

She pressed her palms against her jean skirt surreptitiously pushing down the hem. For a woman who normally wasn't self-conscious about her looks, she felt inordinately insecure about the outfit she'd chosen that morning. Her skirt was considered

94

conservative compared to other ones she'd seen, and since she had smooth and toned legs from all of the walking she did, she had no qualms about showing them from time to time. Her sweater was a last-minute decision. She felt the need to brighten up her day and the golden color always cheered her up, but it was on the older side and showed no awareness of fashion trends. Well it was too late now to make a first impression.

She glanced down at her high-top leather lace-ups that were decent and extremely comfortable but had seen better days. She was tempted to hide the more scuffed one behind her leg, but didn't know how long she would be able to keep the pose. There was also the fact that she was in a line and would have to move eventually. She gave herself a huff of frustration and looked up in time to see the man walking down the line, his eyes on her.

She watched him draw closer and her body went hot then cold then hot again. It wasn't until he stood right in front of her that she actually believed he was purposely headed toward her.

He held out the white bag to her. She glanced down at it wondering if he mistook her for someone else. She looked back at him to double-check that his actions were deliberate. His eyes were clear and hadn't left her face. She found that she was at a loss for words.

"These are for you," he said when she hadn't responded to his gesture.

"Um, what?" She squinted and watched his facial features, hoping they would make the whole situation clearer to her.

It didn't. His answer of wanting to gift her with doughnut holes only made her more confused. "Why?" she asked, hoping desperately that he wasn't some type of stalker or pervert.

She watched him as he explained why he was standing in front of her offering her what she was waiting in line for. As explanations went, it wasn't half bad, and actually downright flattering if she were going to be honest. Something he said caught her attention beyond his deep voice, long. square-tipped fingers holding the bag and the fact that he couldn't be more than three or four inches taller than her own five-feet six-and-a-half inches. It didn't take much effort to look him in the eye, which was both comforting and disconcerting.

It occurred to her that he wasn't just offering her the gift. He wanted to exchange it for her name. She smiled to herself and took the bag, making sure to avoid his fingers.

She gave him her name and he gave a smile that made her insides feel like her organs were playing musical chairs.

He introduced himself, giving her a name other than the one his friend had been calling to get his attention earlier. He held out his hand and she tried to shake off the surrealness of the moment so she wouldn't come off as a total idiot.

"Not Miller?" she said, wincing at herself for the remark while placing her hand in his and marveling at the feel of his fingers wrapping around her hand.

"That's my last name," he said, seeming to take it in stride.

Her stomach roiled at the thought that he might be in the military. She hadn't given it much thought, but she saw what her mom went through and didn't even want to court the possibility of being left for months to years at a time.

"Are you military? I have friends and family in the military. They only use last names or nicknames." *Please don't be in the military.*

The negative shake of his head gave her permission to breathe easily.

"I'm in law enforcement."

"Nice to meet you too, Marc," she said, giving herself a reason to keep her hand in his for just a few seconds longer. The moment she slipped her hand from his, she felt the loss.

The intensity that grew in his eyes made her feel just a little uncomfortable, and she would learn that when she got uncomfortable around this man, whatever she thought would find its way out of her mouth.

"Did you figure it out?" she asked.

He cocked his head to the side. "Figure what out?" "You said you thought I looked familiar, and I have to admit I feel like I have seen you before. It's highly unlikely, since I'm new to the area." She pressed her lips together to stop her runaway tongue.

His eyes that were so expressive and open moments before became hard to read. It struck her as odd.

"Do you take the metro train or go to the school across the street? I was on campus a little bit ago following a lead," he said, but she had the feeling there was more to it. She didn't know why, since she'd never met him, but she'd learned to listen to her feelings.

She leaned back slightly, also noticing a breath later that he gave her a little more space by rocking back on his heels. She felt a modicum of relief in the fact that once he recognized her discomfort, he did something to assuage it. She liked that.

"Both. I attend school, and I sometimes take the metro," she said. But today, just in case, she would ask Katrina for a ride.

"When I figure it out, I will let you know, if I can have your number," he said, taking a sip of his coffee. His expression once again open and full of hope.

She stared at him. Oh, how she wanted to give him her number, but she didn't have a personal phone, and she definitely wasn't going to give him her home number.

She shrugged. "I don't have a phone." She clucked her tongue. "I mean I don't have a personal phone. Maybe you could give me your number?" she asked.

He blinked at her and hesitated for a few seconds before putting his hand in his coat and pulling out a pen.

"Do you have a piece of paper?" he asked.

She looked down trying to remember if she had some paper on her. She patted her pockets with her free hand, and not wanting to give up, she held up her hand to him to write on. He smiled disarmingly at her and nodded to the bag of doughnuts he'd given her.

"May I?"

A little embarrassed, she held up the bag for him to write on since he was still holding his coffee in his other hand.

"I sometimes work late hours, but I'm usually home by nine o'clock," he said after clicking his ballpoint pen closed.

She glanced at the number then back up at him, smiling shyly.

"Are you going to call me?" he asked with a teasing smile that didn't quite reach his eyes. She realized he was actually unsure as to whether she would call him. That knowledge made her want to call him even more.

She opened the bag of doughnuts, peeked inside and took a deep whiff. Seeing that she was next she stepped out of the line to let the next person go.

"I will give it deep consideration," she said, smiling mischievously before deciding it was time to rejoin her friends— then wondered where the playfulness came from.

Marc placed his hand over his heart but didn't say anything.

"Bye, Marc. Thank you for the doughnuts," she said, taking a step in the direction of her booth.

"Bye, Melanie. Hopefully, we'll talk soon," he replied.

She sent him her biggest smile and continued walking until she slid in her booth.

"Is he watching? I didn't want to look back," she asked when her unusually quiet friends just stared at her. They looked up then back at her, nodding in unison.

She smiled, emptied the bag of doughnuts on the plate, and folded it up before placing it between two sheets of her favorite notebook.

When she was done, she looked up to find her friends staring at her with expectant expressions.

"What?" she asked, then ducked when Rickie picked up a doughnut hole and threw it at her.

Chapter 9

And here he was again, Marc thought as he stood waiting in Luca Sable's office. Of course, it wasn't the same office since he was now in Atlanta, but it was decorated much the same. There was heavy dark furniture and earth tones on the walls, and carpet to enhance and accent the more expensive pieces. Marc still wasn't sure how much work he would be able to get done in a study such as this. Even though the blinds were open, the dark furniture seemed to absorb much of the light.

Marc chose to stand because all of the chairs in the room had their backs to the door, and he was already feeling at a disadvantage and quite uncomfortable, given his interaction with Melanie two days ago. Two long days that allowed him to get some distance from what felt like a spell he'd fallen under while in her presence.

It would seem that she was the smarter one of the two of them, since she hadn't called him. She was in her first year of college and had her whole higher academic career ahead of her. He could tell that he wasn't the only one affected by their closeness. He felt the electricity arcing between them when she looked at him and it was heady, but it seemed obvious to him by her lack of communication that she recovered faster than he did once they were out of each other's sight.

Once the haze lifted from his encounter with Melanie, later that evening he began to rethink his initial decision to keep her close. He had a job that was nowhere near relationship friendly and had a promising future in said job. From what the surveillance reports showed she'd never had a boyfriend, let alone friends before this year. He didn't know if he had the time to cultivate a relationship with her no matter how tempting it was to know that she was practically a blank canvas in the relationship arena.

Then there was the fact that she was still being surveyed by the FBI. He wasn't sure, but given her mother's past with the FBI, his working for the bureau might be a game changer. It all came down to just being a bad idea. No matter how much he wanted to pursue her or how right it felt just being in her presence, it wasn't worth the heartache he was also sure would come later for her and him.

Funny that he found himself in Luca Sable's office waiting for directions on an assignment that would keep her in his life...or not so funny. He was playing with fire. He wasn't so disconnected from his emotions to think that he would be able to stay away forever, but he also knew walking away completely wasn't an option now that he'd been touched by the warmth of her smile. He glanced down at his shoes, a smile playing at his lips as he laughed at himself and the fanciful thoughts. Finn would laugh at him, too, then send him to the office shrink in search of a cure.

In all seriousness, though, after seeing her in the café he felt inexorably connected to her in some way, and if he wouldn't let himself date or court her, he would make sure she stayed safe.

That was the place he ended up in late last night after his thoughts ping-ponged all over the place for nearly forty-eight hours. It was the only thought that brought comfort and a modicum of peace.

He was drawn away from his thoughts by the sound of footsteps coming down the hall toward the study. Mr. Sable appeared in the doorway a few seconds later.

"I apologize for the delay, Special Agent Miller. It couldn't be helped," Mr. Sable said, closing the door behind him and walking past Marc to his desk. He gestured for Marc to sit as he did so.

"Well, honestly, Special Agent Miller, I didn't think we would have the pleasure of each other's company again," Mr. Sable said, leaning back in his chair. At Marc's obviously curious look, Mr. Sable's eyes narrowed slightly.

"I don't force people, Special Agent Miller. My request was just that. You were allowed to disregard it. Why didn't you, I wonder," Mr. Sable said without a change of expression.

Marc hated it when people talked in circles. Wasn't Marc's presence a giveaway? Marc continued to look at him.

Mr. Sable watched him for a moment. "Just to assure that we are on the same page, I have asked you here to watch after Grace Melanie. Now that you are both in the same city."

Marc nodded, not trusting himself to speak. There was something about Luca Sable's demeanor that made him cautious.

"What changed your mind?" Mr. Sable asked, his gaze zoning in on Marc's.

Marc considered giving him an ambiguous reason, but why not be truthful.

"I met her," he said, giving Mr. Sable back his direct stare.

Mr. Sable's lips thinned slightly, but other than that, he showed little reaction to Marc's reply. "Before or after you received my request?"

"After," Marc replied as he considered a number of reasons as to why that would matter.

"How is she?" Mr. Sable asked, pressing his fingertips together.

It took a moment for Marc to understand the man's question, but from the interest in his eyes he assumed Mr. Sable wanted to know about Melanie's well-being.

"She seemed"—he thought about it for a moment, and her smile flashed in front of him—"happy."

Mr. Sable's eyes never left his, but he nodded and the creases at the corners of his eyes softened.

"What are your intentions toward Melanie?"

Marc gave Mr. Sable a one-shoulder shrug to downplay his response. "To keep her safe."

"Is that all?"

"Yes."

He wasn't surprised by Mr. Sable's frown. He felt like frowning himself after stating out loud that he would have nothing to do with Melanie. It made it more real somehow.

"I'm sorry if this offends you, but I think you're lying."

Marc wasn't sure how he felt about that. Though he wished things could be different, he had no intentions of taking it further and told Mr. Sable so.

"What if I told you that I think you are kidding yourself."

"I'd say you are welcome to think whatever you'd like. It doesn't make it true."

"No, but it does make you dangerous."

Marc stared at him wondering how they'd reached this point so quickly in the conversation when it had taken him the best of two days to reach it.

"You, Agent Miller, are in denial, and until you are willing to admit what your eyes have already confirmed to me, we are done." Mr. Sable picked up a folder from the stack on the corner of his desk.

"You can see yourself out," he said without looking up.

What did this man want from him? Marc's heart stuttered and sped up, causing heat to flare across the nape of his neck. His body broke out in a sheen of perspiration that he knew Mr. Sable would notice. He was desperate. The realization mortified him. He didn't want to be dismissed. He needed to watch after Melanie. He needed to make sure she was taken care of. His mind didn't acknowledge the fact that she'd made it to twenty without incident, just that now that he'd interacted with her he could no longer ignore her.

Marc crossed his legs at the ankles and uncrossed them as his mind ran through different ways he could still keep an eye on her. He refused to leave this man's office until he came up with another satisfactory option. Nothing came though. He couldn't use the bureau to do it. It would raise too many questions. Seeing no other way, he sighed and rubbed his face.

"It would be the best for everyone if I were to watch her from afar."

"Why?" Mr. Sable asked, still not looking up.

"My career isn't conducive to healthy romantic relationships," Marc responded without hesitation.

"Astronauts have careers that aren't conducive to relationships, but they do it anyway."

"The worst-case scenario for an astronaut is that he dies on his way to, during, or coming back from a trip. In my field of work, the worst-case scenario would be for me to watch as my loved ones were tortured and killed."

Mr. Sable nodded in understanding. "So it isn't denial. It's fear."

"Why are you pressing this? Wouldn't it be better if I could protect her with the type of objectivity that comes from keeping a distance?"

"And how much objectivity will you be able to keep when she starts dating. It is inevitable."

The ice running through his veins at Sable's words was quickly replaced with heat at the thought of her looking at another man like she'd looked at him in the café.

He didn't know whether he was coming or going anymore. He'd never reacted like this over a woman. He could see himself serving a life sentence behind bars for killing the man who hurt her.

"Your admission to your feelings for her is as much for her well-being as it is for yours."

"And when it doesn't work?"

"Don't be so sure. Life is full of opportunities that look impossible at first glance but end up reaffirming something deep within your being."

"You sound like a man who's had one of those reaffirming moments."

"I've had to live with both the regret of not taking advantage of an opportunity and the blessing of getting a second chance later in life." Mr. Sable's eyes had grown solemn.

"Melanie is part of that second chance, and I won't let you jeopardize that." Mr. Sable's gaze was laser-focused on his eyes, translating his meaning if Marc didn't recognize the conviction in his words.

"What do you want me to do?" Marc said, no longer wishing to put up a fight.

"Well for starters, answer your phone when she calls you."

"How did you know I gave her my number?"

"If I felt the way you do about a woman I just met, I wouldn't let her get away without some way to stay in touch, and with her household environment, I wouldn't imagine Melanie would be giving you her number."

"What kind of household is that?"

"A controlling one."

"Why?"

"Same rules as last time, Special Agent Miller. If you wish to take on this assignment of watching and reporting back to me everything you believe is relevant in Melanie's life, I will answer your questions and give you the background information you will need on Melanie and her family."

Marc went on alert. He'd read everything the bureau had on the Morganson family. What more did this man think he had, and why would he have it? He asked himself again why Luca Sable was so concerned about Grace Melanie. He took a moment to consider Mr. Sable's statement.

"I have one question to ask first. It's important that I get an answer first. It has been hounding me since the last time we met."

Mr. Sable nodded, seemingly in acquiescence.

"If I were to ask you why you are so concerned about Grace Melanie's welfare even after her mother hired someone to assassinate your grandson, would your answer make watching over her compromise my integrity or influence me in a negative way toward her?"

"Not if you are worthy of her."

"I already know that I am not."

"Then let's hope one day you can prove that you are."

"I told you—"

Sable held up a hand to silence Marc. "You've had her under surveillance and you've met her. What do you think?"

"I think young children are impressionable, especially those who don't receive the attention they need at home," Marc said, watching Mr. Sable for any reaction. He got nothing.

"Ask your questions, Special Agent Miller. This arrangement will work better if neither of us leaves this room with preconceived notions unaddressed."

"You denied being her father before. Were you intimately involved with her?"

Mr. Sable blanched, and Marc let out the breath he didn't know he'd been holding.

"No, Special Agent Miller. I'm old enough to be her grandfather."

Marc shrugged. "It happens all of the time."

"True. I've committed quite a few sins in my time, Special Agent Miller, but that, I am happy to say, is not one of them."

"Once our protection was lifted, why didn't you return the favor and have Grace assassinated. It seems there are quite a few of your former colleagues who would be willing to do it for free."

"For one, it is illegal, and two, hurting Grace would be hurting myself."

"You still have feelings for her after everything she's done?"

"There would be far-reaching repercussions that I'm not sure I could live with," Mr. Sable said, turning the folder he held open in front of him and pushing it closer to Marc.

Marc hated being a foregone conclusion. Mr. Sable had no qualms about making him feel predictable.

He read the nondisclosure and contract before signing them both and sliding them back across the desk.

Mr. Sable glanced at them then closed their folder and set it aside. Marc sat back and watched as he leaned forward and crossed his fingers on the desk. He seemed to be in deep thought for a few seconds before looking up at Marc, his eyes pinning him with an intense gaze.

"Do you believe in God, Special Agent Miller?"

Marc swallowed before answering, feeling the depth of the question. "Yes, I do."

"Do you believe He redeems men to Himself?"

"Yes. But..." He stopped when Mr. Sable held up a finger, but was unable to hide his curiosity.

"Do you think there are some whom God can't redeem?"

Marc hesitated for a moment as he gave the man's obviously serious question the consideration it deserved. "I don't believe that there are men God can't redeem. That would imply that God wasn't able to do so, and He does not fail at anything."

Marc shifted his position as he searched for the right words. "There are men God won't redeem unto Himself, though, and I'm sure that tears at His heart for He wishes that no man is lost, meaning He would like to have all men reunite with Him in heaven for an eternity." Even though Mr. Sable nodded his agreement and was following, Marc paused again to get himself back on track. His conversations with his mother came to the forefront of his mind.

"God is a gentleman. He will not force His will on anyone. Therefore, if we don't ask forgiveness or come to Him willingly, He won't force us to. There are situations He will use to help get our attention, but ultimately it is up to us if we want to be redeemed."

Mr. Sable placed his forefingers to his lips, his eyes downcast for a moment. He was as still as a statue for a few heartbeats before heaving a great sigh and seeming to come back to himself.

"Thank you for your candor."

"I'm just repeating what I've read and learned," Marc said with a shrug.

"You should use it more. In your line of work. What most see as realistic tends to overshadow the invisibles or the supernatural as your denomination calls it. It can cloud your belief."

Marc didn't know if he were insulted at the intrusion into his personal life or impressed by the depths at which this man had gone to vet him.

"Which *is*?" Marc asked

"That no matter what the current situation looks like, love wins in the end. Therefore God wins," Mr. Sable said.

"Do you believe that?" Marc asked, truly curious.

Mr. Luca paused before answering. "I may not see it in my lifetime, but I do believe it."

Mr. Sable nodded once before he began speaking. "I met Brenda during a pivotal part of my life. I had everything: a beautiful wife, children, a successful business with thousands of people working for me and the ability to obtain anything I wanted.

Marc watched Mr. Sable's eyes glaze over momentarily as if he were remembering that era in his life.

111

"It's funny how God will show Himself to you at times when you mistake your good fortune as a right and give you chances to pull your head out of...well, you know," he said ruefully.

"He will give you chance after chance in hopes you will listen before the devourer steps in. I didn't listen. I was too full of myself. I can see it all now that it's too late to undo it. Too late to be the faithful husband my wife adored, the father my children looked up to and wanted to emulate, and the man a young woman, with incredible potential and a heart bigger than my empire, could admire. I destroyed it as directly as if I were Satan himself." Mr. Sable stopped at the knock at the door, and Marcus wanted to shoo the person away.

After being given permission, in walked Mr. Sable's butler carrying a tray of what looked like tea and slices of a variety of pastries. Marc's mouth watered reminding him that he hadn't eaten yet that day. The tray was set on the corner of Mr. Sable's desk, and at his nod the man poured them both a healthy cup of the sweet-smelling dark brew.

When he left, Mr. Sable continued. "Brenda was a junior accountant for the accounting firm my company contracted to hold and invest our assets. She caught a discrepancy that our direct accountant either overlooked or was too afraid to bring to our attention since it had been happening for a few years. I took her from the company and made her the accountant over my business and some personal accounts. She was a genius when it came to numbers. Her intellect, for lack of a better word, was alluring. Combined with her beauty and uncanny wisdom, she was almost irresistible." The self-deprecating smile that lifted his lips saddened Marc, though he wasn't sure why.

"The first few years she worked for us, I made sure to keep my distance outside of regular work hours. If she worked late, I made sure she had company and that we were never in the building alone. I loved my wife. I considered my vows to her and God sacred, but I got too close, tempted myself one too many times, and it nearly destroyed everything I'd worked for and held dear."

Marc listened to Mr. Sable bare his soul wondering why this man would trust him with such secrets, until he got to Grace Melanie and with two sentences stripped him raw and showed him his own weakness.

"Grace's hatred for me overrode any love she could have given to her daughter. She manipulated her child and my grandson into cultivating a physical relationship. I suspect it was so she could blackmail me with my own great-grandchildren."

"Wh...when?" Marc said, barely able to put enough breath behind the word to make it audible. He felt like he'd been punched in the gut.

"My grandson was fourteen, and Grace Melanie's true age was twelve," Mr. Sable said without preamble.

Marc wondered if it were possible for him to swallow his tongue just from overreacting gag reflexes. She was twelve and had a child. Wait. Mr. Sable said grandchildren.

"You said children. How long did this go on for?" Marc tried to remember if he'd seen more than the little girl who showed up in pictures with Grace Melanie. *What was her name?* Marc mentally scanned the reports he'd read so many times. *Paige. Her name was Paige.* He thought she was Melanie's sister, but he guessed that's exactly what they were led to think.

"It went on for a year and a half. Just long enough to destroy their innocence and break their hearts. Grace Melanie gave birth to twins: a boy and a girl. Brenda wanted to use the boy as some type of emotional blackmail against me." Mr. Sable stopped to take a sip of his tea, and Marc waited, albeit impatiently, for him to continue.

When he didn't, Marc tried to prompt him. "What happened to him?"

Mr. Sable blinked at him as if he'd awakened from a trance. "He was gone before Brenda could use him."

Marc was suddenly at a loss for words. His mind hit a wall. That a mother would use her own daughter to exact revenge was pure evil. Now he knew why Mr. Sable preferred that he watch Grace Melanie close rather than from afar. The person he was really protecting her from was her mother.

"In many ways, Grace Melanie reminds me of Brenda, but she's more resilient. She chooses to see the beauty in people, and it would be a tragedy if she lost that desire." The man seemed to age right in front of Marc's eyes.

"I don't expect that my more recent works will pay for all of my misdeeds or remove the regret from my heart, but it's all I have left. Will you help me?" Mr. Sable asked, and Marc couldn't help but nod his consent.

"Just tell me how you want it done."

STOLEN PROMISES

Chapter 10

"Have you called him yet?" Rickie asked Melanie as they lay on the floor of her dorm room going over ideas for writing projects.

"No," Melanie responded, not looking up from one of the many business magazines she'd been perusing for a story.

"Why not?" Rickie asked as she reached for an encyclopedia from the pile next to them.

"I don't think I'm ready." Melanie flipped page after page, scanning the contents and rejecting the ideas forming in her mind. She wasn't lazy, but she wanted to make sure whatever she chose would give her the motivation needed to finish quickly. She had two other projects coming due around the same time, and she figured the quicker the better.

"To call him?" Rickie asked, glancing up before going back to her book.

"For what comes after," Melanie replied, putting down the magazine and choosing a newspaper.

"What will come after?" Rickie asked, reaching between them for a pretzel from the bowl.

"You know..." Melanie said, shrugging, starting to feel hounded.

"I don't. You haven't called him," Rickie said, giving Melanie her undivided attention. "The man is fine. He's Philip Michael

Thomas and Blair Underwood all rolled into one, so I know that isn't the case."

Rickie's eyes became as big as saucers. "If I am your first friend since you were young, is he going to be your first ki**?"

"Nope." Melanie held up her hand and looked away, stating, in no uncertain terms, that the topic of her innocence would not be up for discussion.

Melanie pressed her lips together to keep from smiling. Rickie had a huge crush on Thomas' character on *Miami Vice*. The fact that Marc was worthy of a comparison rated him high in Rickie's book.

Melanie rolled to her side giving voice to the thoughts running back and forth across her mind over the last few days.

"If I call him and we hit it off then he'll want to date me, and if I accept, and the date is good, then I'll want to see him again. If I see him again, then I will want to see him more, and I don't have time to see him more. I barely have time to study and hang out with you and the girls now. I have obligations at home. I don't think me telling my parents that I'm too busy dating and going out with my friends would be a good excuse for not finishing my chores."

"First of all, if I am your first friend since you were twelve, as you mentioned, your parents owe you a life. Second, you are eighteen. You are no longer a minor. They have to give you some freedom."

Melanie spread her hands out wide. "This is it. I have the freedom of choosing my classes and hanging out until four or five o'clock every day even though my classes sometimes end at two."

Rickie got really serious for a moment. "Was your family part of a cult before you moved here?"

Melanie was about to deny it when she saw the small twitch of Rickie's lips.

She sucked her teeth at her friend. "Whatever."

"You know there was one word that you used over and over in your reason for not calling Marc that I find telling," Rickie said with a smug look.

Melanie wasn't sure she wanted to know where Rickie was going with her sentence but asked anyway. "What word?"

"If. You used the word 'if' like eight times to explain why you don't want to take a chance on a very beautiful man who dresses nicely and is obviously into you." Rickie sat up and scooted closer to Melanie.

"Do you not like beautiful, nicely dressed men who are obviously into you?"

Melanie pushed at her friend to get her both out of her face and out of her business, though neither worked. "Number one, I only used 'if' three times." She'd gone back to her sentence and counted. "Two I like beautiful, nicely dressed men just fine. I just don't have time for them."

"What if he can take you away from your life of Cinderelladom?"

"What? Is that really a thing? I think you've been reading too many fairy tales." Melanie laughed.

"Think about it, Mel. You are taking more than the average number of courses."

"My point exactly. No time."

Rickie held up a forefinger. "Did you really just interrupt me?" She made a circle with her head and neck, making Melanie wonder if all of her vertebrae were attached.

Melanie raised a hand in surrender. "Go ahead."

"Your course load makes me think that you are either rushing through your courses, or you have nothing better to give your attention to. You leave campus by four or five each day, and you don't come back for any of the games or parties. You say you have to be home in time to cook for your dad and sister since your mom works nights. Can't he cook a night or two? Then there is that thing called takeout.

It would be a little different if your sister was your daughter, and you had to get home to take care of her, but I think this is just them taking advantage of you."

Melanie worked to keep her reactions to herself. Rickie was way too close, though Melanie did take in some of what she was saying. It had been that way for so long, Melanie had just gone with it. She didn't want to rock the boat since she had more freedom than she'd ever had before. She resigned herself to taking it step by step. Right now she would concentrate on school and having new friends. The whole dating thing would need to wait.

"Rickie. I'm here to go to school. My scholarship is for taking classes, getting exceptional grades and graduating with some type of honors that will prove to my sponsors that they made a good choice by investing in me. My scholarship does not cover meeting men in cafés no matter how hot they are, then developing a relationship that will take time from those studies."

Melanie watched Rickie's face fall as she continued to talk, and felt guilty. Then she felt angry for feeling guilty about disappointing Rickie.

"Okay, before you make up your mind and consider this conversation moot, may I say something?"

"Sure. It's your dorm," Melanie said, trying to give Rickie the impression of nonchalance.

"You two look like you had a serious connection. He couldn't take his eyes off you from what I could tell, and you didn't seem to fare much better. I'm not saying that your reactions will automatically lead to a happily ever after, but I want to tell you that your type of chemistry isn't common." Rickie lay back down, face up.

"I know I might seem like I have it all together, but things aren't always what they seem." Rickie diverted her eyes from Melanie. "I have three sisters and three brothers, all of them younger than me. I'm the first in my family to go to college, and I almost didn't come." Rickie's voice took on a trancelike quality.

"My family doesn't have much, but we are close. My dad owns a consignment shop and a small store in our town outside of Buffalo. My mom runs the shop, and my dad manages the store. The rest of us float in between. I'm the second oldest. My brother

Samuel helps make deliveries between the two businesses while he goes to the community college at night.

Isabella and Estell are two years behind me in school. They are identical twins, but they couldn't be more different. Isabella plays soccer, and Estell is our mathematician. She's been doing the books for the family businesses for a couple of years now.

Raymond and Hector do most of the stocking and some sales now that they are thirteen and fourteen respectively, and little Martha, at ten, is our fashion expert so you can usually find her dressing a mannequin, working on the consignment shop displays or selling women things they don't need." Rickie smiled wistfully to herself.

"I miss them every day. When I got the letter stating that I received the partial scholarship I needed, I still had to think about coming here. I was afraid more than I was happy. If I hadn't gotten the funds, I would have happily joined my brother in community college this fall, and I would have continued to help my dad in the store. I changed my mind almost daily from the moment I received the letter of acceptance. I knew this would change my life, hopefully for the better, but I would be farther from my family and everything I knew than I'd ever been."

Melanie listened to her friend, wondering if she forgot that she was arguing against her decision to keep her academic career a priority to the degree that she would forego a personal relationship for the present.

"Two days before I had to make my final decision on whether or not to go, my mother came to my room and told me that she'd been in much the same position when she'd met my dad. She'd known of him for years in their small town. She might have even had a crush on him, but it was known that he was going to leave Puerto Rico for the continental United States, and she couldn't imagine leaving her family and home.

When he approached her, she told him she wasn't interested in him even though she said he made her heart beat faster and stomach do flip-flops."

"Are you sure she just wasn't allergic to him?" Melanie said with a giggle. The look Rickie gave her silenced her quickly.

"Anyway," Rickie said with a roll of her eyes, "My dad kept asking and doing things to show her that he really liked her. He finally convinced her to go out with him and allow him to court her. He promised to give her a family of her own so she wouldn't be so lonely, but also to do what he could to either bring their families to live close or have my mother visit her family on occasion.

When telephone lines were put up in their town in Puerto Rico, he made sure her and his family had phones so they could talk every week. He also saved so after the first year, her mother and father could come and visit once a year. Once she was pregnant with their first child, he didn't want my mom traveling by herself. It was a pull on their savings but it was a promise he kept.

My mom said it was the best decision she'd ever made. Was she lonely and afraid at first? Sure. But she said her mother told her that regret was a thankless bedfellow that sucked at the life in you while you were asleep."

Melanie thought Rickie's grandmother may have been putting too much on it, but who was she to say so.

"My mom told me much the same about accepting the opportunity to go to school at a four-year university. It's hard. At night it's way too quiet, and I want to call to just hear their voices, but I can't use all of my money on long-distance bills."

Melanie was more than a little envious of the closeness of Rickie's family. She could feel the love in Rickie's voice while she told the story. When Rickie paused, Melanie blinked at her.

"What do you think?"

"I think it's a great story. Your dad must really love your mother and vice versa."

Rickie smiled dreamily. "Yes. They are still very much in love, but the point I was trying to make was more about taking a chance on the things you want. I don't want you waking up one day to realize that you regret never calling this guy."

Melanie opened her mouth, but Rickie stayed her with a hand. "I'm not saying this is a match made in heaven, but I think you owe it to yourself to at least give him a call."

Melanie considered Rickie's story and words, but the heaviness of guilt that had been slowly releasing its grip on her heart over the years was back with full force. She would rather stay by herself than subject someone else to her mother.

Melanie agreed—regret was a kicker—but she just couldn't risk the regret of accepting Marc in her life outweighing the regret of rejecting him.

Melanie thought of a love that would give her the courage to reach for the dreams she'd set aside in her mind, but no matter what Rickie had said, her life was nowhere near a fairy tale. She recited what she'd told herself the year after it became clear that her knight in shining armor wouldn't come back to rescue her: *happy endings are what she makes for herself.*

Chapter 11

Marc sat in his car five houses down from Melanie's home. He'd watched as she walked to the subway line after class and had driven to the station where she got off to walk the few blocks home. She seemed preoccupied today. She didn't watch her surroundings as she usually did. She looked as though she were daydreaming. As soon as the thought entered his mind, he wondered if she'd met someone else. Maybe there was someone from one of her classes. It was a possibility, since she hadn't called him.

After his visit with Mr. Sable, Marc welcomed the time to come to terms with what he'd learned about Grace Melanie's past. He'd been tempted to visit the café daily to confront her and try to convince her to use the number he'd given her. He didn't go anywhere near the place even when Finn invited him to join him for lunch. He knew if he could approach her he would, but he really wanted her to come to him.

He watched her round the corner to her street. Fall was giving way to winter, and she was dressing with more layers. Today she had on a pair of stonewashed jeans and a pink button-down shirt with a cream cardigan and brown boots. Her eyes were downcast, and he wondered if they shone against everything she wore.

Her steps slowed a little as she neared her home, and he wondered, not for the first time, if her mother was the cause. From what Mr. Sable had shared she was a piece of work. He had a hard time seeing her through the same lens as Mr. Sable, since she was the main cause for Melanie's haunted eyes.

Once he'd heard the front door close behind her, Marc drove away. He needed to go by the store and pick up a few items his mother asked for earlier in the day before going over for dinner. He wondered if he was really careful about the details, if he could ask his mother what he might do to get Melanie to call him. He'd been thinking about it since she'd called him the day before.

By the time he pulled in front of his parent's home, he decided not to bring it up. If she saw something different about him, he would explain his dilemma at that time.

   ***

Dinner was animated. His eldest sister, Laura, arrived with her husband, Ben, and their two children: Katherine, a precocious five-year-old named after his mother and currently in love with astronauts, and Benjamin Jr., still in a carrier but gurgling and smiling at Marc whenever he came into view.

Noana, Marc's youngest sister opened the door giving him a wonderful surprise, since the last time he heard, she was working for a think tank in Virginia that focused on analyzing arms control and nuclear reduction.

"How's the thinking going, sis?" he asked as he gave her a long hug. "Have you made the world a safer place yet?"

She stepped out of his arms, a huge smile on her face. "Getting closer every day."

He gave her another quick hug. "Good."

He followed her through the house, grocery bag in hand.

"Ma. Marcus is here," Noana practically yelled through the house.

"Girl, I told you about that yelling," his mother said, peeking out the kitchen door.

Noana glanced at Marc, giving him one of her mischievous grins.

"Why do you do that when you know you're going to get in trouble?"

"I'm only here through the weekend. I have to make every moment count," Noana said in a stage whisper.

"You are still a little stinker."

"Yep, and don't you forget it," she said, leaving him at the kitchen door as she went back to set the table.

He walked in the kitchen right up to his mother and planted a kiss on her unlined cheek. She kissed him back on his cheek. "How're you doing?"

"Good, Ma," he said, placing the bag on the formica countertop and setting its contents out in a row.

He moved to the oven, lifting a lid off one of the pots on the stove to take a deep whiff. It smelled like love. He adored his mother's cooking. There were many days that were made better by her meals. Today was no different.

"Good?" Katherine Miller asked, standing in the middle of the kitchen watching him.

He turned to catch her intense gaze on him. He often wondered how she could create such different expressions than his with eyes identical in color to his.

"Yeah, Good," he said, giving her his most convincing smile.

"Hmph."

"What's that supposed to mean?" he asked, curious about what she was getting at as he leaned against the counter.

"When I ask my children how they're doing, I usually expect them to tell me the truth. Well…" She paused to think for a couple of breaths. "I do when they aren't lying to themselves. Are you lying to yourself, son?"

Marc reluctantly shook his head in the negative.

"So?"

"So I'm just not sure how to express my dilemma." He looked over at the sliced vegetables on the counter to avoid her eyes. He reached for one.

"Touch that, and you owe me a full explanation," she said, turning back to the stove.

"I'm hungry," he replied, trying to lighten the mood in the suddenly claustrophobic room, but from the look she gave him when she turned back, he'd failed.

"Don't sass me, boy." Her stern look made him feel contrite.

"Sorry Ma," he said, a hand still hovering over the carrot.

She nodded at it, and he picked it up and took a bite, taking advantage of the small reprieve.

Katherine Miller was a woman small in stature but huge in faith and presence. She was the disciplinarian in the family, and many times that didn't mean raising her voice or her hand. She had this beauty and love about her that she wielded, not like a sword but like a magic wand. It probably wasn't the best illustration since the word magic didn't have anything to do with the way she affected people.

He, like her other children, loved her so deeply. They revered her because she didn't only teach them to be courteous, honest, generous and give their all in each part of their lives, she lived it. She was also one of the wisest women he had ever known.

"Your brother and sisters are not going to be too happy with you delaying dinner, so I suggest you start talking if you want to leave here tonight with some sort of solution."

Marc pinched his lips together to keep from smiling. It must have been quite a while since he'd come to her with an issue, because she was milking this.

"There is this woman," he said before realizing he was starting in the middle of the story. It was too late though. He'd gotten his mother's attention.

She turned to him, ladle in hand, sauce dripping. Her lips tilted up at the edges, but the gleam in her eye had him stepping back.

"Noana, come in here," his mother nearly shouted. His mother didn't shout. She barely raised her voice above the octave it took to be heard across a room.

Wait. What was she calling Noana for?

Noana appeared in the doorway. "Yes?"

"I need you to come stir this sauce for me and put those vegetables on the platter on the table. Do you think you can do that?"

Noana glanced at Marc probably assessing how much trouble he was in, then back at their mother. "Yes, ma'am."

"If I'm not back in ten minutes, I need you to take the roast out of the oven. If it burns, we are having curry chicken from that small restaurant on Middleton Street, and you're paying."

"But I don't like curry, Noana said, looking perplexed.

"Exactly," their mother said before moving to the door leading to the den.

"Are you coming?" she said, directing her gaze at Marc.

Marc wiped the smile off his face and followed after his mother. He ignored the snicker coming from the kitchen.

They were seated in his mother's favorite room, on couches sitting adjacent to one another.

"Okay, so you met a girl," she said when they were situated.

"Well, actually I've seen her before. She was a child I had to run surveillance for."

"Child?" Her brows furrowed.

"Child, as in sixteen, four years ago, and I hadn't seen her since until two weeks ago," he explained until her brows relaxed.

"Go on," she said with a nod.

He was a little surprised she didn't ask him why she was under surveillance four years ago, but who really knew what went on in her mind.

"Like I said I saw her again two weeks ago and talked to her for a moment." He couldn't keep his neck and face from heating when he remembered what Grace Melanie looked like, and caught his mom watching him.

"We seemed to hit it off, but she never called."

"How do you know you two hit it off, as you say?"

Marc scratched his chin trying to explain the fireworks that went off when he came face-to-face with Grace Melanie. "Well, uh, besides the chemistry, we had a brief conversation while she was in line waiting for her order. It wasn't much time, but I felt the connection, and I could see by her body language that she felt it too."

"So with all of these feelings between the two of you, why do you think she didn't call you?" His mother's steely-eyed gaze made him feel more like a person of interest being interrogated than her son.

"There's a little more to it," Marc said, then shared as little as he could about being hired to watch her and why. When he was done, his mother was shaking her head.

"You are setting yourself up for a hard time, Marc," his mom said with worried eyes.

"I would like to show you a clear path on this, but there are so many crooked lines in this story I would rather warn you against getting involved with her."

Marc shrugged. "It's too late."

"Too late?" his mother repeated.

Marc nodded solemnly.

"Oh," his mother said quietly.

"Yep."

She took a deep breath. "All right. Why do you think she didn't call you back?"

"She's smarter than me?"

"That's definitely a possibility, but if her mother is half the character you describe, then she's probably very cautious about letting anyone into her life."

"So how do I get her to change her mind?"

"You don't."

"What?"

"You continue being the man I know you are, and she'll see that you are worth taking a chance with."

Marc wondered if she were speaking in code. That could take weeks or months depending on how many opportunities he had to interact with her. He considered her words some more, and an idea began to form.

"Thank you, Ma." He leaned forward and kissed her cheek.

She patted his hand, but the worry didn't leave her eyes.

"I'll be careful," he said, trying to appease her. He didn't like feeling that he'd caused her undue concern.

She gave him a shadow of a smile, letting him know she would be spending extra time praying for him that night, and he wasn't sure it wouldn't be warranted.

His mother's discernment had served them all well. If she were bothered by something, there was a good reason.

"Ma?" he questioned when she hadn't moved.

She raised a hand. "I'm fine. Come on, let's get back in the kitchen before Noana ruins dinner."

She rose from the couch and took the arm he offered. "Why you can't do things easily, I don't know."

Marc shrugged. "Me either, Ma. Me either."

Chapter 12

Melanie noted to herself that almost three weeks had gone by since she'd accepted one of her friend's invitations to the café. She knew she was being a coward, but if she ran into Marc, she didn't know which would be harder on her—him forgiving her and asking her again to give him a call, or him giving her the cold shoulder, believing she'd snubbed him. Well she had, hadn't she? It just wasn't that cut and dried. She really wanted to call him and would have if she thought talking to him and going out with him would be lighthearted fun. There was nothing lighthearted about the way he looked at her or the way she reacted to him. She'd light up like fireworks, and being in his presence any length of time would either burn her out or set everything around them on fire including her future.

Melanie scanned the café as they walked in and sighed in relief when she didn't see Marc or his friend. They walked to their table where Rickie and Sophia were waiting.

"I'm so glad you joined us today," Sophia said with an overly bright smile.

"I said I would, but your giddiness at my presence is a little suspect," Melanie said, giving Sophia a small frown.

"You caught me. I wanted to show you someone."

Melanie froze at Sophia's words. Her face must have shown her horror because Sophia reached out a hand, laying it on hers in a calming gesture and whispering, "For me."

Melanie's whole body warmed and melted. The smile she gave Sophia, she felt all the way to her toes.

"Okay." She looked around the café trying to guess at whom Sophia was talking about.

"Who is he?" Melanie asked when her perusal around the room rendered no clue.

"He's on his way," Sophia said shyly.

Melanie looked around the table at Rickie and Katrina. "Have you met him?"

"We've seen him but not officially met him," Rickie said. Melanie looked each one of them in the eye then looked back at Sophia.

"How did you meet him?" Melanie asked.

"He's the teaching assistant for my French literature class," Sophia replied.

Melanie sighed, a little relieved that he was someone that was around and easily traceable.

"What's his name?" Melanie asked, wondering why none of the other women were asking questions. Weren't they interested or concerned?

"Allen Resnick," Sophia said.

"What's he like? How did he approach you?" Melanie asked, looking around again. Rickie and Katherine looked interested but kept quiet.

"He's nice and crazy intelligent. He's extremely handsome. He totally doesn't look like a man who knows anything about

Vulgar Latin, and he told me that I'm one of the most beautiful women he's ever seen."

"How long has he been a teaching assistant?" Melanie asked, starting to feel like she was the last one to the party.

"Two years, but this is his first year working here."

"Really? Where was he before?" Melanie asked.

"Michigan. No. Missouri," Sophia answered, sounding unsure.

"Okay. How old is he? Where's he from?" Melanie asked and would have continued if it weren't for Sophia's look.

"What?"

"Why are you interrogating me?" Sophia asked, sounding defensive.

"What? I'm just asking you questions about him." Melanie looked at Katrina and Rickie before looking back at Sophia.

"Maybe it seems like an interrogation because I'm the only one asking questions. Why am I the only one asking questions?" She looked to Rickie and Katrina.

Rickie shrugged. "Because you're doing such a great job of asking questions. We'd don't know much about him either except that Sophia met him in her French literature class and has been talking to him for about a week now."

"Don't you want to know more about him?"

"Yes, but you seem to be asking all the important questions, so we figured we would just let you continue."

"Important questions? What questions do you have?"

"If he is as fine as Sophia says he is, does he have any brothers? It's kind of risky to date your TA. What if things go wrong? Will that have an effect on your grades?"

"You two were right to let me ask the questions," Melanie said, looking pointedly at Katrina and Rickie. They looked back at her sheepishly, which had alarms going off in her head.

"Okay. What's going on?"

"I would really like you to go out with us tonight," Sophia said, her voice raising in a plea at the end of her sentence.

"What?" It was the last thing she expected to hear but was still oddly disappointed it wasn't her first assumption.

"Allen is giving a party, and I would feel more comfortable if all of you are there."

Melanie's first thought was to respond with a resounding, "No," but as she looked at her friends' faces and considered Sophia's request, she wondered when she would truly start living.

"What time's the party?"

"It starts at nine," Sophia said with hope in her voice.

Melanie thought about it. That would give her enough time to finish dinner, put Paige to bed and get back to this part of town. "Everyone's going?"

She watched all of her friends nod. "Okay. Could you give me a ride if I meet you here, Katrina?"

"Sure," Katrina said, looking at her in surprise.

"Um. There's something else," Sophia said even more hesitantly.

Melanie blinked, not sure she could take much more suspense. "Okay."

"We all have dates for the party."

"Huh?" She shook her head. "What?"

"Allen has a few friends he works with. He asked if I had some friends and I told him I would ask. You don't have to pair up with anyone. I told him I would ask though."

"I don't feel comfortable with the blind quadruple date, but I'm still willing to go to the party," Melanie said as a consolation.

Sophia shrugged and smiled. "I think we will have a great time."

Melanie looked again at Katrina and Rickie who were now looking toward the door.

The man walking through the door was supermodel material with jet-black hair cut low on the sides and long enough at the top to hang over his forehead. She couldn't tell what color his eyes were from this distance, but the rest of his face was so perfectly asymmetrical that it didn't really matter. He was tall with broad shoulders and an equally broad chest. His physique tapered down to a slim waist and hips, then to long legs. He was gorgeous.

Melanie pulled her eyes away from the man to see if he were who Sophia had been talking about. With one glance she knew by the dreamy-eyed look her friend was sporting that the Christopher Reeve look-alike was Allen Resnick.

He walked over, his long strides bringing him to their table with a fluidity she'd not seen a man use before. To be fair, she didn't make a habit of watching men walk. Marc had a nice walk. She shook her head to rid herself of the thought.

Melanie blinked around a low ray of sun blocking her vision and blinked again when he stood in front of it, giving her a clear view. She didn't know if she expected him to be even better looking up close, but he wasn't. He looked artificial. She had a hard time putting her finger on it.

Sophia introduced Allen to Rickie and Katrina. When Allen turned and held out his hand to her, his eyes roamed over her face and body in the oddest way. It wasn't like he was leering at her, but sizing her up like a piece of meat. She shook his hand then quickly pulled away, not liking the feel of his limp hand in hers.

His lips lifted, and she saw her mother's smile. It was predatory and...wrong.

Melanie looked around the table to see if any of the other women saw it, but they had much the same expression as Sophia.

She kept a benign and open expression on her face as he slid into the booth. Rickie, Katrina and Sophia took turns asking him questions, and he was very charming, but she struggled to ignore what she'd seen so she could fully participate.

She concentrated on listening to the conversation instead of getting stuck in her cycle of thoughts, and managed to garner a few smiles from Sophia when she asked a few poignant questions of her own.

"How did you come to work at the university?" Rickie asked after taking a sip of her hot chocolate.

"I transferred over after last year. I was a TA for an English literature class which was all right, but my first love is the French classics. I've been waiting for quite a while for that class, and now I've found even more worth waiting for.

The sighs around the table sounded like a television sitcom soundtrack. It was a sweet sentiment, but in his line of work, he had plenty of material. Melanie mentally smacked her hand for being so cynical. He could be genuine.

"Is it your full-time job?" Katrina asked him, bringing Melanie back to the conversation.

"I work with a group of guys. We have started a security system company for bigger corporations. It's not like sitting at Victor Hugo's feet but it pays the bills," Allen said with a boyish grin, putting a sparkle in his grayish-blue eyes.

Melanie watched Katrina's eyes dilate. The first line of defense was gone. Melanie mentally shook her head.

"Do you have family in the area?" Rickie asked.

"No. I had a small family," he said, and Melanie saw him squeeze Sophia's hand a little.

"I lost them in a bombing, but that was a long time ago. I have a new family now in my friends." He rubbed his cheek against the back side of Sophia's hand he'd been holding as if the movement soothed him.

Melanie didn't even have to look at Rickie to know he'd won her heart.

She was the last woman standing.

"Have you dated students from any of your other classes?" Melanie asked him.

Though his eyes showed surprise for a couple of seconds, he didn't seem offended in the least.

"I'm afraid I didn't date much in high school or college. I've been a bit preoccupied with my studies and work to date." He looked at Sophia in a way that made Melanie blush.

"Sophia's actually the first woman I've dated," he said with a sheepish grin that would have had the most hardened heart melting.

Melanie hoped for Sophia's sake that she was wrong about what she'd seen those first couple of seconds, but she wasn't holding her breath.

"Do you hold parties often?" Melanie asked, wondering if she could get any peek into his lifestyle.

"No, I'm thinking of this party as a celebration of finding Sophia," he said, taking Sophia's hand. The contrast between her ebony skin color and his fair complexion was striking. Melanie watched as Allen linked his perfectly manicured fingers with her lean, purple-tipped ones.

The thought of Sophia in the beginnings of a new relationship sent a small pang of envy through Melanie. It was only natural, she told herself, but it made her even more protective of her friend and at the same time hesitant about telling anyone what she felt.

"I was hoping you all could come. I think it would be nice for my friends to meet you. Sophia's friends and my friends. It's a perfect match since I have three and she has three," he said, glancing at all of us.

"We're all coming," Rickie said with a wide grin.

"Ah. That's wonderful. I'm going to have to break out the champagne or apple cider," he added, when the light shining in Rickie's eyes dimmed a little.

Melanie worked hard to keep her smile in place and the thoughts at bay.

  ***

On the ride home, Melanie went back and forth regarding her decision to go to the party.

She just felt like something was wrong, but she didn't want to be the one to rain on Sophia's date night as it were.

On her way home, Melanie considered a few different safety plans in case things went wrong at the party. She could tell her dad where she was going but maybe not tell him any of her concerns. Sure, she might get grounded until she was fifty if it came out that she had a bad feeling.

She could tell her father where she was going as well as share her concerns, but then she didn't think he would allow her to go, which would keep her friends in trouble.

Marc said he was in law enforcement. Though she didn't know what kind, she assumed he was a policeman or a detective since he was dressed in plain clothing the day that she met him. She could maybe give him a call and let him know about the party. But that would be awkward since she hadn't called him back in the last three weeks. Her mind continued to work through different scenarios. Maybe she was just being paranoid. Maybe it was just another side effect of growing up with her mother. An image of Allen's smile came to her and reaffirmed her commitment to have some type of backup plan.

As Melanie walked through the station, she considered telling Sophia how she felt, but it could easily be mistaken jealousy or pettiness and ignored—then they would all be right back where she was at the moment.

During her walk, she discarded the thought of contacting Marc. Calling Marc for the purpose of garnering protection sounded selfish and completely inconsiderate and might ruin her chances with him if she decided to change her mind.

She could. It had only been three weeks. She could still call him. She took a few more steps. She was kidding herself. She wasn't going to call him.

By the time she turned onto her street, Melanie had chosen to tell her father that she was going to a party with friends. She would give him the address and let him know what time she would be back. The thought of the protection it would give her friends this evening gave her a modicum of relief.

Melanie nodded her head, feeling better about the evening to come. She was so preoccupied with her thoughts, she never saw the car sitting at the end of her street.

Chapter 13

Melanie pulled her coat a little closer around her as they walked up the short but wide-set steps to one of the most beautiful homes she'd ever seen. She wobbled a little on the high heels she borrowed from her mother's closet. They went with the wine-colored velvet dress that she also borrowed. She had to admit when she tried it on, she was pleasantly surprised by her reflection. After years of hiding her figure underneath layers of clothing, she'd begun to wear outfits that fit and complimented her medium-sized frame.

It was odd how her perspective had changed over the last month and a half. She had worked so hard to disappear after having Paige. The baby weight had come off easily with her daily walks on the old roller-style treadmill in the garage, and then constantly running behind Paige.

She'd inherited her mother's curvy shape, but the three inches of height she had on her mom gave her a more proportioned hourglass figure.

The dress had a short skirt that swished around her legs. It outlined her curves, but at least it wasn't as snug as the little black one she'd tried on first. It had long sleeves and a satin collar which she thought was ironic, since her bare legs were now cold.

The four of them were dressed much the same way. Rickie's dress was also on the shorter side but it was a deep-blue knit dress that stopped just above her knees. The matching bolero jacket accentuated her small waist. Katrina wore a black sheath dress with short sleeves and Sophia wore a sleeveless cream dress with a cream lacey-knit overlay with long sleeves. The color enhanced her darker complexion.

Melanie had worn her long coat back to the café, thankful it stopped near her ankles. She was surprised to see Rickie and Sophia in the back of Katrina's car when she opened the passenger door. She was relieved to know that they would all arrive together, which to her meant they would all leave together.

Melanie was the last one of their group to walk through the door at the party. She wanted to make sure the four of them stayed together and that she was in a position to watch everyone.

It was hard though. The place was opulently decorated. The front door opened to a vaulted ceiling entryway with small diamond-shaped mirrors on the walls making the area look like it sparkled. Their jackets and coats were exchanged for tickets at an alcove under the stairs. They walked under an archway and followed those who'd arrived just before them through an open door to the left. Three steps down, and Melanie found herself in the sunken living room that rivaled the size of the first story of her home.

The décor was done in ivory, cream and woods of all shades. This house was not just a home, it was a showpiece. A very expensive showpiece. Much too expensive for a teaching assistant. *The security systems business with his friends must do well.*

If Melanie had not been on alert before, she definitely was now.

She kept close to Katrina who was in front of her as they made their way through the small gathering of people.

Melanie noticed there were more women than men, and the men were dressed in expensive suits ranging between mid-to-late twenties and early fifties. She also noticed that there were very few people of color. She was sure she and her friends stood out like the United Nations they were. She scanned the room as her heels sank into the extremely thick carpet. She looked toward, hearing Rickie say something to Sophia, but the music accompanied by the hum of conversation made it hard to comprehend.

Melanie felt exposed as she passed a few men sitting on a set of couches facing one another. She smiled briefly, not wanting to come off as too friendly or rude. She was hoping not to make much of an impression. The slow nods and leering stares taking in her person from her uncomfortably high heels to her curly hair told her not to hold out hope.

Still, she fought back the warning beating in her heart and continued to move forward with her friend. This was an unfamiliar world, so she would reserve judgment for later.

Melanie's attention was pulled toward the small laugh she recognized as Sophia's and watched as Allen came forward, giving her a long hug. He was accompanied by three other gentlemen who looked close to his age. These must be his friends he wanted them to meet. Melanie had been so preoccupied with the party as a whole, she'd forgotten about Allen's friends.

They were all as beautiful as he was, but only one of them shared his predatory gaze. She would make sure to steer clear of him.

Melanie pasted a friendly smile on her face and watched as Allen made introductions. Claude was tall with intelligent green-hazel eyes, dark brown hair and a friendly enough smile. His focus narrowed on Katrina right away, and Melanie felt no qualms about it either way. Nor did she feel any dissidence when Paul, a young man with dark blond hair and brown eyes, locked gazes with her. He seemed nice enough, and his studious, almost nerdy appearance made her feel a little more comfortable.

It was Ward, the man whose gaze zeroed in on Rickie, that had her alarm bells ringing. He wasn't overt with his appraisal, but she saw his eyes rest just a little too long on her friend's chest when Allen was making introductions for others, and he looked around the room as if he were gracing people with his presence. She was not impressed.

Allen's stare had cooled some when it came to her. It probably had something to do with her questions earlier that day, but he was still friendly enough when he introduced her to his friends.

Try though she might to keep all of her friends within earshot, as the night drew on, the girls separated as their male companions got them drinks, introduced them to more friends, and they took to the dance floor in another room.

Around eleven thirty, Melanie's energy began to lag, and she turned Paul down for another dance. Paul might have been someone Melanie would have befriended if they were in class together. He was easy to talk to and pretty much catered to her the whole evening. It did little to assuage her concern over her friends, especially when they were out of her sight.

147

Melanie faked having to go to the restroom so that she could set eyes on all of her friends. She found Sophia on the dance floor dancing with Allen. Rickie was near the bar she'd sent Paul to three times that night: each time for a Shirley Temple. She loved the cherry-flavored Sprite drink. It took some searching to find Katrina, but Melanie spotted her sitting on a lounge chair near the pool talking with Claude and a group of people. Melanie smiled to herself. The way Claude was hanging on her every word, Katrina wouldn't be able to get away without giving him someone's number.

She headed back to Paul, taking the long way to stretch her legs. She entered the room behind the bar with the intention to wave at Rickie when she saw Ward slip something into a drink. Melanie paused to watch for a moment, wanting to make sure she wasn't imagining anything. Her mind spun. It was one thing to expect deceitfulness and another to witness it.

She moved forward with deliberate strides, her vision tunneling in on the glass being carried by Ward. She stared, unable to take her eyes off the glass as Rickie's hands closed around it and brought it up to her lips.

Unable to think of a better plan, Melanie forced herself to stumble but had a hard time catching herself in her heels, and instead of knocking the glass free, the glass and its contents ended up all over Rickie. Melanie righted herself, covering her mouth in horror.

"Oh my gosh. I'm so sorry. I really am," she said, reaching behind Ward for a napkin. Rickie looked at her wide-eyed for a few seconds then burst out laughing.

"Girl, you should see your face." It wasn't the response Melanie had expected but she would take it.

"Come on. Let me take you to the bathroom to see if we can get it before it dries," Melanie said, taking her hand. She glanced up at Ward briefly, seeing the hard set of his mouth. She was going to apologize to him, too, but changed her mind when she saw his eyes narrow.

It was time to go home.

Melanie guided Rickie from the room, holding her elbow so they didn't get separated. She accompanied Rickie to the bathroom and retrieved a couple of hand towels to help dab the liquid from her dress.

"I'm so sorry. What were you drinking?" Melanie said as she dabbed.

"Ginger ale," Rickie said, which explained why she wasn't panicking.

"Oh," Melanie said, straightening and handing Rickie the other hand towel.

"Good, because we need to go, and I would have felt bad about ruining your dress on top of ruining any hopes you may have for a match with Ward."

More than a few expressions crossed Rickie's face. "Wait. What?"

"I saw Ward put a pill in your drink when you weren't looking. I tripped on purpose to knock the drink out of your hand, but I couldn't catch myself before running into you." Melanie waited for Rickie to absorb her words.

149

"What? What kind of pill?" Rickie asked, halfway between confused and affronted.

"The white kind you don't want a woman to know you are putting in her drink," Melanie said.

Rickie's eyes rounded. "No."

Melanie just nodded.

"That rat," Rickie said between clenched teeth, her face turning red then pale.

"What about Katrina and Sophia? We need to make sure the other guys don't do anything," Rickie said, putting more effort into drying her dress.

"I was coming back from checking on them when I saw what Ward did," Melanie said, not feeling the assurance she was trying to give Rickie.

Rickie started moving quicker.

"Come on, I think I need to find a phone," Melanie said, walking toward the bathroom door.

"Why?" Rickie asked, straightening her dress.

"Because I believe in having a plan," Melanie said in a whisper.

"Who're you going to call?" Rickie asked, whispering back.

"No one yet, but if Katrina or Sophia have been harmed I'm calling my dad," Melanie said, wondering why Rickie was whispering.

"Who's your dad?" Rickie asked with hope in her voice.

"A colonel."

Rickie frowned. "I don't understand. Colonel of what?"

"Colonel in the air force," Melanie said, trying to convince Rickie of the relevancy of her reasoning.

Rickie blinked at her and opened her mouth.

"Never mind. We need to go," Melanie said, grabbing Rickie's arm and pulling her out the door.

Melanie looked into two rooms as they walked down the hall to the back of the house to the pool. In one room, she spied a phone sitting on a huge desk and noted which way they'd come.

They walked out to the pool area, and Melanie scanned the place where she'd seen Katrina before. Her friend was nowhere to be seen and neither was Claude.

"I thought you said she was out here?"

"She was."

Melanie and Rickie walked over to the group and asked if they'd seen where Katrina went. One of the girls said Katrina wasn't feeling well, and Claude had just taken her to the bathroom off the side door.

Rickie and Melanie walked as quickly as they could to the side door, finding the restroom exactly where the girl said—empty.

Panic rose in Melanie, and her forehead broke out in perspiration. *Where was Katrina?*

Melanie turned almost in a circle when she heard a sound that didn't go with the laughter outside or the music streaming from the makeshift dance room. She strained her ears to hear what the sound was and where it was coming from. There was a thud against the door they were passing. Melanie looked at Rickie before placing her hand on the doorknob. At Rickie's nod she turned it and opened the door just in time to see Katrina throw up on Claude.

"Oh no, Katrina," Melanie said as they rushed in. Melanie moved Katrina away from the vomit and looked in her friend's eyes. They were glassy, and her pupils were dilated.

Melanie looked up at Claude, anger rolling through her like a fire that just found a newspaper warehouse.

"What did you do?" she asked, her voice a near growl. She opened her mouth to order him to answer, but Rickie's voice interrupted her

"You're ill, honey. Let's get you cleaned up," Rickie said, placing herself under one of Katrina's arms. Melanie took her lead and placed Katrina's other behind her neck. They half walked, half dragged Katrina back down the hall to the bathroom. Melanie was torn between cleaning Katrina up and going to get Sophia.

They sat Katrina on the commode, and Melanie wet a cloth, handing it to Rickie.

"Do you think I should go get Sophia? She's out there alone with Allen," Melanie asked, some of her anger waning in the wake of the fear that filled her.

Rickie looked at Katrina who was blinking rapidly. "Katrina. Do you know who I am?"

Katrina looked at Rickie and smiled. "You're little Rickie." Katrina reached out and patted Rickie on the head like one would a little girl.

Rickie turned to look at Melanie and shook her head when Katrina tried to pinch her cheek.

"Cute little Rickie," Katrina singsonged.

"She seems to be doing good," Melanie said, backing toward the door.

"Don't you leave me in here with her. Just help me clean her up enough to drag her out of here," Rickie said, her voice turning into a hiss.

Melanie came back and helped Rickie clean Katrina and supply her with tap water to rinse with. By the time they were ready to leave the bathroom, Katrina could stand on her own, even though she was a little wobbly. Rickie and Melanie helped her out of the bathroom and started down the hall toward where she last saw Sophia. She half expected Claude or Ward to come out of the woodwork, but no one tried to stop them.

They reached the doorway of the room with the dance floor and came face-to-face with a red-eyed Sophia. "What's wrong?" Melanie asked.

"Where have you been? I've been looking for you guys everywhere. I thought you'd left me," Sophia said, looking to be on the verge of a panic attack herself.

Melanie sent Rickie a huffy look. "We've been tending to Rickie. She isn't feeling well. We came to find you because we need to go."

Sophia seemed to realize that she and Rickie were half-carrying Katrina. "Oh no. What happened?"

153

"All I can say is we think Katrina was drugged, but we can't talk about it here. We need to go," Melanie said before she and Rickie turned to head to the door.

"I need to tell Allen that we are leaving," Sophia said, hesitating.

"No we don't," Rickie said over her shoulder.

"What? Why?" Sophia said, slowly following them.

"We will explain it to you when we get in the car," Melanie chimed in.

"I don't think she should be driving," Sophia said.

Melanie and Rickie slowed. "Katrina may I drive you home?" Melanie asked her.

"You take the subway. You don't drive," Katrina retorted.

"I know how to drive; I just like taking the subway," Melanie said defending herself.

"Who likes to take the subway?" Katrina asked no one in particular, slurring her words.

"May I drive your car, so we can get out of here?" Melanie asked.

Katrina was quiet for a moment and looked thoughtful as they reached the coat check. Melanie and Rickie handed their tags to Sophia. Katrina almost started swaying as she patted her hips as if she had pockets.

"I have your ticket, Katrina," Sophia said. "You gave it to me when we arrived because you had nowhere to put it."

Sophia exchanged the tickets for their coats, and Melanie and Rickie helped Katrina to the door.

They were halfway through the door when Melanie heard Sophia's name.

"Come on. We need to go," Melanie said, trying to pull Katrina and Rickie while pushing Sophia through the door. She'd made it down one step when she came up short at the sight of Marc coming up the walk.

Chapter 14

Marc sat in his car calling himself all kinds of coward. He was an FBI agent. He ran into situations that would turn most people's hair white just thinking about them. However, with all of his bravado, he couldn't get up the courage to approach Melanie again.

He didn't like rejection. Not like anyone did, but it was really rough when the woman who monopolized your thoughts didn't want anything to do with you. He couldn't even send her presents to bring her around to his way of thinking because he wasn't supposed to know where she lived. From what Luca had revealed about her home life, he may want to avoid sending anything to her home anyway. He was a mess. Even his thought process was convoluted and the call he received from Luca as he sat in his kitchen trying to digest yet another unappetizing frozen pizza didn't make things easier.

Melanie rarely went anywhere outside of school and home, which made running into her "by accident" anywhere else almost impossible. When she stopped frequenting the café he figured she was purposely avoiding running into him again.

Her lack of social life was the very reason he had left her street a few minutes after making sure she had safely entered her home. He'd spent hours watching her home after her mother left for work, the heat in his heart making him almost desperate to see how Melanie had fared in her mother's presence. He'd tried to think of any scenario that would allow him to come to her house, but when he couldn't think of one, he began leaving after making sure Melanie was in for the night.

If it wasn't for Luca's call, Melanie would have been out with her friends without proper cover and that meant the kind where he could intervene. It was one of the stipulations of his contract with Luca. If Melanie found herself in trouble, he could step in, whereas the two other men he had on Melanie were only ever to observe, if he were present. It seemed that Luca kept his business close to his chest, only giving out information as needed.

As soon as Marc was given an address to the party, he felt uneasy. It was pretty far from campus in a very upscale part of town. The person holding the party didn't ring any type of bell, but how would a teaching assistant of a college class have the funds for a house in that area. Something didn't add up.

He called headquarters, giving them the address and the person's name to see if anything could be found in the database. When neither yielded satisfactory information, he told the resident researcher, Mitchell, to keep digging and call him on the mobile phone he'd had installed for such instances. Meanwhile, he headed to the home so he could do some light reconnaissance and be there when the girls arrived.

Almost three hours ago, he'd watched Melanie follow the three friends he'd seen her with at the café into the house. Her hair was down, the curls moving as if they had a life of their own. The cool of the night and the high-heeled sandals accentuated what he could see of her ankles around the movement of the long coat she wore. His imagination had gone wild for a moment, but he stopped the images of her outfit as if cutting out part a film. He was here to gather whatever information he could about the nearly impenetrable home and keep her safe.

The sound of the car's mobile phone ringing pulled him out of his thoughts.

Disengaging the receiver, he answered, "This is Miller."

"I received information on that address you gave us," said Mitchell, his voice grave.

Marc's alert level went up a couple of notches. The unease in his gut became an alarm, and he had to tamp down on the instinct to go running into the house without all the information he needed.

What had Melanie stumbled into?

"Go ahead," Marc said with an impatient efficiency that hopefully resonated through the phone.

Mitchell let him know that the home at the address he'd given was up for sale. Marc did a double take at the house with lights shining inside and out, and listened to the low hum of music coming from some of the windows that were covered with what looked like expensive curtains. Earlier when he'd walked around the perimeter of the home looking for anything amiss, he could see some of the furnishings that made up the lavish décor.

He double-checked that the agent had the right address then told him to keep going. The initial information on Allen Resnick didn't yield satisfying results either, and his frustration grew in leaps and bounds.

"You said you had information on the house, Mitchell?" Marc said, working hard to sound calm.

"I was trying to pull up anything I could about Mr. Resnick. I checked out his credentials with the school, and no Allen Resnick works as a TA, but Marshall Colmes does."

"Who is Marshall Colmes?" Marc asked, not recognizing the name.

"One of the heavy hitters in the Wright investigation," Mitchell said.

"How do we know we have the same man?" Marc asked, gathering his keys.

"You are at the address of the brother he put on his emergency contacts." Marc's blood ran cold. He had his hand on the door when he heard Mitchell's voice go up a couple of octaves.

"You have to be careful. It was flagged when I went into the system. This is Merryman's territory. You can't compromise the investigation. It looks like they've been working on this drug trafficking ring for years."

Marc ground his back molars as he thought of a viable explanation for him crashing a party in this area.

How did Melanie get mixed up in things like this? Was she a magnet for the nefarious sort? Sure, Luca was looking out for her, but he was no Santa Claus.

How did he get himself into situations like this? Oh yeah, watching a woman without her knowledge while harboring a deep crush on her. I'm just one paycheck short of being a stalker.

"I won't compromise the investigation, but if I get arrested I need you to vouch for me," Marc said, coming up with a plan. Not a great plan but a plan nonetheless.

"I got you. Who's the girl? Is she one of ours?"

"Um. I gotta go, Mitchell. Tell Merryman I'm not touching his men," Marc said then hung up. He hoped he wouldn't have to touch the man.

He glanced both ways before crossing the street to the house. He had his foot on the first step, when the door opened and out walked Melanie's friend Sophia with Melanie and Rickie following, half holding up a swaying Katrina. He'd made sure he could recognize them in case he needed to find Melanie.

He watched Melanie's eyes scan the street, pass over him and come back. He saw when she recognized him, shock registering on her face. He just took in the sight of her like a thirsty man catching his first glimpse of water. She was beautiful. She'd only had time to don her coat but it hung open, showing the velvet dress she wore.

"Wait. What is he doing here?" he heard Sophia ask in bewilderment. Melanie dragged her gaze away from him and looked at Sophia.

"I haven't seen him since the café."

They both turned and looked at him, waiting for an explanation.

For a heartbeat he was speechless, then his training kicked in, and the urgency of the situation came back to him.

"Young lady, could you close the door?" he said, pointing to Rickie. "I'm here doing surveillance. A number of these cars were being cased. I was coming to see who the owner of that car is." He pointed to the car they'd all arrived in.

Rickie's eyes bugged out. "That's Katrina's car."

"And Katrina is?" he asked.

"It's me. Figures," Katrina said, looking as though she'd had one too many.

"I don't think you're in any position to drive, miss," he said, eyeing her, wondering if it was drugs or alcohol that had her so unsteady. He walked up the steps to help steady her and relieve Rickie and Melanie of her weight. He began assisting her down the stairs, trying to get the women away from the house to avoid any confrontations with the "owner."

"Is anyone else capable of driving her car?" he asked but had to bite his tongue on the retort that wanted to come forward when Melanie raised her hand. After what he'd recently learned about the type of peril they'd just been in, he wasn't pleased about letting her out of his sight.

Katrina stumbled, drawing his attention back to her. "You look a little worse for wear, but I don't smell alcohol on you. Are you okay?" He watched all of the women exchange glances.

"We don't want any trouble—" Rickie began.

Melanie interrupted her. "Katrina just isn't feeling well. I think she ate something that didn't agree with her."

"Okay. Well, do you mind if I make sure that all of you get home safely?"

Three "no's" and a "yes" rang out simultaneously. Everyone turned to Melanie.

"That's all right." All of the women continued to stare at Melanie. She finally shrugged her shoulders.

"I guess that will be fine," she said, a small frown marring her forehead. He watched as she bit her lip in hesitation. At this point they were at Katrina's car.

"No offense because we really appreciate the offer," Melanie said, walking around to the driver's side of the car.

"But we don't know you from Adam. You've shown us no badge or shield, so how do we know you're legit."

Marc actually wanted to smile at her cautiousness, but he pursed his lips. He reached into his back pocket, wishing that he could have revealed this part of his life to her after they started dating or at least once she willingly called him. He would have liked to have won some of her trust first, but he uncovered and showed the women his badge.

While Sophia, Rickie and Katrina visibly relaxed, the sight of his badge had the opposite effect on Melanie. His heart sank at the realization that he might have just hammered the nail in the proverbial coffin of their relationship.

"You said law enforcement," Melanie said, almost in accusation.

Marc nodded at her. "Yes. The FBI is also part of law enforcement."

She seemed to catch herself and try to take on a nonchalant air.

"I thought you just meant the police department."

"Well, sometimes we work together," he said, trying to elicit a smile from her. It didn't work.

"I think we will be fine."

162

"Will you be taking your friend to the hospital?" he asked, seeing another way to keep her in his sights a little longer.

The women looked at each other, seeming to wither under the weight of that decision. "Do you know what it was that she ingested that did not agree with her?" he asked, purposefully using the same language Melanie used.

The women looked at one another again and sighed in resignation.

It looked like they were headed to the hospital. He wanted to clap and rub his hands together. Instead he helped Katrina into the car and waited until everyone else was seated and buckled before he walked around to Melanie sitting behind the wheel.

"Will you please follow me. I know the quickest way to the emergency." He glanced behind her at Katrina, whose head was resting on Rickie's shoulder. All of them looked solemn.

"I don't think there is a great deal to worry about, but I wouldn't be able to sleep without knowing that she is all right," he said, focusing on each of the women in the car.

"That *you* are all right," he said in a softer voice to Melanie. He watched her swallow then nod her acquiescence.

He tapped the door and jogged across the street to get in his car.

He started his engine and turned around on the street so he could lead them out of the neighborhood. He made a call from his mobile phone to get an idea of how busy the ER was. He was assured that if it were drug related, she would be seen right away.

Confident that he would have a few minutes to talk with Melanie, he began feeling better than he had in two and a half weeks.

Chapter 15

The car was quiet for the first few minutes of the ride to the hospital. The girls seemed to be in deep thought until Sophia spoke up.

"Will you tell me why you think Katrina was drugged and why we had to leave in such a hurry?"

Melanie glanced back at Rickie, checking to see if she wanted to answer the question. Rickie shook her head once and looked out her window.

Melanie took a deep breath and began to relay the night from her perspective when she faked going to the bathroom to check her friends. Every now and then she glanced over at Sophia who gasped or made a noise of distress. Sophia was openly sobbing by the time she was done.

"I'm so sorry," Sophia said between breaths.

"It's not your fault," Rickie said, trying to soothe her.

"No one knew what they were like. We were all dreamy eyed over your man," Rickie said.

"Not Melanie," Sophia said. Melanie could see her looking her way, but she kept her eyes on the road.

"Melanie was right there with us. She just happened to see Ward drop something into my drink," Rickie said, still trying to assuage Sophia's guilt while keeping her spot next to Katrina.

"No. I think Melanie saw something in him. I think that's why she asked those questions about his job," Sophia said with a quivering voice.

"You knew something," Sophia said more in resignation than accusation.

"I wasn't sure, and I wasn't about to say something when I wasn't sure. You were so happy. I wanted you to be happy until…well, you know." Melanie prepared for the words of censure or incrimination for not saying anything sooner but they never came. Instead she heard a quiet "thank you" from the passenger seat.

"You're welcome. We're friends. We look out for each other," Melanie said with sincerity, keeping her eyes on the road. She would do just about anything for her friends.

After that, the car grew silent as the women returned to their thoughts. The night had been more than any of them had bargained for. Katrina moaned, drawing everyone's attention to her, but other than that everyone remained preoccupied with their own thoughts.

Melanie's thoughts ricocheted between her encounter with Marc and the realization that they had been invited to a party to be drugged and who knew what else. At one point Sophia let out a sob, and Melanie briefly lifted one of her hands off the steering wheel to squeeze one of Sophia's.

She wondered if Marc was telling the truth about his surveillance assignment with the men casing cars. She shook her head at the fanciful thought of having a real-life knight in shining armor. He had no other reason for being there. She'd rejected him,

166

and she'd been taught that men handle rejection well. Oh, she really wasn't going there.

Melanie told herself to face facts. There was no way he could have known that she was at that party unless he'd followed her. Her heart rebelled, wanting to hold on to the idea of that type of loyalty and adoration directed at her. Melanie thought back to earlier that day and couldn't recall a moment when she felt like she was being followed during her walk and ride from home to the café. It was just a very fortuitous coincidence. Well mostly fortuitous.

She was sure he would want to speak to her, and she didn't know what she would say. She had tried so hard to avoid him, and for what—just to be brought right back into his presence. She knew she was feeling vulnerable. Who wouldn't after a night like that. She was afraid that if he were half the gentleman that he had been as he ushered them to the car, practically saving their lives, she would cave.

He seemed to be able to take care of himself. He was an FBI agent, after all. But that could cause problems rather than resolve them, especially if her mother found out. She was a wreck. She couldn't honestly say whether she wanted him to try again or not. Of course, life would be safer if he left her alone. Safe and boring. She replayed his parting words and the look he gave her, in her mind. *Yeah, you will try again.*

"He was really nice." The words came from Rickie, slightly startling Melanie who had been concentrating on Marc's brake lights.

"Yes he was," Sophia agreed.

"And he smelled good," Katrina chimed in, surprising all of them since they thought she was asleep.

They all started giggling and couldn't stop. It helped to release some of the tension from the night.

"If he asks you again, will you go out with him?" Rickie asked, voicing the conversation Melanie had just finished with herself.

"I've been asking myself the same question," Melanie replied.

"Say yes," Rickie volleyed.

Melanie glanced at her in the rearview mirror. Rickie gave her a reassuring smile but it did little to help.

By the time they reached the emergency dock, Melanie's nerves seemed wired for sound. She was ashamed to admit that it was more at the thought of being near Marc for any length of time than for Katrina's well-being.

Melanie was surprised at how quickly Katrina was seen once they entered the ER. She sat on one of the hard, plastic chairs next to Rickie while they waited to find out the results of Katrina's examination.

Marc had gone in with her. Maybe he was getting her statement while she was being examined. Did the FBI take statements like that? She looked around the room at the people in various states of dress and obvious pain waiting to see the doctor. She hated hospitals. Too many bad memories.

Not a minute later, Marc strolled up to the three of them with a cardboard carrier filled with drink containers.

"Ladies, I thought you'd like something hot to drink. There weren't too many choices so I took the liberty of buying hot chocolates all around." He bent forward so they could each take a cup, and they thanked him for his thoughtfulness.

He took his cup out and set the holder aside as he sat down next to Melanie. She took a sip of her hot chocolate, relishing the taste of the sweet warm liquid and the heat that coated her insides.

"Good?" Marc asked.

"Melanie opened her eyes and turned to see him watching her. She couldn't help the flush that stole over her at his look.

"Yes. It's exactly what I needed."

She turned the rest of her body toward him because what she said needed to be done face-to-face.

"I want to thank you for what you did tonight. I'm not going to question how you came to be there at exactly the right moment. I don't really care. I'm just happy you were there, and you got us safely away from that house." She didn't look away. Instead she kept his gaze so he could understand how much his actions that night had meant.

He smiled a little sheepishly, but allowed her the moment. "I'm glad I was there." He took a sip of his drink, turning away slightly.

"Did I embarrass you?" she asked, teasing him.

He turned, staring at her for a moment as if he were trying to figure her out. Finally, he raised his hand with his forefinger and thumb about an inch apart.

"Just a little," he said with a small smile. She liked that smile. It seemed like it was reserved just for her.

"So I'm sorry to have to do this, but I borrowed one of the rooms the hospital caseworkers use. I've already interviewed Katrina, and I would like to ask each one of you questions separately. Do you mind? I need it for the case we'll be building on these guys.

Each woman nodded her head, and Marc chose to speak to Sophia first as Melanie watched him guide her around the corner. The remaining girls looked at one another but didn't speak.

Melanie was nervous by the time her turn came around, but Marc was efficient, and his questions were quick and to the point. Twenty minutes later, they were all sitting back in the emergency waiting room. He joined them, looking around at those who were left.

She looked at him, feeling safe to take in her fill while he scanned the emergency waiting area. Again she was hit with a feeling of familiarity, and she stared harder trying to figure out what it was about him.

"It's rude to stare," he said, not looking at her as he continued to scan the room.

She shifted so that she was sitting straight again, only slightly abashed at being caught.

She felt a little jab at her ribs and looked over at Rickie who winked at her and held up the okay sign with her fingers.

Melanie sat back in her chair and looked ahead, refusing to look left or right.

A few minutes went by before Marc spoke again.

"I like your dress. It looks beautiful on you," he said, quietly leaning close so she could hear him.

His compliment made her feel beautiful. "It's my mom's."

"Really? You two are the same size?" Marc sounded surprised.

"She's shorter so this dress comes down farther on her," she said, feeling bad about borrowing the dress now without asking permission. She pulled at the hem.

"I'm thinking you probably look better in it. I can't imagine a woman doing it more justice," he said, then sat back as if he'd revealed too much.

She couldn't help but smile. There was something adorable about his guilelessness. It was almost as if he couldn't help telling her how beautiful he thought she was. That it flattered her was only the icing on the cake.

His posture changed, and she looked around to see the cause.

"Does anyone need to call their emergency contacts, whether it be a friend or relative?" he asked, looking at each of them.

She checked her watch and dread filled Melanie. She had forgotten about her courtesy call to her father. She didn't want to give him any reason to worry. She got up immediately, searching for a pay phone. Marc stood up with her, and Sophia and Rickie directed them around the corner where there was a row of pay phones in the hallway.

It was just a little after one o'clock. It seemed like the whole experience lasted all night. She relaxed a little, knowing that she hadn't made her dad wait up too much longer than her twelve-thirty check-in time.

As she dialed her home number, she noticed that Marc stepped back, giving all of them privacy as they made their calls. Out of the corner of her eye she saw him leaning against the opposite wall preparing to wait.

When her father answered the phone her attention shifted to her call. "Hello."

"Hi Dad."

"Melanie? Where are you?"

"I'm at the hospital. A friend of mine is in the emergency."

"Name and precise details please," he said clearly with a sharp edge to his voice.

"I am at Parker General Hospital in the emergency wing where Katrina Reece is being examined and treated for being drugged at the party we attended." She paused briefly to organize her next thoughts.

"I was not drugged. I intercepted an attempted drugging of my friend Francesca 'Rickie' Rosario. We retrieved Katrina Reece as she regurgitated on the person of Claude—no last name—who we believed drugged her. We cleaned Reece up and assessed her. We then found Sophia Monafee as she searched for us. We were met outside the front door by Special Agent Marc Miller who ushered us to Katrina Reece's car and escorted us to the hospital." She blew out a deep breath during the pause.

"Why was Special Agent Marcus Miller at the party?"

"It was a coincidence. He was doing surveillance for a case involving carjackers," she answered as precisely as she could.

"Did you request to see his identification or do you know him?"

"Yes, I asked for his ID, and yes, I met him briefly three weeks ago at the Café on the Corner near the university campus."

"May I speak to him?" he asked, even though they both knew it wasn't a request.

"Yes sir," she said, breathing out, and turned to Marc, holding out the receiver to him with an apologetic smile pasted on her face.

When he reached her, she whispered, "My dad." She handed him the phone.

She watched his face go blank and his shoulders square as he took the receiver, but he didn't turn away from her.

"Hello, this is Special Agent Marcus Miller."

She kept her breaths shallow so as not to distract him while he listened to her father even though he still hadn't looked away from her.

She could just barely hear the rumble of her father's voice as he spoke.

"You're welcome, sir."

She winced and his eyes narrowed slightly.

"Why is that, Colonel?" She pushed down the temptation to lean forward as she strained to catch any clear word from her father's side.

"I am an agent for the FBI, Atlanta branch," he said, glancing behind her for a couple of breaths before pausing.

Marc began reciting numbers. She assumed it was his work ID." Heat began crawling up her neck in an embarrassed flush. His eyes shifted back to hers when he started reciting numbers she recognized. It was his phone number. She fought not to look away and lost when he grinned at her.

Rascal.

"Child Abduction Rapid Deployment."

"Certainly, Colonel. You're welcome. Good evening." Marc handed the receiver back to her.

Melanie placed the receiver back to her ear. "Yes, sir?"

"Are you feeling well?" She paused, slightly confused by the question.

"Yes," she responded slowly.

"Do you feel safe with Agent Miller?"

"Yes," she said, bringing her eyes back up to Marc's.

"Good. I will see you when you get home. Goodbye," her father stated.

"Goodbye." Melanie turned to hang up the phone. She didn't know what she was hoping for, but she was left feeling wanting.

"You father sounds...intense," he said as they moved away from the line of pay phones to the wall and waited for Sophia and Rickie to finish their calls.

"He's military," she said with a shrug of one shoulder.

174

"He sounds like he really cares about you" he said, stepping around her so he could keep both her and her friends in his line of vision as he leaned against the wall. He looked so relaxed, but his eyes scanned the hall often.

"Really?" she said, then could have kicked herself at his puzzled look.

"He isn't a man given over to a great deal of affection." *That sounded objective, didn't it?*

Marc nodded. "I guess that's to be expected. He can't go around hugging his soldiers. People might talk."

Melanie couldn't stop the laughter that burst forth at the picture his words evoked. She covered her mouth thinking an ER hallway wasn't the best place to give into peals of laughter.

Marc chuckled at her expression. "It's okay to laugh. It's way too heavy in here. Understandably, it is a serious place with hurting people, but don't you think there should be some type of entertainment to take people's minds away from their problems at least while they are waiting and can't do anything about it?"

"Honestly. I could tell he was very concerned. How many times did the phone ring when you called?"

She stopped to think. It had only rung once before she heard his voice which was alert and awake.

"Once, maybe."

"He was waiting. He was definitely concerned. Plus, he did let me know, in no uncertain terms, that if I didn't see you home, he would come looking for me."

"He didn't." She gasped even as he started nodding, not knowing whether to be embarrassed or pleased by her father's actions. She gave herself permission to be both.

"And I quote: "I'm going to need you to bring my daughter home safely, and if she doesn't make it, I need to know where I can find you.""

"I would do the same if my daughter called me in the middle of the night from an ER with a guy claiming to be any type of law enforcement, and I couldn't get to her right away. I would make it as personal as possible," he said, glancing down the hall again.

"What do you mean?" She had a good idea of what he meant, but she still wanted to hear him express it.

"I would let the boy, man, or person know that there would be consequences for not doing everything they could to bring my child safely home. If I didn't get my child back in one piece, they may lose something they valued."

"He didn't sound like that. Did he?" she asked, her heart beating rapidly while the little girl in her blew at a dandelion hoping every last bit of white fluff released.

Marc nodded seriously. There was no hint of teasing in his eyes.

"I heard you giving him your phone numbers. How did he make it personal for you?"

Marc tipped his head to the side staring at her for a moment. "Melanie, as soon as I saw you it started out personal."

A lump formed in her throat at his words, making her thoughts come out in a mere whisper.

"But, I didn't call you."

His lips lifted in a wry smile. "It didn't keep me from thinking about you."

"Ha," she said, letting go of an involuntary chuckle.

He didn't ask but looked at her with curiosity.

She raised her hand. "Me too. Thinking about you," she added for clarity.

His shoulders seemed to slump, but a relieved look took over his features.

"Good. I was hoping I wasn't making a fool of myself."

"You helping us tonight, getting Katrina to the ER quickly, and assuring my dad that I'm in good hands doesn't sound foolish," she said, feeling particularly warm under his gaze.

"Are you fishing, Ms. Morganson?" he asked, the just-for-her smile back on his lips.

Her face heated at the idea that he would think she was looking for…for what exactly? She opened her mouth and closed it, opened it again and closed it just as quickly.

He placed a hand on her shoulder, bending his knees so he was on her level looking at her eye to eye. "I was teasing. It's a little bit of a defense mechanism for me when I'm nervous."

"Nervous?" she said, this moment feeling surreal. She hoped she didn't mess it up by saying something stupid.

"Obviously I'm not doing a good job at spelling this out. I was trying to tell you that I was still very interested in you without putting myself out there," he said, taking his hand away.

"Oh," she said, but nothing else came to mind. She had just gotten her wish. Too bad she hadn't planned out what she would do if she got it.

"I was hoping you would give me a call if I gave you my number again, but not in gratitude or with some misguided need to pay me back. I was hoping you would call me because you wanted to."

"You don't know me too well if you think I would call you just to mollify some need to show you gratitude," she said kind of flippantly.

"Exactly!" he said, throwing up in his hands in a mock gesture of exasperation.

She laughed again, thrilled by his humor.

She raised her hands in surrender. "Okay. Yes. I will call you."

He sobered. "You will?"

"Yep," she said without hesitation.

"Why now when you didn't before?"

"I had some time to think about it," she said, hedging. She was not ready to admit that she'd made up her mind before they got to the ER.

"And...?" he prompted.

"And that time plus some of our interaction tonight has led me to change my mind." She waited while his eyes skimmed her face looking for the truth in her features. He must have found it because the intensity of his stare lightened.

"When are you going to call me?" he asked.

"What?" She had a problem following the swing in his mood.

"When are you going to call me?" There was a little excitement in his voice which made her feel good.

"That's for me to decide," she said, joining in his enthusiasm.

"I won't argue with that. I just want to make sure I'm home when you call."

She considered his answer and her schedule then told him.

"What are we going to talk about?" he asked. His eyes lit up like a child's with a new toy.

"How old are you?" she asked half-jokingly.

"Twenty-eight. Why? Is that too old for you?" Some of the light left his eyes, and she was sorry for causing it.

"No. That isn't too old," she said quickly.

"Good. Now tell me what we will talk about," he asked again

I don't know," she said, half laughing as she scrambled for a topic.

"Quick, before your friend stops pretending to be on the phone," he said.

Melanie turned toward the row of phones. Sophia was turned away from them, but Rickie had the receiver up to her ear with a huge smile on her face.

Chapter 16

"What are you studying?" Marc asked as he turned down the main street leading to Melanie's parents' home. It was nearly three in the morning, and he was both relieved and regretful that their evening was almost over.

Katrina had been released after an hour of tests and a dose of charcoal to absorb what was left of the drug in her system. The attending nurse and doctor both considered it fortunate that she had vomited almost immediately. She received a much smaller dose of the Rohypnol Claude had slipped in her drink. It was enough to make her feel inebriated since she hadn't been drinking, but she was dehydrated so they put her on an IV to counteract the affects and her upset stomach.

Since her family was still on another continent and her roommate didn't drive, Marc was fine with having everyone wait until she was released. He was glad that she wouldn't be going home to an empty house.

He followed Melanie as she drove an almost despondent Sophia and suspiciously wide-eyed Rickie to their dorms then drove Katrina to her apartment, parked her car and assisted her upstairs. The moment he put the key in the lock, Katrina's roommate, Shirley, opened the door. She was an older woman who took Katrina in her arms. He could hear her mothering the young lady through the door after she closed and locked it. He breathed easier knowing Katrina had someone to take care of her.

Melanie called her father again right before they left the hospital, and he wondered if it was something she offered or he had requested. It was smart either way. It was way too easy for her to disappear after dropping off the other women.

She had quite a few men in her life taking care of her, but she didn't seem to be aware of it. It made him wonder just who she was, but he was hesitant to dig any deeper because she was obviously being cloaked. She seemed like any other young woman starting college except for the manpower seeing to her well-being, and he was just another addition...for the moment.

It's my first year, so I'm taking most of my general education courses. Creative writing, anthropology, Algebra II, Biology 101, African history—which I really love—and Communications 101 which is more like Toastmasters.

"You know Toastmasters?" Marc asked, surprised. His mother had been in Toastmasters to help with her speaking in public, especially when she was asked to speak on behalf of her church auxiliary.

"I was homeschooled during some of my grade-school years. My mother taught me both life applications and academics," she answered, and he had to give it to her. She didn't lie, but she told him very little.

He wouldn't push. If he played his cards right he would have time, and the more he was in her presence, the more time he wanted with her. It was a new feeling for him. There were moments he thought himself headed for a life as a bachelor even as he wished for what his parents had.

"Do you know what you want to major in?" he asked and caught the jerk of her head as she turned to him. When she was quiet for a few heartbeats, his curiosity was piqued.

"What?" he asked, sparing her a brief glance.

"Aren't you going to ask me why I'm carrying so many units?" Melanie asked.

He was curious, but he could tell that she was an intelligent and responsible young woman who seemed to know herself. He figured it was safest to make light of it for the moment.

"Why? Don't you know?"

There was another pause before she answered. "Yes, but I seem to get that question as soon as I reveal how many units I'm taking."

"Do you know what you're doing?"

"I believe so."

"Are you feeling like your workload is too heavy?"

"No."

"Do you think you will have time to go out with me once a week?"

"Maybe." He heard the smile in her voice.

"Well, that settles it. You need to drop a class, maybe two, because you owe me a call, and I'm not going to take your college career being important as an excuse for why you can't spend more than fifteen minutes on the phone with me."

She snickered but didn't rise to the bait.

"You didn't answer my question. Do you know what you want to major in?"

She was quiet again. He really liked that she didn't just blurt out answers. She wasn't afraid to take her time with her thoughts.

"I've been thinking of some type of communications lately, but I'm not sure. When I was younger I wanted to be a teacher."

"Really? Why is that?"

"Well, when I was in the eighth grade I had a teacher, Ms. Lend, who was very attentive. She really went out of her way to make sure that I got the attention I needed in class. She equipped me with a certain way of looking at things. A logic that didn't always follow the norm. She said she recognized why I was struggling and gave me tools to get around my very fast mind."

That made so much sense to him. What a strong sense of discipline she had to have.

"I understand. My favorite teacher was Mr. Fagan, my tenth-grade science teacher. He made science click for me. He gave us an understanding of what we were learning and how it applied to life. He was also a deacon at my church. It was weird seeing him outside of the classroom. You tend to think that teachers have no life. That they are there just to get you to learn something. He is a great guy."

"You still go to church?

"Yes. Both because I love it and because my mom says so."

Melanie didn't know how to react at first. She wasn't sure if he was kidding or not.

He smiled at her, letting her know that he was kidding, even if it was only a little.

"I love and respect my mother, but I'm not a mama's boy, if that's what you're thinking. She does expect us to nurture our relationship with God though."

"Huh. You don't seem like a zealot," Melanie said then pressed her lips together as if she'd not meant for that to come out. He was glad though. He wanted to know what she thought.

"Know many zealots, do you?" he asked, winking at her while taking note of her nonexistent spiritual walk.

He wasn't offended. Some nonbelievers thought you had to be a fanatic or extremist. If she saw him pray or speak to God in his car sometimes she would swear he was just that. As much as he loved it, he couldn't face the sickness in the world every day if he didn't have God to ground him. He wondered who she went to. He wondered if she still kept in touch with her teacher.

"Do you still talk to her?"

"Who?" Melanie asked.

He realized she'd gone quiet the past few seconds.

"Ms. Lend sounds like a very special teacher who was able to recognize it in someone else," he said, not exaggerating one bit.

"You talk like you know me," she said, sounding wary.

"No. I just like what I do know," he said with all sincerity.

"Which is?" she asked.

"You are intelligent, beautiful, and have a keen eye and an awareness most people don't. You are courageous, loyal to your friends, and you laugh at my jokes." He glanced at her when he was done catching her with her mouth open.

"We've only spent two hours together," she said with astonishment.

"Can you imagine how much longer the list would be if we spent more time together?"

"Well, you gave us at least one more minute," she said, smirking. "You just missed my street."

"It's all part of my ultimate plan to seem normal so I don't intimidate you with my razor wit and intellectual prowess." He let go a maniacal laugh that used to make his younger siblings shiver.

He made a U-turn.

Melanie laughed. "That was great! It sounded real."

"What do you mean? It was real," he said, sounding offended.

"You laugh like that when you find something funny?" she said, pointing to her street then watching him to wait for his response.

He drew out the moment then finally answered, shaking his head. "Nah."

She laughed again, making him feel like he'd won a prize.

"Right here," she said, pointing to the house on their right.

"I would like to make a request before I walk you to your house," he said, pulling to the curb.

"Okay." She watched him.

At the last second he realized that he wasn't supposed to know she walked home. "Do you get a ride to and from school?"

185

"No. I walk my sister to her bus then I take the transportation system to and from campus."

"Would it be possible for you to get a ride to and from campus for a few weeks?"

"Why?" she asked, only curiosity showing on her face.

He didn't want to scare her, but he needed her to be aware that the men who tried to drug her friends might not be in jail by the end of the next day.

"Just in case any of the boys at the party get any ideas, I would rather you not be alone." He saw fear cross her face, and he wanted to take back his words.

"There is always bail," he said for want of another explanation, since he couldn't share that they were part of an ongoing investigation.

"Do you think they will retaliate?" Her voice trembled slightly. "For what, not successfully drugging my friends?"

He nodded.

"Ugh. Monsters," she said with more frustration than fear, and he wanted to pat her on the back for her bravery.

"Will you call me if you need a ride?" When she opened her mouth, he interrupted.

"Please?" he said.

She heaved a sigh. "Okay."

He knew she didn't like asking for favors, but this was way too important.

He pulled over, and she reached for the handle. "Hold on. Let me come around and open the door for you."

"You opened it for me when I got in. This isn't a date," she said with a little snark. *That* wouldn't be on his list of things he liked about her.

He became serious. "A man who only opens the door for you when you are dating is not a gentleman. He is an opportunist."

"My mother taught me that my opening the door for you isn't a sign of weakness but worth," he said, watching her.

Melanie slowly inched her hand away from the handle, and he nodded before he opened his door to come around to hers.

He walked her up the stone path to the two-story, single-family home. It was on the bigger side for the street, but it was still a nice representative of a home owned by a middle-class family.

The light was on over the door, and Marc put his palm out for her key. "May I?"

"Really? My dad is probably on the other side of that door," she said, sounding a little impatient but more intrigued.

She handed him her keys, holding the door key away from the rest. He unlocked the door and opened it for her. He stepped back, remaining on the outside of the threshold.

Melanie smiled up at him and opened her mouth but turned at the last second and shifted out of the doorway. She was replaced with whom he assumed was her father.

"Special Agent Miller?" Colonel Morganson offered his hand.

"Yes," Marc said in his most professional voice as they shook.

Melanie's father looked to where she'd disappeared. "You've had a long night. You've got to be tired."

"I am, but Special Agent Miller promised to give me his number so I was just waiting for it," she said loud enough for him to hear.

He hid his smile as he reached in his back pocket and pulled out his ID case. He pulled a card free then took a pen from his jacket pocket and wrote his home number on the back.

Melanie appeared back in the doorway in front of her father and reached for his card. "Good morning."

"Good morning."

She flashed him a smile that raised his heartbeat and slipped back to the side and out of sight.

When he raised his eyes back to her father, he wiped the smile from his face.

Colonel Morganson stepped forward, closing the door behind him. Marc could tell he was sizing him up.

"As I said on the phone, I appreciate you coming to my daughter's aid along with her friends. Melanie told me this wasn't your first meeting. She met you in a café near her campus, was it?"

"Yes. The Café on the Corner."

"Was that the first time you've seen her?"

"No," he said, finding no need to lie. "But it was a coincidence."

No expression registered on Colonel Morganson's face.

"Was your presence at the home tonight a coincidence?"

188

Marc expected the question. He'd planned to lie, but the man's tone changed and his eyes betrayed him. *What was that? Hope.*

"I do not have the authority to answer that," Marc said, wishing they could speak openly. *Did Colonel Morganson know about Luca?*

"You gave my daughter your personal number."

"Yes," he said, even though the man hadn't posed a question.

"Why?"

"That is a personal matter," Marc stated with as much respect as he could.

The colonel nodded his head. "One thing about Melanie. She equates lies of commission and omission with being manipulated. She will not tolerate it. If you want your personal matter to go beyond a phone call, be completely honest with her.

Colonel Morganson moved as if he were going to go back inside. If Marc wanted an answer to his question, this was a good time to ask.

"Did your phone call bring me to that home tonight?" Marc asked.

Melanie's father looked him in the eye. "How could I? I don't work for the FBI."

His comment would have been convincing had he not paused longer than needed before going back inside.

Marc stood there for a moment wondering what he really was involved in.

Luca showed remorse over his part in the affair with Melanie's mother and possibly some other unfulfilled promise that caused Brenda/Grace to seek revenge on her own. Sure, Luca and Melanie shared a common bond now in Paige which made Melanie and family worth protecting, but there was something Luca hadn't shared. He could feel it and he trusted his feelings.

He prayed for direction. He knew right from wrong. There was no need to pray about whether to be honest, just what to expect when he was.

Chapter 17

Melanie was up early despite the late night. She slowly ate her cereal across the table from Paige who barely acknowledged her. Her little girl was growing up right before her eyes.

If she knew how to pray, she would pray that her daughter found peace in the middle of their family storm. She would pray for her daughter's life to be spared the troubles she had, and Paige would find a love to last a lifetime. She would pray for God to protect her mind and soul from the type of anger and hate that devoured hopes and dreams.

"You've been doing really good in school this year. I was wondering if there was something special you wanted." Melanie said between bites.

Paige looked up from her book at Melanie. She chewed slowly. "I've been saving up for a desktop word processor. If you could help me with the rest…"

Melanie shook her head. She'd been saving up too. Paige had mentioned the word processor a couple of times in the last few months while she was in the room.

"Save your money for paper. I've got you. Just show me the picture of the one you want."

"Really?" Paige's smile lit up the whole room. It was rare these days, which saddened Melanie, but when it came out it was nothing short of breathtaking. Paige was made to smile. She laughed and giggled a great deal as a baby and toddler, always wanting to play.

Melanie tried hard to come between Paige and their mother's disdain. She tried to love Paige enough for the child not to miss her mother's attention. She could see each day that Paige lost herself in a book, which kept her from dealing with family life.

"Really."

"Thank you, Mel." Paige came around the table and hugged Melanie. It was the first one in way too long, so she wrapped her arms around her little girl and breathed in her fragrance with a deep breath before letting her go. Paige smiled at her again before going back to her seat and breakfast.

Melanie watched her daughter for a few seconds more. She was the last Melanie would carry. There was no going back. She couldn't press a button and redo her past. There would be no growing up before she experienced the parts of life she wasn't truly physically or emotionally ready for. She could tell herself that she should have lived in the moment and taken in the feel of being pregnant, but she was twelve, for goodness sake. She'd walked through most of her pregnancy in terror.

She was pulled from her thoughts by her father's voice. "Melanie, will you come here, please?"

Paige sent her a sympathetic look before going back to her book and cereal.

Melanie took one more bite of her cereal before getting up to see what her dad wanted.

"So how are you really doing?" her father asked, as she sat across from him at the dining room table.

"I'm okay," Melanie said, more curious as to why her father had called her away from the breakfast table than his odd question.

"Now that the emotions have ebbed from the moment, I would like a full recount of last evening." This was her father. Down to business and wanting the facts.

Melanie took a deep breath and recited how she felt meeting Allen Resnick in the Café on the Corner. She did not share how all of the women were starry-eyed and that he had a charisma that seemed to blind people to whom he really was. It was one of the reasons she insisted that Sophia tell her the address so that she could share it with her father.

She replayed the night again along with her unease with being separated from her friends. She recounted how she faked having to use the restroom so she could check up on all of her friends, which was when she caught one of the men dropping a pill in Rickie's drink.

When she caught her father up to the point where she called him from the hospital, she went silent. The quietness in the room did not serve to calm her nerves but rather the opposite.

When her father finally looked up from his hands that were folded on the table, what he said could have knocked her sideways if she were standing.

"I'm proud of you. You followed your instincts and made sure you kept an eye on your friends without causing a scene, even though part of their modus operandi was to separate you and make you more vulnerable," he said matter-of-factly.

"You and your friends were relatively unharmed due to your quick thinking and courage." He paused for a moment.

Melanie could not have said anything if someone held a gun to her head. She knew her surprise was written clearly on her face, but there was nothing she could do about it.

"I need you to ask your friend Katrina if she can bring you home from school for the next few weeks."

She smiled to herself, knowing where he was going.

"If you will take Paige and me to school today, I will see if Katrina is in class. If she is absent, I will call Special Agent Miller. He asked me last evening to call him if I didn't have a ride home," she responded with as little emotion as possible.

Her father's hawk eyes watched her, and for a moment she thought they softened a little.

"Do you like this Special Agent Marc Miller?"

Stunned, Melanie was momentarily speechless. His pointed look reminded her whom she was speaking to, or not speaking to, as it were.

"I barely know him," she said, hedging.

"You barely knew Allen Resnick, but you saw something in him that your friends didn't."

Melanie thought about that for a moment. She tried to think back to what she felt the minute she met Marc. She felt awkward about sharing some of the emotions with her father. The heat that suffused her neck was probably not lost on him.

"He is..." She stopped speaking while she searched for better words than nice, beautiful or timely to describe him. They only skimmed the surface of how she felt about Marc.

"He makes me feel safe. He makes me feel important." She paused again.

Should she tell her dad that she thought Marc was extremely handsome, and when he looked at her sometimes she felt a warmth inside her that spread from the tips of her fingers to her toes? No. She would keep that to herself.

"He's really funny. He seems to be able to make me laugh when there's nothing to laugh at. Do you know what I mean?"

Her father stared at her for a moment before nodding.

"And here I thought you didn't know him." He gave her a wan smile and patted her hand.

Melanie was having a hard time keeping up. The whole situation was surreal. Her father had complimented her, wanted to make sure a plan for her safety was in place, and he touched her with affection. It had been so long since she'd experienced those things from him, she was more confused than elated.

"If your Special Agent Marc Miller isn't available, call me. I will send a private to drive you."

She blinked at him.

"What?"

She didn't want to make too big a deal about it. It could anger him, and they would be right back to square one.

"Nothing. Thank you very much, Dad. I'll go get my things so we don't make you late." He waved her comment away and she stalled. Who was this man, and what had he done with her father? Wait. Never mind. She would gratefully take this one.

"Oh, and I have already bought Paige's word processor. You aren't the only one with ears, he said, smiling ruefully. "You can buy the ribbon."

She offered him a tentative smile and left the room with wings on her feet.

Chapter 18

Marc bit the inside of his cheek. He knew he had a personal stake in this, and he was trying to talk himself down, but he was having a hard time getting his emotions under control.

He'd been debriefed on the role he played the night before. Merryman wanted to make sure he hadn't jeopardized their case. It seems he had a man inside at the party, undercover, who had clocked Ward's and Allen's movements but not Claude and Paul. They were just two more men thinking their money and contacts entitled them to women and anything else they wanted.

It made him physically ill to think of what could have happened if Melanie hadn't told her father where she was going. It was obvious to Marc now that Mr. Morganson knew all about Luca Sable. He'd called the number Mr. Sable had given him for reporting these situations, but he'd not received a call back yet.

His report to Merryman yielded nothing as far as he was concerned. Since the men were part of an ongoing investigation, Merryman didn't want to spook anyone by charging them for their actions the night of the party. The drug they used on Katrina was one of the ones they were under investigation for selling. The fact that Melanie intervened before any real harm was done sadly worked against the women because the men couldn't be charged on their intentions.

He couldn't wait for those good-for-nothing men to be brought in. The frustration in knowing that it wouldn't be for another week had him both frustrated at the system and concerned for Melanie's welfare.

The only good thing that had come from this situation was the time he got to spend with Melanie, and he had the opportunity to do it again. She'd called him a couple of hours ago letting him know that Katrina wasn't in class. Neither were Sophia nor Rickie. It seemed the women were recovering slowly from their night and possibly heartache or embarrassment.

He'd made a few calls up to the school to speak to the dean of literature. He wanted to see if Mr. Resnick had the gall to show up for his TA session. The woman let him know that he'd called in sick. Marc muttered a few choice words under his breath regarding her response. He wondered if the guy was just going to wait for things to die down or if he would try and slip away.

After another hour and half of calls, he glanced at the clock then at the open file on his desk. Melanie wouldn't be out of class for another two hours. His mind drifted to what class she was presently in. He'd memorized her schedule after leaving Mr. Sable's a few weeks ago and was happy he'd done so. Knowing where she was helped to put his mind at ease.

He shook his head to get himself to focus back on his work. He tried not to think of Melanie during his job. One thought usually led to another and that thought led to daydreaming. Next thing he knew, minutes would have gone by and whatever work he'd begun would still be there waiting on his desk. It had happened quite a few times.

He set thoughts of Melanie aside and began reading through the file again. He'd gotten through three pages when the thought of asking Melanie out crowded the words from the boring report from his mind. He wondered if it were too soon. She had just been through a bit of a trauma. It probably wasn't right to offer her a ride and then ask. She might think he would consider going out with him a form of payment, when that was the last thing he wanted.

On the other hand, they did have decent conversations last night, and he'd made her laugh a few times. He needed a good but objective opinion. His mom wouldn't work; she'd been wanting to see him date for the longest time. His sister Laura was touch and go. It usually depended on whether or not she was mad at Benjamin. Noana would probably give him all the reasons why he shouldn't. His brother was no better at dating than he was. He would call his dad.

He couldn't remember the last time he gave this much thought to a woman he barely knew. It was probably because it had never happened. He really liked being in Melanie's presence. She was like a breath of fresh air. If half of what Mr. Sable revealed to him about her past was true, it was a wonder that she wasn't bitter and angry like her mother. It was a deep betrayal to manipulate and guide children to act like adults the way that woman had. To have done that to her own daughter was downright wicked no matter what Mr. Sable said. At some point people had to take responsibility for their emotions and circumstances. She could learn a thing or two from Melanie who had lost more by age twelve than most people lost in a lifetime.

He wondered if the woman's obvious love and concern for her friends would extend to a more personal relationship. Had she been in a relationship since Sable's grandson? She gave him the impression that she was a loner, but she was also really good at being a friend.

"Miller. How far have you gotten with that report?" Marc blinked a few times to bring Finn into focus. He looked down at the file he'd barely touched and blew out a frustrated sigh. He rubbed his forehead.

"Not too far, I'm afraid. Was there something in particular that you were looking for?" he said, laying the folder out on the desk.

Finn leaned a hip against Marc's desk. "Was there any connection between Beth Bryant and anyone else involved with Travenski's organization?"

"Not from what I've been able to read so far," Marc said. "But I haven't gotten far."

"Why?" Finn said, watching Marc carefully. "Does it have to do with the girl you helped last night?" Finn asked.

"Maybe," Marc said.

"I spoke to Mitchell this morning. How did you manage to get yourself entangled in that? Did she call you? Mitchell said you knew nothing about Merryman's case before you approached the house," Finn said, half asking.

"No, I didn't know anything about the occupants of the house or who was attending the party outside of Melanie and her friends," he said, looking back at Finn.

Finn sat on the edge of Marc's desk and stared at him. "Are you getting in deep, Marc?"

"I don't know what you mean, Finn," Marc said, staring back at him.

"Did you almost compromise Merryman's case by going after the girl?" Finn asked.

"No. I was nowhere near compromising anything," Marc answered.

Marc noticed Finn giving him his interrogation stare. He could tell his partner was curious about his connection to Melanie so why wasn't he asking him about her?

"Why aren't you asking me questions about her?" Marc asked.

"Maybe I hoped you would offer the information, seeing as I'm your partner for most of our cases," Finn said without moving.

"It was a case of being in the wrong place at the wrong time. And that goes for all of us." Marc wasn't sure he would tell Finn about his watching over Melanie even if he could. "It was a personal matter that unfortunately crossed into investigation territory."

"What do you know about her?" Finn asked.

"More than enough to know that her being at the party last night was pure coincidence," Marc said, not taking his eyes off Finn.

The man stared back at him for a few seconds then something shifted in his eyes and the beginnings of a smile touched his lips. "Oh, I think you're in deeper than you know," Finn finished with a chuckle.

Marc didn't go for the bait. "I'll finish reading this report and get to you as soon as I can. You got here early if you talked to Mitchell. What time are you heading out?" Marc asked, checking his watch.

Finn raised up off the desk. All humor erased from his face, and Marc could see his mind working.

"I'm out in half an hour. If you find anything worth mentioning you can give me a call in an hour," Finn said, and Marc nodded his agreement.

"Be careful, okay," Finn said before walking away.

Normally Marc would pay heed to Finn's warnings, but this wasn't work. It was personal.

***

Marc waited in the parking lot he and Melanie had agreed upon earlier. He'd made a quick call to his dad before leaving the office giving him a quick rundown of the last few weeks without revealing his connection to Mr. Sable. No need to worry his dad.

Once he was done, his father gave him an answer that had his knee nervously bouncing and fingers tapping on the steering wheel.

There was a knock on his passenger window, and he looked over to see Melanie peering in at him. He got out wondering where she'd come from.

"Hey," he said, looking at her over the car roof.

"Hi." Was he imagining it, or was she a little nervous too?

He walked around the car and held up a finger when she looked like she would complain. She closed her mouth and stepped back so he could open the door for her. She glanced at him but said nothing before getting in.

"How are you doing?" he asked as he slipped back behind his wheel.

"I'm doing surprisingly well for the night I had," she said, still sounding surprised.

"How was your day?" he asked without hesitation.

"It was uneventful. Exactly what I needed. We had a lecture and film in anthropology. There was a quiz in Algebra II that kept my mind occupied, biology was on a subject I was already familiar with, and communications was decent. Uneventful," she finished with a nod.

"How was your day?" she asked him while pulling on her seat belt.

"It was an exercise in discipline and futility," he said, pulling out of the spot.

"How ambiguous. I'm going to take a guess and say it didn't turn out as you wished," she replied.

"The day's not over yet," he said, pulling out of the parking lot.

"Oh. Are you going back to the office after you take me home? I didn't mean to be an inconvenience." She turned to him with a look of regret.

"No. My day is over at the office. You're right. It didn't go as I'd hoped, but they can't all be moneymakers," he said, hoping to soothe her guilt.

She turned quiet on him after that, and he tried to think of something that would bring the conversation around to his favor. It was Friday, and unless he got his courage up in the next twenty

203

minutes he wouldn't see her until Monday, which seemed a long ways away.

"Have you eaten?" he asked, turning right to take the scenic route.

"I had breakfast and a late lunch," she responded.

"What about on the weekend?" he asked.

"Yes. I eat on the weekends too," she answered quickly, cutting him off.

"Funny, funny," Marc said, glancing over at her.

"What I was going to say or ask anyway, was if you would like to go to lunch with me tomorrow." He dared another glance and saw her biting her lip.

He looked back at the road hoping her silence had more to do with her contemplating his invitation than considering a way to reject him.

"I would really like to, but I usually do the grocery shopping in the afternoon. My mom works nights and sleeps through most of the day. When I started driving, I would help out when I could," she said apologetically.

He was disappointed, but he didn't let that discourage him. "Do you mind if I join you? I need to do a little grocery shopping of my own. I've been putting it off because I haven't had time." He took his eyes off the road to check her expression but didn't relax until she spoke again.

"Okay, if you're sure. I'm not quick at it," she said. He turned to her but couldn't read her expression.

"If that was supposed to be discouraging it has the opposite effect," he said.

She remained quiet, but when he looked her way again a secret smile played at her lips.

"Good. This way I can turn a chore into fun," he added, giving her a grin.

"No pressure there," Melanie said after a few more seconds of quiet.

"Ah. I don't think you have to worry about that. If I didn't find your company pleasant, I wouldn't ask for more." He gave his most charming smile.

She laughed, startling him.

"I said yes. You don't have to try to disarm me with one of your pretty-boy smiles," she blurted.

He wanted to laugh himself but cleared his throat. He liked her quick wit and the fact that she wasn't afraid, even at this early stage, to call him out for trying to dazzle her with his charms.

"You think I'm a pretty boy?" he asked, teasing her.

"I think your smile is what you use to make women think you are a pretty boy," she responded as if she'd known what he'd say.

He shrugged. "Fair enough. What time, and which grocery store tomorrow?"

"How about one o'clock. The big supermarket on the corner of Maryland Ave. and Waters Street."

"Perfect." He was familiar with the market. It was a little out of his way, but that was nothing compared to spending an hour or two with her.

"What do you normally do on Saturdays?" Melanie asked, opening her purse.

"I help around my mom and dad's house. My brother and I usually take turns, but he's been preoccupied with wedding plans," he said, turning into her neighborhood. The drive was coming in way too soon for his liking.

"That's nice of you. Are you going tomorrow?"

"I am. It's time to winterize the house," he replied.

"Winterize the house? What's that?" She turned toward him.

"Getting the house ready for winter. Making sure the caulk around the windows is good, changing out the light drapes for the heavier ones, and replace weather stripping around the doors." He liked the interest in her eyes about something as mundane as winterizing a house.

"From what you've said about them, you seem close to your parents." When he checked, she hadn't changed positions.

"I am. My whole family is close," he said.

"Brothers and sisters?" she asked right on the heels of his answer.

"One older brother, one older sister and one younger sister."

"That's nice."

"I was the only child in the house until I was ten," she offered.

"I suspect you got used to being an only child before that."

He saw her shrug out of the side of his eye.

"Actually, it was nice when Paige came along. There was less attention on me."

"That's a first. Most children love their parents' attention unless it's abusive."

She shrugged again.

"You haven't talked about your mother, but your dad seems decent," he said, pulling up to her house and turning to look at her.

Her eyes clouded slightly. It was heart-wrenching to watch.

"So tomorrow at one o'clock?" she said after a long blink.

"Yep. Are you still going to call me this evening?" he asked, referring to her promise the night before in the hospital.

"But I'll see you tomorrow," she said, grinning and frowning at the same time.

"And?" he said without looking away.

She smiled, seeming delighted. "Okay. I'll call you at the scheduled time."

He nodded before unlocking the car. When he straightened from exiting the car, he was startled to see her peek at him over the roof. He narrowed his eyes, and she slowly slid back down into the car. He chuckled to himself as he headed around to her side. He was really looking forward to tonight and tomorrow.

Chapter 19

"I have a date tomorrow with Marc," Melanie said excitedly over the phone.

"What? How'd that happen, and what happened to the whole 'If I call him, and we hit it off, then he'll want to date me and marry me'?" Rickie teased.

"No one said anything about getting married," Melanie replied.

"Yeah, but that's where you were headed. Could still be," she murmured.

"Enough. I just called to see how you were doing and tell you the news," Melanie said.

"I still can't believe you went to class today after last night and this morning. Aren't you exhausted, or are you high on Special Agent Marcus Miller?" Rickie spoke his name lowering her tone.

"Shush, you. Don't make me regret telling you about him."

"Okay. Do you know where you're going on your date?"

"We are going shopping," Melanie said, unable to keep the giddiness from her voice.

"He's taking you shopping?" Rickie's voice rang in confusion.

"No. We're meeting at the supermarket tomorrow. I have to go grocery shopping, and he needs to do his own, so we're going to do it together."

Melanie waited for Rickie's response for a few seconds then a few seconds more. "Rickie?"

"Yeah. I'm here. Did I hear you right? You're going grocery shopping together?" Rickie sounded incredulous.

"Yes. He asked me to lunch, but I had to do the weekly shopping. I thought he would want to reschedule, but he asked to join me. He said being with me would make the chore of shopping fun. I'm paraphrasing."

"Wow. I've never thought of grocery shopping as romantic, but he may have something there. I would draw the line at cleaning floors together though. There is nothing romantic about wax buildup," Rickie said more to herself than Melanie.

Melanie laughed. "What?"

"Never mind. Will you go out to lunch before or after?"

"No. I don't think so. After we shop I will have to get the food back home and in the freezer."

"Mmm. Well, I guess it's better than nothing," Rickie said, not at all impressed. "Did he really say shopping with you would make it fun?"

"Yep."

"That was nice."

"Yes." Melanie's voice took on a dreamlike quality.

"He also won't let me open my car door. He insists on opening it for me."

"My dad still opens the door for my mother," Rickie said a little breathlessly. "That's nice."

209

"I agree."

"So what are you going to wear?"

"Wear?"

"Yes you need to wear something comfortable but slightly more than casual."

"I don't understand. We're going shopping," Melanie said.

"Yes, but you're shopping with Marc."

"If I'm too dressy, he might get suspicious."

"It's a delicate balance. Maybe a pair of jeans and a nice top."

Melanie considered her friend's idea and decided to look through her closet later.

"Have you talked to Katrina or Sophia?" Rickie asked, and the conversation turned toward their friends and recapping what happened the night before.

It ended on a good note, much the same as how it had begun.

"I want to know everything that happens tomorrow. I think it's safer to live vicariously through you for a while," Rickie said.

"Don't be like that. I don't think you will get through this year without being asked out."

"Oh, I've been asked out. It's just not with anyone I want to go out with."

Melanie was surprised, though she didn't know why. Her friend was beautiful, with dark hair down to the middle of her back; she was vivacious and full of life. Any man would be fortunate to date her.

"I'll call you tomorrow evening and tell you all about it."

"Thank you. We'll talk tomorrow. Bye," Rickie said, signing off.

"Bye."

Melanie checked her watch. She had fifteen minutes before her call with Marc. She hoped they could keep it light. They'd been brought together by an intense situation. It would be nice to talk about something light.

***

Melanie waited outside the market in her mom's car. She was early, but she needed the time to regroup and deal with her nerves. It didn't make sense. She'd just seen him yesterday and spoke with him last night. She kept it to a half hour, not wanting to monopolize the line especially since her mother was off.

The air in the house this morning had been thick with tension. Her mother had picked at Paige during breakfast, acting like she'd forgotten the birthday party Paige had been invited to. It was the first one since the child had turned five. It was on the scheduling board the family kept on the refrigerator, and Melanie had overheard Paige reminding her mother about it Thursday night before her mother went to work.

Her mother had Paige in tears thinking she wouldn't be able to go, until Melanie stepped in, which turned her mother's attention on her. After a few threats and a rant that Melanie refused to let bother her, their father stepped in. He asked Melanie to get Paige ready, and take her out to get the present her mother was supposed to take her to get then drop her off at the party before going grocery shopping.

It was fine with Melanie. She and Paige escaped the oppressiveness of the house and spent some time together at the mall before Melanie dropped Paige off at the party.

She would have enough time to grocery shop with Marc, get it home before certain items melted, and go back out to get Paige.

Melanie wondered what set her mother off. Lately, she spent less and less time at home—which no one was complaining about—but when she was home she was almost cruel.

She set aside the book she'd opened ten minutes ago and not read. Thoughts of Marc and their call had been foremost in her mind. He'd basically read her mind and kept the conversation light, asking her about her favorite foods, color, television shows, music and books.

His were anything Italian, the color blue, cop and detective shows because he liked to find the holes in the storylines, R&B, Jazz and contemporary Gospel for music, and *The Vision* by Deann Koontz. Melanie found it in the mall bookstore and purchased it while Paige took a few minutes in the music store. She could see why he liked it. She was caught after a couple of pages.

Melanie liked Marc. He was real. He didn't put on airs, and he loved his family. He also loved God and mentioned Him a few times in their conversation, but she didn't have the courage to ask him about that yet. Neither one of her parents were religious. Brian and his parents were Catholic, but they didn't do much beyond going to Mass.

It was curious the way Marc spoke of God and Jesus. It was like they were…friends, but he reverenced them too. She could hear it in his voice. She didn't think he was a fanatic, but that had a little more to do with the fact that he was an FBI agent than the way his features softened when he spoke of God.

Melanie checked her watch and glanced back at the entrance to the store to see Marc standing to the side scanning the parking lot. He was early. She couldn't help the smile that came to her lips. Her heartbeat quickened, and she forced herself to take a few deep breaths. She double-checked that she had her list, coupons and money in her pouch and exited the car.

She watched him as she approached the store. It only took him a few seconds to spot her, and the smile that took over his face when their eyes met was breathtaking. Why did he have to be so good looking and nice. She might have had a chance if he were just nice. She'd met nice guys before whom she had no interest in. Marc's looks, quick thinking and kindness were a lethal combination for her heart. She would have to tread lightly.

"You're early," they said in unison. She laughed as he smiled. He lead her to the carts and disengaged one for her.

"Do you start on any particular side?" he asked.

"I usually start with drinks and water so I can put them on the bottom," she said, at least feeling confident in this.

He held out a hand. "I will defer to your expertise."

"I thought you said you shop for yourself." She looked at him out of the side of her eye.

213

"I do, but if you have a plan for how you shop, you are definitely more experienced with this than I am," he said, looking around the store.

"Is that something you do automatically, or is there a reason why you seem to be looking for all of the exits?" she asked as they headed toward the drink aisle.

"Uh, well, since I was unaware that I was doing it, I guess it has become automatic," he said sheepishly.

"Cool. That must make it hard for people to sneak up on you," Melanie said.

"Um, I guess so." He shrugged as he looked at the variety of waters, sparkling waters and sodas.

She got the feeling he wasn't in the mood to talk about his work skills, so she decided to change the subject.

"What's your favorite drink?" she asked, placing a twelve pack of soda in the cart.

He turned around in a circle, perusing the aisles. "Um, cranberry juice, but it has so much sugar I only allow myself to have a glass every few days."

"Are you a health nut?"

"Far from it. Right now I have in my kitchen, two frozen pizzas, a bottle of ketchup, bottled water, tea, an orange and an apple," he said.

She blinked wondering if his list was an exact itemization of what was in his kitchen but had a feeling it was.

"The cranberry juice is in the juice aisle. Why they separate liquids like that, I don't know."

He looked at the wonderment on her face. "Huh, I guess I have more to learn than I thought."

He reached over, picked up a twenty-four pack of water and placed it in his cart. "Well let's get this party started. Do you want one of these?"

She nodded and held up two fingers. He placed the water at the bottom of her cart and went back to his.

She watched him as they slowly continued down the aisle. He seemed to be in deep thought. They were halfway through the next aisle when she stopped. He rolled a few feet then stopped to look back at her.

"If I wanted to shop alone I wouldn't have met you here," she said and stared at him.

He watched her for a moment then took a deep breath and looked everywhere but her. "I hate feeling lost. It is not an emotion I'm used to. Actually, it's quite foreign."

He rocked back on his toes and heels once. "I'm lost in here. I usually come in, head to the freezer aisle, pick up some produce and somehow find the juice aisle. I also shop at a much smaller store."

He suddenly stopped as if he'd said too much.

She watched him intently. Was he being serious with her? It was shopping, for goodness sake. She wasn't going to share that with him though.

"When I came out of that party the other night under Katrina's arm I had no clue what I would do if those guys came after us." She stepped around her cart to stand in front of him.

"When I saw you—well, I must admit I was surprised at first—but once you opened your mouth, I went from lost to safe, and I have continued to feel safe every time I'm with you. I feel safe with you now." She sucked her teeth.

"I am probably giving away way too much right now, but so are you," she said, watching his eyes dart to hers.

"I don't need you to know where everything is on these shelves and in these aisles. I already know that. I want to spend time with the guy I was in the car with yesterday."

She stepped in closer and looked up at him. "Is he in there?"

She watched him as he watched her. His expression didn't shift for a couple of seconds and her heart dropped. He blinked slowly and nodded.

"Where are the hot dogs? I need something to go with the ketchup in my fridge," he said before giving her one of his charming smiles.

She shook her head. "That's unfortunate."

She went back to her cart. "There are two kinds of people in this world. Those who put ketchup on their hot dog and those who put mustard, relish and onions on their hot dogs."

His smile faltered. "So, what does that mean?"

She pushed her cart past him. "You aren't perfect."

She hadn't gotten five feet before she heard him chuckling. "Sassy mouth."

She laughed out loud at the reference. She had been called "Black Ice," "Regal" and "the Golden Princess." None of them were meant to be a compliment, and they all spoke of coldness, detachment from other kids and lack of emotion. It was quite the opposite though. She'd felt every word, look and sneer deeply.

Sassy mouth. She liked it. It said she had fire and maybe a zest for life. One day she would tell him how much that meant to her, but not today.

"Come on. Let's see what we can find out about each other in the next aisle."

***

For the next hour and a half, they slowly walked up and down the aisles as she went through her list and placed item after item in her cart. They continued their conversation from the night before, asking each other semiserious questions like what they had wanted to be when they were young. She found the light conversation soothing. If they spent more time together—and she had a feeling they would—the conversations would grow deep soon enough. She hadn't even let herself contemplate how she would tell him about her childhood or her mother.

Things had gotten better after those first few minutes in the store. They played around a little bit with each other's carts and secretly snuck food in there when the other wasn't looking. Yet there was still an underlying tension around him. Their conversation continued from the night before, and she learned they had a lot more in common than she first thought. She really enjoyed spending time with him.

As it always was by the time she was almost done, her cart was extremely heavy. Marc switched carts with her since his was nowhere as full.

Soon after that they made their way to the cashier, and he helped her place her bags in her car. She checked her watch when they were done. She still had plenty of time to get the groceries home and go pick up Paige. She slid behind the wheel, and he held the car door open.

"So, I'm wondering if you might like to go out with me again," he said, trying to look relaxed.

She thought about the date they were ending and how much fun they'd had grocery shopping. Grocery shopping. She wondered what a more traditional date would be like.

"Sure," Melanie said, looking up at him.

He seemed to let out a deep breath.

"Good, 'cause I have to go shopping for my niece's birthday present, and I thought you could go with me."

Her mouth didn't drop open, but it was close. She turned to stare at her steering wheel while she thought of what to say. To say that she was flabbergasted was an understatement. Yes, they had fun, but still.

She looked back up to see if he were really serious, and she saw a slow lazy grin take over his features.

She burst out laughing, maybe more in relief than actual humor.

"Oh, you think you got jokes," she finally said.

He placed his forefinger and thumb two inches apart.

"How about dinner? Maybe Wednesday. It may have to be late. Maybe eight o'clock or eight thirty?"

"That sounds perfect." She knew she was beaming. She didn't care.

He reached down to brush his knuckles against her cheek. She felt the feeling all the way to her toes.

"Will you call me?" His voice seemed to be coming from a long ways away. She responded as soon as the words worked themselves into something that made sense in her head.

"Sure. Tomorrow night?"

"How about tonight?"

"Yep. Tomorrow night it is," she said, nodding her head and smiling.

He looked a little disappointed but nodded in agreement.

She wasn't about to tell him that if she called him tomorrow she wouldn't have the same time constraints.

He closed her door. "I'll follow you home to make sure you get there in one piece." Then he was gone before she could discourage him. She paused, trying to think if she should get out and tell him no, but that would look suspicious. She would just hope he didn't get out to talk to her when she made it home.

She hoped hard all the way. Maybe her mother was taking a nap or in the back of the house. She drove with her fingers crossed the last mile home.

Marc only slowed down as he passed her home and waved. She breathed a sigh of relief and carried the first set of bags to the house.

She stepped in the house only to come face-to-face with her mother.

Chapter 20

Marc closed his door and walked up the now familiar steps to Mr. Sable's home.

He'd received a call the day before, letting him know that Mr. Sable would be able to see him this morning. He took an early lunch just in case Melanie was in need of a ride later and drove as fast as the speed limit would allow.

He had some questions, and he hoped Mr. Sable was in a giving mood.

He knocked and only needed to wait a few seconds before it was opened.

"Good morning, Special Agent Miller," the elderly gentleman said as he stood aside to allow Marc inside.

"What is it going to take for you to call me Marc?" he said as he crossed the threshold.

"Marriage," the man said.

It struck Marc as funny.

"But I don't even know your name," Marc said with a chuckle and was met with nothing but a bland expression.

Marc nodded his head both in recognition of his failure to elicit a smile and in apology to the servant.

"Mr. Sable is this way," the man said, leading Marc through the house straight to the patio.

Marc walked through yet another door onto a patio with floor-to-ceiling windows giving a person the feeling they were outside without having to deal with bugs or heat, in the summer, anyway.

He was sure the view was gorgeous with summertime blooms, but they were almost in winter.

Marc was shown to a small table laden with what looked to be lunch fare, and wondered if he were interrupting a meeting Mr. Sable was about to have. He checked his watch. He was exactly on time.

He sat down in the seat the man gestured to. It was positioned with its back to the wall, allowing him to see the room in its entirety.

Once he was left alone, he scanned the room, taking in all of the exits and furnishings, which were light.

"Special Agent Miller?"

Marc raised himself from the chair in respect and watched Mr. Sable enter the room. He was dressed in a linen tunic-style top and loose pants. It made him look relaxed.

"Mr. Sable," he said, giving a slight bow before returning to his chair.

Mr. Sable sat down at the table and took a napkin from his place setting. "I know it's early for lunch, but I was hoping you haven't eaten yet."

"No, I haven't." Marc wondered if Mr. Sable had an idea why Marc requested this meeting and was trying to appease him. Then he wondered why he wouldn't know. He knew everything else.

Marc slipped his napkin from the table and opened it on his lap. He followed Mr. Sable's movements and partook of the fresh fruit and began constructing a sandwich of roast beef and pastrami. He'd always wanted to mix the meats.

They were in the middle of their meal before Mr. Sable spoke again. "How is Grace Melanie doing?" The use of her full name struck Marc as odd. He'd come to know her as Melanie, separating her from her mother.

"She's doing well. She recovered faster than I expected for her ordeal," he said honestly.

"I suspect your presence that evening and even now has something to do with that. She has something else to focus on?" Mr. Sable said before popping a grape in his mouth.

Marc shrugged. No need to deny what he hoped to be true.

"May I ask how the investigation is going regarding the man who lured them to the party and his friends?"

"All I can say is it is going slowly because of their ties to a more heinous group the FBI is investigating. It should be over soon."

"I hope so," Mr. Sable said, wiping his mouth. "I received your report. It was thorough, so I was curious as to why you sought an audience with me."

Marc smiled to himself. It was a good thing he never let his guard down in this house.

"Thank you for inviting me to break bread with you. The food was delicious," Marc said, straightening up in his seat.

Mr. Sable nodded.

"Is Colonel Morganson how you found out about the party?"

Mr. Sable looked at him for a moment then nodded again.

"Does he communicate with you often?" Marc asked.

"When needed." Mr. Sable folded his hands together.

"Who is he?" Marc asked.

"He is a colonel in the United States Air Force, and he is Melanie and Paige's father and Brenda's husband."

"I thought you said Melanie was Paige's mother?" Marc asked without thinking.

"She is Paige's biological mother and sister for all intents and purposes, as he is Paige's father for all intents and purposes."

Marc went over Mr. Sable's initial answer. "Is he Melanie's biological father?"

Mr. Sable smiled. "You are the real deal, Special Agent Miller."

Marc waited for an actual answer but it never came.

Marc tamped down the irritation. "Why is Melanie's protection so deep? Why is she being guarded so heavily without her knowledge?"

"I cannot share that with you. To do so would be placing yours and Melanie's life in jeopardy.

"So, what you're saying is if you tell me then you would have to kill me?" Marc said half joking.

"No. I am saying, if I tell you it could get you killed," Mr. Sable said, leaning forward in his chair, all relaxation gone.

"There are some things that I have not revealed. Not because I harbor any illusions that I can control life or people, but because if I tell you, there is a very good chance that the information will get into the hands of the wrong people. Please know that this truly is for your safety and Melanie's. The fact that I have told you that Brian is alive could very well put his life in danger." The older man said with severity.

"Then why would you tell me that?" Marc asked, his curiosity piqued.

"Because Melanie knows, and a day may come when you need to protect her from those who would try and use that knowledge against her." Mr. Sable answered. "She's an accessory to a cover-up, or is faking one's death no longer a crime." He continued as he leaned back in his chair again.

"She may not share that with you now, but there will come a day, a dark day, when Melanie will need to contact him, and you may be the only one who can encourage her to keep going when it looks like she will hit a dead end," Mr. Sable said.

Marc opened his mouth to speak, but Mr. Sable held up his hand.

"I am working to delay that day from coming for a very long time."

"Do I need to be on the lookout for someone?" Marc asked.

"If you don't find them, they will not know you exist."

"What?" That concept went against everything Marc had been taught.

"You never know when there is someone listening for what they can sell instead of who that protects. Please, for your sake, stop digging."

Marc stared at Mr. Sable for a few moments and never saw a flutter of movement. He wasn't going to budge.

"I'm used to being the planner. If I don't know what to look for how can I plan?"

"You can know everything, or you can stay in Melanie's life," Mr. Sable said quietly, but the sound put Marc on edge rather than soothed him.

He continued to stare at the man, knowing he wasn't bluffing. There was no reason for it.

"Brian was given the same choice," Luca said with a weariness in his voice that surprised Marc. "Are you really going to take another person from Melanie's life?"

Marc sat there congratulating the man on playing the only move that would make him back down because he couldn't leave Melanie."

"No." Marc didn't feel the need to elaborate.

Mr. Sable nodded, and the light returned to his eyes.

Ha. Marc thought. Mr. Sable hadn't known which he would choose.

Mr. Sable checked his watch. "Unless you have any more questions, this meeting should end because your lunch break is almost over."

Marc got up, refusing to lament the fact that he didn't get the information he wanted.

Just before they reached the door, Mr. Sable placed a hand on his arm. "You have permission to tell her everything you deem necessary. Couples shouldn't have secrets from one another."

Marc had nothing to say. He just nodded and left.

All the way to work he went through what was said during lunch. By .the time he stepped through the office door, he was resolved to let it go until he couldn't let it go.

***

That evening Marc found himself sitting at another table sharing a meal. It was just his mother, his dad and himself for dinner which was common, especially when he ran out of food. This evening he came more for comfort than anything else.

Marc put the food on his fork, placed the food in his mouth, chewed slowly and swallowed. He did it over and over until he was done. He was in a place where he could think and muse over his day.

After dinner he washed dishes with his father.

"So, who did you come to talk to?"

Marc looked up from the plate he was drying and answered with a sheepish smile. "Mom."

"Ah. It's about that young lady," Marc's dad said, handing him a glass.

Marc wasn't surprised. There wasn't much his parents didn't share with each other.

"Yes."

"Okay, but don't count me out. I got that woman to marry me," his dad said, letting water out of the sink.

"I will never forget that. You are one of the smartest men I know," Marc said and meant it. "But I need a woman's point of view."

When they were done, Marc walked into the den and sat across from his mother. She glanced at him and put her book down.

"I'm about to make a big decision." He rubbed his hands together.

"It sounds like you already have," she said.

"I may have, but I haven't acted on it, so I could change my mind. I never thought I would be in this position. I thought my job would be my life.

"That isn't much of a life," his mom said. He'd heard it in different ways over the last few years.

"It was the one I'd always wanted," he said, looking at his hands.

Are you telling me you want her more?" Her eyes danced.

"I could be," he said.

"What's your reservation?" his mother said, leaning forward.

"There is a bit of intrigue surrounding her. She has protection like Fort Knox, but no one has told her anything," he said, looking up to meet his mother's eyes.

His mother's eyes clouded a little as she thought about his words. "Is she dangerous or careless?" "No. She's the most careful and disciplined young woman I've met," he said emphatically.

"So what is the real reason for your reservation?" she asked.

"I'm not sure if she thinks I'm the one"

"Well, you do have to remember that you have a four-year head start. Your feelings may have evolved where she is concerned, but you said you had a profound feeling of protection for her which was some kind of connection. Tell me why you think she may not share your feelings."

"Why?"

He shared what he could about the night he came to Melanie's rescue, their interaction afterward and the car rides they shared. He held back the information about Luca Sable. He wouldn't even bring the man up until she asked him point blank.

"I think she is more grateful than anything else." He said.

He started sharing his date with Melanie on Saturday, and his mother stopped him.

"How was it?" she asked, interest showing in her eyes again.

He shrugged. "It went well." He thought about that and rephrased his answer. "It went better toward the end than it did in the beginning."

"Why, what did you guys do?"

"Well, she had some grocery shopping to do, so I asked to join her since I had a little bit of shopping to do myself."

"Wait. You went into a grocery store?"

"Yes."

"How many times have you been in a store before Saturday?"

He gave the question serious consideration. "Twice."

"Twice in how much time?" she asked, the pain of the subject showing in her eyes.

"Twice in the last two years." He started to ask himself what he'd been thinking.

"What do you do? How do you get your grocery shopping done?" she asked.

"I get it delivered," he said.

"So you went to the store," she prompted.

"It was okay until we entered the first aisle. Well, almost okay. I hadn't been in that store before so I wasn't able to see all the exits," he said, breathing out.

"Were you able you use some of the exercises Dr. Stance gave you? I know it's been a long time…" His mother's voice faded.

"I did. I was so busy breathing and pretending I was somewhere else she got a little miffed with me."

"You didn't tell her?"

He shook his head.

"Oh, honey."

He just shrugged.

"What did she say?"

He glanced at his mom, wondering how she knew.

230

"You said you pretended you weren't there. That gets pretty obvious after a while."

"She called me out on it and told me she could shop on her own."

"Makes sense. What did you say?"

He gave his mother a rueful look. "In essence I told her I felt lost in the place and felt uncomfortable not knowing where everything was."

"So you told her you were a control freak instead of being honest about your anxiety from being in grocery stores?"

He nodded.

"So instead of receiving sympathy for something that wasn't your fault and sharing a vulnerable moment that might have brought you together if she is a woman worth having, you decided to lie and look like a control freak?" she asked.

He felt dumber than a rock at the moment, but he didn't want his first date to be a therapy session with the woman he really wanted to date again.

"Okay. What did she say?" his mom said with a sigh.

"She told me that I didn't have to play her rescuer all the time, even if that was how we started this relationship. She said she felt lost the night she had to get all of her friends out of the house, and seeing how I handled the situation made her feel safe anytime she was with me."

His mother's eyes were glistening when he was done. "I think you need to give the woman more credit. I believe she knows her feelings." Before he could ask her what she meant, his mother asked another question. "How did it go after that?"

"I powered through. I was able to relax enough to play with her a little and hold conversations, but I suspect she noticed that I was still tense. I think I breathed my first full breath when we got outside."

"So, not your best impression." She seemed to be in deep thought. "Did you ask her on another date?"

"Yes. We're going out to dinner on Wednesday."

"I suggest you have a long talk after and share everything. Until you do so, you can't really know if this is going to work."

"What if she decides this is too much trouble?"

"Then it's better to know now."

"I think my heart is already invested," he said solemnly.

"What did you receive during your prayers?" she asked.

"She's the one," he said almost reluctantly.

"If she's the one for you then why are you acting like you don't know?"

"Is she a believer?" his mother asked.

"No. Her parents never talked about God."

"Well, I guess that's better than someone who has been hurt by someone misrepresenting God. I want you to invite her to church on Sunday."

232

"It might be a little soon—" Marc stopped at his mother's look.

"If your heart is invested then I want to meet her. I can meet her at church, or you can bring her here."

"Will you be going to the first or second service?" Marc asked, choosing quickly.

His mother smiled.

***

That evening, Marc lay in bed contemplating the different ways his talk with Melanie could go wrong and then how it might go right. His mother was right. He'd lied. Not intentionally. He had felt lost in the grips of his memory, and the place was huge and mazelike, but he let her think it was because he felt uncomfortable being in a place that he hadn't already cased.

Hopefully, she would be able to forgive him for his deception. That was all he could really call it. He didn't even want to think of what would happen to him if she didn't.

He'd not had these kinds of feelings for Sheila. Everything was so easy and comfortable with her. It was also lacking, and until he saw Melanie again he hadn't realized how much he'd compromised in his personal life.

Sheila was nice. She didn't play games. She had very clear aspirations, and even he could persuade her to deviate from them. They had a lot in common, and she went to church with him on occasion, but still…

He'd been back in Atlanta for two weeks when he was helping his father clean out in the attic. He found the box of journals he kept until he moved to take his job with the FBI. He had sifted through them, reading about Bible studies that caught his attention and the thoughts of a much younger him. The one on top had been the most recent. It held the list of things he wanted in a wife. He knew at the time it was a long way off, but he listened to his heart and God when he was making the list. He moved the boxes with his dad but took the journal home with him.

He took it out once more the day he'd run into Melanie again. She'd come close to matching the characteristics he'd listed. All the ones he'd known. When he'd spent time with her, he'd gotten to know more she'd continued to match the items. All except one. The biggest one. She wasn't a believer.

He'd prayed about that. He'd prayed about her. How could he not. She was always on his mind. He'd quieted himself and listened, which wasn't too easy those first few days when she didn't call him, but as one day dragged into the next, he began to welcome a no, so he could let the idea of them go. Instead, he received a yes that confirmed itself deep in his soul.

This didn't make waiting for her easier, but it kept him just short of hounding her.

Now he was making dumb decisions that could cause her not to trust him. His very last intention was to hurt her, but some old scars were not good with being poked.

Marc considered again the differences between his feelings for Sheila and Melanie. He should have known that the need to maintain a certain amount of separation between Sheila and himself was not a sign of a healthy relationship. With Melanie, he wanted no such thing. He would have been fine with not letting her out of his sight from the moment he saw her walk out the door of the party.

He liked being near her. He liked the way he felt when he was near her. He also liked the fact that if she were meant to be his wife, she would one day come to know Jesus Christ as her Lord and Savior, and she would have an opportunity to have eternal life. That thought made him smile.

The smile slowly fell as he remembered what he needed to reveal to her on Wednesday. He had really wanted more time to court her before he told her everything. It may give him an advantage if her heart was also invested.

Chapter 21

Melanie found her mother's hovering almost suffocating. She hadn't been given this much attention by her mother since her first month back in public school. Melanie went about her regular schedule, hoping her mother's keen nose for anything fishy was broken.

Saturday, when she'd walked into the house to set her purse down, her mother was on her like a probation officer in a transition home.

She was so surprised at her mother questioning Marc's presence—as quick as it was—it took a moment to come up with a decent half-truth. It had been so long since she'd had to lie; she was gratefully out of practice.

"I asked you a question, young lady." She could remember her mother's mouth fixed in a line and her eyes going from curious to calculating.

Melanie had stumbled over her explanation that the man in the car was a friend she'd met at the café near her school. He'd honked at her, getting her attention at the stop sign at the end of the street, then slowed once she reached her house to wave hello.

Her mother's gaze was piercing, but it did nothing to prepare Melanie for the woman's next words.

"Was he the reason why you were late coming in last Thursday?"

Only years of hiding her emotions from her mother kept her jaw from dropping. How did she know?

Her mother's smile sent a chill up her spine.

"You're losing your touch, little girl. I read you like a book."

Melanie had taken a deep breath and told her mother that she'd gone to a party where she'd caught a guy trying to drug one of her friends but didn't get to her other friend's side in time to prevent her from ingesting some of whatever drug was being used. They'd spent a few hours in the ER until her friend was released.

Her mother had warned her against borrowing her clothing without asking, then dismissed her, telling her to bring in the groceries before some of them melted.

Since then her mother would "pop in" to talk at all times of the evening until she was ready to leave for work, which she also started going to later. She'd been going in early for so long, Melanie had forgotten that her mother worked from 9 p.m. to 5 a.m.

Melanie let Marc know that she wouldn't be ready until nine o'clock for dinner. Marc seemed to take it in stride, and Melanie was relieved.

Melanie was really looking forward to their date. She'd shared her date on Saturday with Rickie as promised, and her friend had "oohed and aahed" so much, she sounded like a sitcom soundtrack. Though Melanie wasn't as ready to swoon over Marc's help or desire to continue to protect her, it did touch her heart as had every other thing Marc had done just for her.

She wondered what he would come up with to make her laugh tonight. She couldn't remember the last time she laughed so often. She was given to smiling in the middle of doing her homework because a phrase or word reminded her of something Marc said or did. With each conversation she was becoming more attached, and when he rubbed his knuckles along her cheek before closing her door she wanted to lean into his hand to prolong the feeling of warmth and well-being that flowed through her. A man who could do that with just a soft caress was appealing to the woman hoping for the real-life happy ending to be detrimental to the shield around her heart.

***

Melanie had taken Rickie's advice on what to wear, settling for a pair of nice wool slacks and a silk blouse she'd bought for her college interview. She'd slowly turned in front of her full-length mirror and finally decided that things would get no better or worse the longer she looked.

Marc rang the doorbell exactly at nine o'clock. Melanie was walking around the banister when Paige appeared in her doorway. Her eyes widened and a smile crept across her face.

"Where're you going?" she said in a stage whisper.

Melanie decided to own this. "I'm going on a date."

Melanie heard her father walk to the entryway and open the door.

"A date? With a guy?" Paige's eyes got wider.

"Was he the reason why you got home so late last week?" Paige asked and Melanie wondered if she'd said something to Grace.

"No, I had a friend who got sick so I went to the hospital to make sure they were all right," she said as she began descending the stairs.

"May I see him?" Paige asked, trying to get a peek of Marc from her position.

Melanie bit her tongue on her retort. Marc wasn't an animal in a zoo to be gawked at. "Yes. You may come and meet him," Melanie said.

Paige's eyes lit up. "Let me change my shirt."

"Why?" Melanie asked.

"First impressions. If I look good, it looks good for you," Paige said, stepping back in her room.

"Why?" Melanie repeated, truly puzzled by the girl's thought process.

"One second," Paige said before disappearing behind the door.

Melanie checked her watch. She counted to fifteen and slowly started making her way down the stairs again. She was halfway down when she heard Paige's door open and listened to her scramble down after her.

"I am going to ask you to try not to embarrass me," Melanie said right before she knew she came into view of those standing at the door.

"Like how?" Paige whispered.

Melanie saw Marc's smile grow wider as she reached the bottom step. It made her feel beautiful.

She took in his suit and tie and thought he looked devastatingly handsome. She felt like the luckiest woman in the world.

"Hi." He breathed out more than he spoke.

She opened her mouth to respond, when he continued.

"You look beautiful."

It hit her right then that she got it all. Even though she'd missed her winter formal junior and senior proms, watching Marc's response gave her the best part of each of those experiences.

"Hi, and thank you," she said, unable to keep the smile off her face.

Her father's light cough reminded her that they weren't alone. Melanie turned to her dad. "We are just going to dinner. Did he tell you where, because he wouldn't tell me," she said, turning back to Marc. He'd told her the place he was taking her was a surprise, which made dressing for their date challenging. She guessed she nailed it by his expression.

"He told me. He also promised to have you home inside of the twelve o'clock hour since you have class tomorrow."

Melanie nodded. "Fair enough."

She felt a nudge at her side and remembered Paige. "Oh, Marc. This is Paige."

Paige leaned forward to shake Marc's hand.

"Very pleased to meet you," Marc said, stepping forward to meet her, and Melanie was about to release a sigh of relief when Paige spoke again.

"Very pleased to meet you too. Wow. You are gorgeous. Do you know that?"

Melanie wanted to cover her face with her hands. Instead she sent her father a pleading look.

"Well, I seem to be in good company. It's not often that a family is blessed with two beautiful women."

Paige shrugged like she heard that all the time. "Thank you, but I'm not a woman yet but I am a young lady and I have eight more years to get even more beautiful.

Marc chuckled. "I stand corrected."

"Come on, Paige. You and I have a date with a pint of Chunky Monkey," Melanie's dad said, reaching for the girl who was still making goo-goo eyes at Melanie's date.

"Bye," Paige said, finger waving as she was ushered down the hall to the living room.

"Bye," Marc replied, holding up one hand.

When Melanie turned back to Marc, he must have seen the astonishment on her face.

"What?" he said, taking her jacket from her hands so he could help her into it.

"Paige was flirting with you," she said, hovering somewhere between shocked and mortified.

"Really. I thought she was charming," Marc said before opening the door for her.

She stared at him a moment before walking through the door. She turned to lock the door herself, glad at least that Paige's performance was brief.

She turned back around thinking Marc had moved away and bounced off him. He reached out to steady her then kept his hand on her upper arms.

"I meant what I said. You look very beautiful this evening, but then you look more beautiful every time I see you. It makes it nice since I only have eyes for you," he said as his eyes scanned her face. Then he stepped back and dropped his hands.

"Are you ready to go to dinner?" he asked.

"Yes," she said because she couldn't think of anything else to say. His words had sent her heart into her throat.

She let him guide her down the walk and to his car in a bit of a daze. She was sitting snug in the passenger seat watching him focus on the road, rearview mirror, side-view mirrors and then finally her.

"Why are you looking at me?" he said, his lips twitching as his gaze returned to the road.

"I think my sister was right. You are gorgeous." She smiled when he glanced over at her in amazement.

"Are you flirting with me?" Marc asked.

She shrugged. "Paige got to do it. I figured I would give it a try. How am I doing?"

He chuckled. "You're a natural."

She bit her thumbnail and smiled as she watched the lights go by outside the passenger window.

"I wanted to ask you something," he said with a couple of deep breaths.

"Ask away," she said, curious.

"I was wondering if you would come to church with me on Sunday," he asked.

Her heart took a stumble then righted itself and beat a healthy staccato against her ribs. Church. She knew nothing of church. She didn't even know his denomination. She felt stupid for asking.

"What do you do at your church?" she asked tentatively.

"Mmm. What do we do," he said.

"So one of the reasons for church these days is for people of like faith to come together to praise God with words and worship Him with songs, to receive encouragement and listen to a sermon from the pastor that is meant to both teach and confirm. Another reason is so we can be encouraged by other people's testimonies, grow with each other and help each other. We are also charged with spreading the gospel in every part of the life we live. It isn't always with words but also with how we conduct ourselves in life."

"Wow. That's a lot. You do all that during service?" How long must that take?

"No, not all. It happens over time, but there is some of it in each service. We praise and worship God in a number of ways: with music, words and sometimes dance—it seems like there

243

should be more words for that act of praise and worship." He said the last part more to himself than her.

"The pastor of our church offers a sermon, and we celebrate milestones in people's lives," he finished.

"You do this every Sunday?"

He nodded. "It's more of an extension of our everyday lives."

She thought about it for a moment. It sounded nice. She'd heard gospel many times. Some sounded like love stories. It couldn't hurt. If she didn't like it she would just let him know, even though it seemed like a good portion of his life.

"Where's your church?" she asked.

"Benson and Vista," he responded without hesitation.

"What time?" she asked.

"Nine o'clock."

"I'll think about it," she said honestly. Melanie wondered if she could get Katrina to go with her. Her friend had been wanting to thank Marc in person.

He took a deep breath. "Speaking of living a life in representation of God and His love…I need to confess something."

She watched his features contort briefly and knew it wasn't something he enjoyed doing. Her whole body tensed.

"Saturday at the supermarket I was having problems," he started slowly.

She nodded, remembering, but hadn't he already explained himself?

"I told you I was lost, and I was—to a degree. I was more lost in a memory rather than feeling lost in the store," he said. She could see his hands gripping the steering wheel.

She said nothing as he went on. "When I was six years old, I went with my family to the grand opening of one of the first big box stores. I don't think anyone thought there would be that many people. Getting into the store wasn't an issue. It happened when I stopped to look at something. I wasn't supposed to let go of my brother's hand, but I was awestruck. I don't even remember what I was looking at now, but it was enough to draw my attention away long enough that when I took the hand next to me and looked up, it was into the eyes of a stranger."

Melanie found herself holding her breath. Her heart clenched as she listened to Marc.

"All I saw were legs. At six I was terrified. I walked around looking for anyone who looked familiar for what seemed like hours. There was one man who saw me. He told me my parents were looking for me and guided me to the front of the store. I was relieved and shaky, but as we got closer to the exit and I didn't see my parents, the terror set in again. I pulled at his hand, but he clamped tight on my arm. He pulled until I began struggling with all of my might. I finally started screaming and he let me go. That was it. I kind of left the situation in my head.

"My mom said they found me three hours after I disappeared, hiding under a display. I wouldn't come out even for my dad. They said my eyes were open, but I don't remember anything until two days later when I woke up in the hospital. My mind had shut down to protect itself.

"I went to therapy for a few years, but even now I'm very uncomfortable in grocery stores. The bigger they are, the worse it is," he said.

Melanie was left dumbstruck by his story. She shivered at the thought of what he went through. What he still went through.

"So why did you offer to go shopping with me?" she said almost breathlessly at the thought and memory of his initial quietness.

"Because I wanted to see you when we weren't running from a house or sitting in an emergency waiting room. I wanted to see what you were like outside of a intense moment. I wanted to get to know you and spend time with you," he said earnestly.

She was speechless again for another reason. That was the single most beautiful gesture anyone had ever made for her. She wouldn't let him do it again, but she couldn't wait to tell her friends.

He pulled into a parking lot, and she looked up to see the name of a high-end steak restaurant. She smiled to herself. He was pulling out all the stops.

"Are you okay with this place?" he asked after putting the car in park.

"I've never been here, but I hear they have a decent steak." She grinned at him.

"Sassy mouth," he said, smiling at her before getting out of the car and coming over to open her door. He took her hand to help her out of the car and kept hold of it all the way to the restaurant.

She giggled and noticed that he didn't let go of her hand until he opened the door for her. If it were his goal to make her feel like a princess, he had already met it, and they had just started the date.

Chapter 22

Dinner was more delicious than she expected, and her choice of the Parmesan-encrusted top sirloin was perfectly tender. Marc shared lighter and funnier family memories with her throughout dinner, making her feel like she knew his jokester of a big brother, bossy older sister, willful and extremely intelligent little sister and almost unbelievably loving parents.

There was a nervousness about him, though, that she couldn't understand. His finger fidgeted, and he must have adjusted his tie twenty times. When she asked him about it, he said he had a couple of things on his mind and looked to make a concerted effort to relax.

She tried to shrug it off, but right before they headed toward her home, he told her he needed to tell her something. Now it was her turn to fidget until he took her hand while he drove her home. She hoped it wasn't anything bad. She'd had such a wonderful time.

She started imagining things, and her mind began to run away with her. "Are you married?"

"What?" His head jerked toward her. "I say I need to tell you something, and you assume my news is that I'm married?"

He looked slightly offended but more hurt than anything. She shrugged. She was definitely keeping the rest of her guesses to herself. She had to admit that she felt better that he wasn't playing with her feelings.

248

He pulled up in front of her home, placing the car in park. He heaved a sigh before letting down the windows a quarter of the way. She wondered if he thought they were going to have a heated discussion and laughed at her own joke. She looked at her house. It looked dark, save the light over the front door. When she turned back to Marc his expression was solemn, and she was back on alert.

"I want to let you know that despite how we finally got together, I wouldn't change a thing about the last week. You've consumed so much of my thoughts I feel like we've been seeing each other much longer." He rubbed his hands on his slacks, and she so desperately wanted to calm him, she reached over and laid her hand on his. He blew out a deep breath and shook his head as he chuckled to himself.

"You amaze me. Your heart is bigger than your beautiful eyes, and I've never met anyone like you. You are rare and precious, and that is one of the reasons why I made the decision I have to tell you about now, so that you don't think I take our situation for granted." He rubbed his free hand down his face and took a deep breath.

He turned her hand that was covering his and squeezed it before placing it on her lap.

"I used to live in Colorado. It was my first home office within the FBI. As a new agent I was given a surveillance detail. It was one week, and though I didn't admit it until later, it changed my life." He looked up at her from the steering wheel he'd been staring at.

"My surveillance detail was the Morganson family," he said, not looking away from her.

She heard him speak. She knew she heard him speak. It made sense and it didn't. He was an agent with the FBI, so of course he would do surveillance, but on her family? She blinked at him hoping the movement would help clear her mind.

"You watched my family?" she asked softly.

"Yes," he said, nodding once.

"For a week?" she asked, using the time to wrap her mind around everything.

"Yes," was all he said.

"After the FBI pulled us from WITSEC?"

His eyes widened slightly. She guessed he didn't think she'd known.

"I wasn't there when that happened."

She let go of a big sigh in response. That was something. She nodded for him to continue.

"I saw you going into school one day. That might be the reason I seem familiar. I think you saw me across the street at the construction site."

A younger Marc superimposed himself in front of this man in her mind, and she felt dumb for not making the connection. "The goatee man," she said without thinking.

He smiled at her word but it didn't reach his eyes. "Yes."

"I thought about you for a long time after that," she shared because she couldn't help herself.

"The moment you looked in my direction, I thought you had the saddest eyes. No one with such beautiful eyes should hold such sadness as well. I had the urge to take you away from whatever was making you so unhappy."

For a moment she thought he'd been holding on to some secret and forbidden love for her, but the reality of that would have been disturbing, so she let go of that childish notion.

"Mr. Luca Sable approached me and asked if I would watch after you, soon after that."

"Mr. Sable?" It was a wonder her brain could work enough to help her form words let alone give her the ability to talk.

"You know Mr. Sable? He was in town?" Melanie asked then shut her mouth. *How much did Marc know? Why him? He'd been watching her since she was sixteen?* She frowned at her fingers.

"I turned him down," Marc said.

At his words, Melanie's head shot up. "No. Why?"

"You were sixteen, and after one week I wanted to find the safest town in the United States and hide you there. I think I was afraid of getting in any deeper." He shrugged.

It was a lot to take in, but he was forthcoming with information she wouldn't have known about. It said a lot about his integrity.

"Thank you for telling me," she said to let him know she didn't hold anything against him.

"That isn't all," he said, giving her a rueful smile.

Her stomach bottomed out when she saw his face.

"I moved here a few months before you arrived," he said.

"How?" She started to ask him how he knew, but realized just because they were in a different place didn't mean the FBI wouldn't know where her family was.

"Your case came across my desk when you moved. I offered to take it because I was familiar with your family on paper. No need to bring another agent into the mix."

"Thank you," she said quieter.

"I'm not telling you these things for your thanks. I'm telling you because I need there to be full disclosure between us."

She nodded because he was so adamant.

"I need there to be no question of my motives when I tell you. You are special to me."

Her heart took a leap then settled into place. *Don't get ahead of yourself. You only met him a month ago, and most of that time you avoided him.*

She noticed that the car had gone silent, and she focused back on Marc.

"Soon after your case fell on my desk, Mr. Sable sent me a note," Marc said. "I was pretty sure he wanted to ask me again if I would watch you."

"And..." she prompted, wondering if this was the reason he looked so solemn.

"And I ran into you at the café and was bowled over," he said.

He rubbed his chest, and she wondered if he did it subconsciously.

"I also accepted his offer to watch you," he said.

She stared at him, waiting for him to tell her he was kidding. He didn't. *Why? Why would he do that?* She was finding it hard to breathe and turned toward the open window for air.

"Why?" she asked to the window.

"I wanted to make sure you were protected. If you didn't want to call or see me I couldn't do anything about that, and I wouldn't force you, but I could make sure you were okay."

That seemed so rational. He said it like it made perfect sense and she hated it. She hated not knowing. She didn't want to be rational right now. She wanted to feel, and she felt betrayed. She felt like she was being treated like a little girl who couldn't take care of herself. She didn't know who she was becoming angrier with right now: Mr. Sable, who was in town moving people around like pieces on a board, or Marc, who was willing to be used just so he could stay in her life when she hadn't made up her mind yet.

She told herself to breathe.

"Melanie."

Her name on his lips made her flinch, and she held up her hand to stop him for a moment. She needed another minute of quiet. She concentrated on breathing in and out for a minute to let the information settle in her mind. Somewhere between breath eight and twelve she had to tamp down some of her emotions. She had questions that needed answering.

"What did Mr. Sable tell you?" she asked, keeping her voice as even keel as possible.

"Melanie…" Marc's voice was beseeching, and she wanted the facts.

"What did Mr. Sable tell you about me?" she asked again.

"That Paige is your daughter, his grandson's daughter," he said quietly.

She closed her eyes and laid her head on the window, letting the coolness relieve some of the heat at her temple. It was so unfair. No. She wasn't going to go there. She had questions.

"What else?" She forced the words out of her newly parched throat.

"He told me that he regretted his part in what caused your mother to go to the FBI," he said as quietly. "He hinted at an affair, but it didn't last long."

"What?" She whirled to face Marc. My mother and Mr. Sable had an affair?" The world tilted on its axis. Her dinner rolled around in her stomach threatening a revolt.

"I thought you knew," Marc said, looking horrified at being the one to reveal that information.

She didn't care…she didn't want to care. The heat in her head and chest got hotter.

"Why would I?" Her voice climbed. She couldn't help it. "That's my mom."

"I'm sorry." Marc rubbed his forehead. "I thought you had an understanding with Mr. Sable. I thought that was why he made sure you were protected.

"Protected. Protected from what?" This wasn't making sense.

"I don't know. He wouldn't tell me."

"But he told you he and my mom had an affair?" She was pretty sure she was being unfair, but she was no longer in charge of her emotions. She had tried, but this was too close. Too close to Brian and too close to her children.

"He felt bad about something, and it seems like he's trying to make up for it," Marc said, looking at her with concern.

Too late. Too late.

"He told me what happened when you were twelve."

"Ten," she said, the lie more of a reflex than anything else. "You know that too?" She asked after pausing to look at him.

"Your FBI file has you as twenty now but that your mother kept you back two years. We never knew why. We just chalked it up to her personality. I guess it seemed less likely that a ten-year-old would have a child than a twelve-year-old; though, that is still…" He let the last of the sentence fade.

"What else?" she asked, preparing for the next hit and looking forward.

"That's it." His voice sounded concerned.

"What else? she asked not believing him.

"I don't know." His voice rose then leveled out. "Mr. Sable said he wouldn't tell me any more. He said if he told me more I wouldn't be able to see you again."

"Why?" she asked, turning to him startled.

"It would be too dangerous for you."

"And?" she almost spat.

"I don't care about any of that stuff; I just want you," he said, but his eyes held little hope.

She blinked, feeling the back of her eyes get warm. She would not cry, no matter how much she wanted to.

"Well. It sounds like you got what you wanted. You know all there is to know about me, and I can't get rid of you because you get paid to watch me." She couldn't help the shaking in her voice and it brought the anger back. She was sick of being the one who paid for other people's bad choices. Was it too much to want something not tainted by her mother or Luca Sable?

"That's not you. That is your past," Marc said. He opened his mouth to say more, but Melanie cut him off with her laugh. She knew it sounded like she was on the verge of hysterics—she probably was—but once she began she had a hard time stopping. He had no clue.

"My past. My past?" she said when she was able to gain some composure. She stopped to breathe and swallow down the lump forming in her throat. "You mean my future."

He blinked at her.

She shook her head, feeling some of the anger ebb and allowing the hopelessness of the situation to shine through.

"Paige was my last child. I can't have any more children." *There, that should take care of any thoughts he might have of creating a future for them. She had totally decimated their chances. No man wanted a barren woman.*

256

Marc reached for her, and she pressed herself to the door. If he touched her now, she would truly become unhinged. She pulled at the latch but nothing happened.

"Unlock this door. I want to get out," she said, starting to feel desperate.

"Melanie, I…"

"Open the door," she said quietly, because the only other option was to yell.

He unlocked the door and was out and at her side before she straightened herself from exiting the car.

"Please, Melanie. I know you are angry and hurt, but please try to understand that I told you now so we could go on without this between us."

She didn't say anything; she just concentrated on putting one foot in front of the other until Marc stepped in front of her. His eyes were shining with desperation, but he didn't try to touch her.

"Please, Melanie. I told you because I want a future with you. With *you*.

His words were like bulldozers against her defenses, and she knew if she didn't get in the house quickly she would break down.

"I want to go, and I need you to respect the fact that I need time to think. If you try to influence my decision in any way it will work against you, she said, surprised to be able to get words past the lump in her throat.

"Okay. Okay, Melanie," he said and stepped aside.

She hightailed it to the door and let herself in and locked it behind her. She turned off the light over the door and slid to the floor. She didn't make it to her bedroom but she didn't care. She gave into the pain and let the tears fall.

Chapter 23

"Come on, get up." She heard the words near her ear and winced at the fact that she'd been so lost in her pain that she hadn't heard her father approach.

"This is no place to have a breakdown," he said, holding out his hands to help her up.

"But I made it in the house," she said through tears. "I didn't let him see me cry. I just couldn't get up the stairs."

"Well, no sense in sitting here all night," he said, guiding her to the back of the house. "I'll fix us something warm to drink and you can tell me why your date was so disastrous."

His hand on her back brought the tears to the forefront again, making it hard to talk.

"But it wasn't." She sat on a stool at the breakfast counter. "It was a great date. I had a really great steak."

Her heart hurt so much. She desperately wanted to go to her room and climb under the covers for a few days, lick her wounds, cry some more and climb back under them again.

"He was such a nice guy. It's just not fair," she babbled as she reached for a tissue.

"Oh, Melly, if this is how you react to a good date, I would really hate to see what would happen if you had a bad date," her dad said, momentarily shocking her out of her sobs. He hadn't been intentionally funny in a long time.

"What?" he said, moving around the kitchen.

"You told a joke," she said, hiccupping.

Her dad frowned but didn't say anything.

"Not that it was funny." She shrugged, wiping at her eyes.

"Don't push it," he said, placing two cups in the microwave.

The waterworks continued, but she couldn't help her grin.

The kitchen stayed silent until her dad set her cup in front of her with the tea jar filled with a variety of individually wrapped tea bags.

"All right. Tell me what happened, so I know whether to kill him quickly or slowly."

She looked up to see if he were serious. Her heart stopped at the flat look on his face, but the gleam she'd learned to look for when she was younger, telling her he was teasing, was there.

"So, you don't want me to kill him?" he asked.

The thought of Marc not being in her world made the tears come in earnest again.

Her dad came around the counter and turned her around to envelop her in a hug. It felt good, and it hurt at the same time. How many moments in her young life had she needed this? She held on to him tightly, letting his embrace ease some of the hurt.

After what seemed like hours, he stepped back and handed her a tissue. She saw that she had soaked the front of his T-shirt, but he didn't seem to care. He sat down next to her and drew his cup toward him.

"Okay. What is the problem?" he asked.

Melanie's lip began to tremble, but she pushed back the new threat of tears and told him that Marc had been hired by Mr. Sable. She looked up to see an odd expression on her dad's face.

"Did you know?" she asked him.

Her father nodded. "We shared a few words after you went up to bed."

She didn't know how she felt about that.

"I thought you were trying to warn him away. It's why I got his numbers," she said sheepishly.

"You were willing to defy me to communicate with him?" he asked, his eyes going steely.

She shrugged.

"You like him that much?"

Her heart squeezed and she swallowed. "Yeah." Her voice cracked.

"So he tells you he was hired to watch you. Do you doubt his feelings for you?" her dad asked, and she realized at no time did she doubt that Marc had feelings for her. He'd made it clear that he really liked her. It only made it worse.

"No," she squeezed out.

"Whoa," her dad said when her eyes started watering again.

"I thought I could have someone who was untouched by all of this mess." She threw a hand up in the air.

"Please be more detailed." Her father's quiet voice clued her into her mistake.

261

"What I did with Brian," she said just as quietly, taking the blame again.

"You mean what was done to you with Brian." her father said, rubbing his eyes.

She stared at him. "Wow. You finally admitted it out loud."

Her dad's head popped up, and he stared back at her. He opened his mouth then closed it.

"Mom sure didn't accept any responsibility for her part even after they found the hormones in my blood, and when you got back I thought you were angry at me. You didn't..." She choked on the words and looked away so she could finish. "You didn't talk to me or look at me. We didn't have any more Saturday..." She clenched her teeth. She was seesawing back and forth between pain and anger for bringing it back up.

Her father looked as though he were clenching his teeth too. "I wasn't angry at you, and I never blamed you for your mother's machinations and vengeful nature. I was angry with myself for not protecting you as I should have. That is a hard thing to admit as a father. That you've failed to protect your only child. That you were so busy fighting to protect her from threats from outside, you underestimated the one right beside her." He shook his head, aging right before her eyes.

"It took an embarrassingly long time before I could look at you without the pain almost skewering me."

Melanie took a good look at her dad. There was a lot more gray at his temples than she'd seen before the move to Atlanta, but there was something else. Something softer, if she were allowed to say that about a full-bird colonel.

"I can't take it back, and you had every right to say what you did a couple of weeks ago. You sacrificed a great deal that you had no business sacrificing."

"I'm sorry, Melly. You didn't deserve what happened. You deserved to have a longer childhood, one where your eyes would remain unclouded and untouched by the hatred in this world," he said.

She heard him, but there was a question going around and around in her mind that pushed his words to the background.

"Why didn't you divorce her?"

She'd been told their marital life was none of her business, but they didn't seem happy. Not for a long time.

"I couldn't leave you to her," he said.

"Couldn't you have sued for custody?" she said.

He looked at her with a sadness so deep she wanted to console him. She reached a hand out, but he held his up, causing her to pause.

"I would have lost."

"But I'm half yours…" She stopped at his look.

"Do you really think a judge would have given me custody over your mother with my job and the way I traveled?" he said, watching her.

She thought about it and conceded that her father was right and then where would she and Paige be?

263

She nodded her head.

"You love so fiercely." He stared at her, placing a hand on her head like he did when she was real young. "I've been both proud and afraid for you," he said, not taking his hand away but stroking the crown of her head.

"But your Special Agent Miller seems different," he said.

"Yes, but…" she began, trying to get her feeling across.

"But what? Eventually you would have had to tell him. That is not something you keep from the person you love and loves you" her father said as if he were scolding her.

Love. Who was talking about love?

She could admit that she hoped it eventually got there, but they'd just had their second date and neither was perfect.

"You were saved from that talk because he disclosed everything, so there wouldn't be any misunderstanding later. He wants a "later" with you. What about you?" he asked.

She thought about the question for a few moments then shrugged.

"Well, then, I guess you have a lot to think about," he said, his eyes wet and a little sad. "Baby. Don't let your past overshadow your future. You will end up on the same path as your mom."

"Marc said Mr. Sable hinted at having an affair with Mom."

Her dad's eyes widened before he shut down his features. She always hated when he did that.

Was he right? she asked, her heart beating a mile a minute at the prospect of her mother's true anger being pointed toward someone other than herself.

"That was in the past. It was before you, and it was before me."

"Is that why she did that to me and Brian? She was trying to get back at his grandfather?" she asked, both sickened and lightened by the hope.

"Only your mother knows her real intent, but there's no arguing that what she did was wrong. If I was here I wouldn't have allowed it to happen. The only way to beat her is to find peace, and the only way to find peace is to let it go," he said and got up. He kissed her where his hand had been.

"So you think Special Agent Miller is a good man?" she asked, half kidding, half serious.

"Yes, I do, but what really matters is whether or not you think so," he said, giving her a small smile.

"But you've only met him once," she said.

"If I had to stand on my assessment of him, I would still call him a good man, but since I don't, I did a background check, and I still believe he's a good man," he said.

She stood up and hugged him with all the love she'd been too afraid to show. By the time she pulled away, both their eyes were wet.

"We have an early morning if I'm taking you to school. You better head up to bed," he said as he gathered their still-full cups.

"You are always sending me to bed like a little girl," she quipped.

"You will always be my little girl, Melly," he said, sparing her a glance before walking over to the kitchen sink.

She shuffled out of the kitchen and picked up her purse at the door before walking up the stairs to her room to go to bed.

Chapter 24

It had been a long time since Marc found himself alone in this place. There always seemed to be something going on, but not tonight and he was pleasantly surprised. He was desperate for the peace he'd found here many times in the past. It didn't matter how many times he was told that things would work out for the good—that was the future—and he was sitting right in the middle of the present. His hands had been tied and he was squirming.

He looked around the empty sanctuary with its blue-cushioned pews and dimmed sconces and listened to the silence. He had never been able to find another place with the same kind of silence. He wondered if the walls and windows had been reinforced to allow for complete quiet.

Marc sat in there in the fifth pew on the left for an hour. He prayed for the first half hour and sat thinking about the last two days. He hadn't heard from Melanie and he hadn't expected to. He'd followed her home and waited down the street as long as he dared before her mother left for work. Being on Melanie's street made him feel close to her, so he stayed long after he had to go. Seeing her for the few seconds it took for her to approach and get into Katrina's car and get out and walk in the house wasn't enough, but there was nothing he could do about it until she called him.

Tonight, he chose to come to church instead of waiting at home for a call that wouldn't come.

It wasn't the first time he'd come here without looking for an answer, but it was the first time he'd come here to escape what was going on in his life. He was tired of hearing himself bemoan the fact that he'd done the right thing by telling Melanie everything. He was tired, period, because he hadn't slept a total of eight hours since Wednesday.

Wednesday night after walking Melanie to the door, he stood outside feeling helpless. When he heard her crying he had the urge to break through the door, take her up in his arms and comfort her until she stopped. Her sobs tore him apart, but he couldn't move away.

Her father was his saving grace, otherwise he would still be standing with his hand on the door until her mother came home. He couldn't make out anything that was said, just that there were two voices and one of them was male.

He went home and sat on the side of his bed going over their conversation until the sun came up. He tried to think of any way he could have told her that would have brought him a different outcome and he kept coming up blank. It was probably for the best. He would have beat himself over the head with what he could have or should have done until his ego was pulverized.

He got up, took a shower and went into work where he received the very welcoming news that Merryman's investigation was at an end, and they were preparing to raid the "party" house from two weeks before, as well as six other residences of men involved in drug and sex trafficking. He wished his own case was going as well, but as Merryman had invested two years in that case, and he and Finn were now on month five, he wasn't going to beat himself up about it.

Of course, he wanted to tell Melanie the great news but chose instead to make a call to Colonel Morganson. The man was very cordial when he came on the line, which made Marc wary. If Melanie's father wasn't in favor of their relationship, then it was easy to be civil in light of the fact that Melanie was upset with him. If he were in Marc's corner, either he wasn't doing a very good job of convincing his daughter to call him or she was stubborn.

Marc gave him a surface update on the investigation. He shied away from details but let Melanie's dad know that everything should be resolved soon. Once he was done, it was all he could do not to ask about Melanie. He said goodbye but paused before hanging up.

"I commend you on your restraint," the colonel had said.

"Excuse me?"

"If I were in your shoes, I would do what I could to find out how she's doing." Marc took a moment to swallow before doing just that.

"She's a little tired and quiet which means she's thinking. Melanie thinking is a good thing for you," Colonel Morganson said.

Marc would have liked more, but that had been enough at the time. Marc thanked the colonel and asked if her father would simply relay the fact that he had asked about her. Her father agreed and ended the call.

The rest of Thursday was uneventful until he caught a glimpse of Melanie that evening. He went home hoping she might be done "thinking," but there was no call. He'd pushed around his heated frozen pizza until it was cold again and turned on the television so that one of his favorite shows could watch him sulk. Marc wasn't a good brooder. Some people made it their life's work. Not him. Marc liked being happy. He was used to being happy. He was used to seeing what he wanted, creating a plan on how to get it and executing that plan. This time there was nothing to implement, nothing to work on, just an exercise in the discipline of staying away from the one person he'd wanted most. Even the news that she couldn't have children hadn't weakened his resolve to be with her. His mother might not be ecstatic about the prospect, but one, it was none of her business, and two, if Melanie was agreeable to adoption, the problem was solved where he was concerned. He never had an overwhelming urge to contribute to the gene pool. He did want children eventually, but that was a bridge to a country called tomorrow.

As much as it went against his nature, he would wait. He would wait and pray. He would pray as he always had the first day he saw her walking into the junior high school building. He prayed that the peace of the Lord would envelop her. That His love would surround her heart like a fortress, keeping her safe until she accepted Jesus Christ into it. He prayed that God would guide her to people who knew and loved Him so that she too could have a personal and intimate relationship with Him. He prayed that God would heal her and make her whole: body, soul and spirit.

He prayed some variation of it over and over that night until he was tired enough to go home and go to sleep.

***

Sunday dawned just as Thursday, Friday and Saturday had—slowly, and with him watching. Though he'd gotten a little more sleep than the night before, he was starting to feel punchy. He'd been on stakeouts and undercover assignments that had him up at a second's notice, but the energy coursing through him kept him alert. He had nothing to use his restless energy on except the gym, which he chose as a remedy for last night's sleeplessness.

Marc prayed for strength as he got ready for the service. It would be nice to at least have the question of whether Melanie would come or not, out of the way. Since he hadn't talked to her since that Wednesday, he figured it was a no-go.

He'd spent most of Saturday cleaning his apartment then cleaning out the rain gutters at his parent's home. He had a brief lunch with his parents that he tried not to brood through, but his mother wasn't fooled. He was tempted to tell her that he'd done exactly what she'd said, and it blew up in his face, but he knew that was only the anger and self-pity talking. Things would just be okay if he kept busy, and that was what he'd done until late into the night, but he'd still woken up before dawn with a pain in his heart.

Marc walked into the sanctuary after being greeted by a couple who gave everyone a hug at the door. He wondered briefly at how they made it work. They'd been married for at least twenty-five years because that's how long he remembered seeing them right here every morning giving love.

He walked down the side aisle to where his mother, father, brother Malcolm and his fiancée sat. After hugging and kissing everyone, he caught his mother looking behind him, and he saw the moment she realized he was alone. She quickly veiled the disappointment and gave him an encouraging smile. He smiled back then straightened in place, gritting his teeth against the temptation to blame Melanie for his mother's disappointment when one had little to do with the other. Melanie had no clue that his mother wanted to meet her. He shook his head briefly and placed his attention on the speaker who began their service by exulting Christ.

He thought on the goodness of God. The many years that had gone by before his parents were even conceived, and he had to revel in the vastness and perfection of God's plan. It only took one thing not to happen to keep him from being here at this moment, and many things could have happened to prevent him from being in the place he was with the family he had, surrounded by the love that gave him the courage to love others. God was amazing. He lost himself in worship and pushed all his cares away.

By the time their pastor stood before them to give the sermon, Marc was feeling much lighter.

"I debated whether or not to give this message today. With Thanksgiving fast approaching I thought a sermon of love and the family would be fitting, but God seems to have another idea, and since this is His house, I am going to be obedient and share the message He has been prompting me to give today. Please turn your books to Hosea." Their pastor looked down at his notes for a moment.

Marc took the opportunity to turn his Bible to the Book of Hosea. It wasn't a popular book, nor was the subject it told, but his pastor had never given a message that wasn't timely to some or all the members. Marc assumed it would be a message of warning not to forget God during the upcoming holiday season, that material things couldn't buy love, replace love or be loved. Marc knew God was a jealous God, and He was very firm about there not being any other gods besides Him, which was anything they used to replace their time with Him.

He waited as everyone else found their place, and anticipated being right about his assumption. He couldn't be more wrong. His pastor didn't use Hosea's life as an illustration for the upcoming holidays, but dealt straight with the heart of God for His people. The continual drawing God did with the children of Israel. Their time of prosperity as He blessed them and proclaimed to all that they were His. Their disobedience and want for worldly power that led them to worship other gods. God's chastisement so that He could redeem their souls back to Him and crown them with His love once more. The parallel story of Hosea who was charged to marry a harlot whom he clothed, sheltered, loved and gave children to. Her leaving him to go back to her life and then falling upon hard times and coming back to him. God's command that he take her back in his house and life, and be open to loving her again.

Marc, along with the congregation, was speechless when the pastor paused the first time.

"How do you love? Do you love like God with compassion, utter patience, adoration, loyalty, undying devotion? Or do you love when it is convenient, when it feels good to do so, when things are going good, and the person has done all the things you desired they would. Is your love attached to acts of kindness, beautiful faces, big wallets or perfect proposals, or is it interwoven with joy and sorrow, victories and failures, agreements and disagreements, health and sickness. Have you placed limits on your love? Is there an expiration date, restrictions on offenses or a margin call on good deeds?

"How many of us would be on the other side of the ground forever lost right now if God had limits?

"Treat those you love the way God loves you. Aren't you happy we serve a God that can love us with an everlasting love? Take the cap off your love."

Their pastor closed his Bible on his notes before continuing to speak. "May the congregation say 'Amen.'"

Marc sat there for a moment stunned by the message. Had he been trying to put limits on his love for Melanie?

Even after they were dismissed from the service, he worked his pastor's words over in his mind. It seemed the congregation was doing the same, as the usually jovial and loud conversations of people trying to hear over one another were muted.

He kissed his mother and hugged his father as they passed him into the aisle. Still in somewhat of a daze, he promised to come by for Sunday dinner later. He shuffled his feet, not in a hurry to go home but didn't want to draw attention to himself. He made his way down the aisle, deep in thought, and was halfway down when he realized he'd forgotten his Bible. He looked up, and there Melanie was sitting next to Katrina, four rows down and to the left.

He stopped and stared, wondering if he were just seeing what he wanted to see. There was a cough behind him, and he moved into the space between pews to get out of their way.

Melanie got up with Katrina trailing behind, looking a little uncomfortable. He watched, still not certain she was really there.

"Hi," Melanie said when she stood in front of him.

It wasn't a figment of his imagination. She was really there. She was speaking to him. *Oh, man what had she said. Hi. She said, "Hi."*

"Hi," he responded.

"Hi, Katrina. It's good to see you. How are you doing?" he said out of politeness and needing a moment to get his thoughts together.

"I'm good. Thank you so much, for everything," she said, and he could see the sincerity in her eyes.

"You're welcome. I was happy to be there," he said automatically.

"I was happy you were there too." She smiled.

He returned it before turning back to Melanie.

"So..." Melanie said then cleared her throat. "I didn't know...I mean I thought the Bible only had holy people in it."

"Nope. There are killers, rapists, thieves, prostitutes and kings. God doesn't love people because they don't sin, He loves them through their sin."

"It was a very encouraging message," she said. It's like He loves you no matter what."

Marc was dumbstruck by Melanie's perception of His pastor's sermon. She saw God's love where he saw his shortcomings. He was humbled by it. He didn't have any words.

Chapter 25

Melanie was more nervous than she had been on her first day of school. Marc could very well tell her he was done waiting, but when she considered walking out in the middle of the service, the man standing at the pulpit, who her program said was Pastor Edgar Roan, started talking about loving, no matter what. She figured if his pastor was talking about unconditional love, Marc might listen, and give her a chance to apologize for taking her time in approaching him.

It had been a long week. She didn't have highs and lows, just decent moments and low moments. Her talk with her father went a long way in soothing the initial pain of her conversation with Marc. She went from blaming him to realizing that he had done exactly what she would have wanted him to if she had the luxury of objectivity. He'd actually handled the situation better than she might have. She wondered how long it would have taken her to broach the subject of Paige and Brian. A great deal longer than it did for Marc to tell her about working for Mr. Sable, that's for sure.

The more she thought about Marc and the week they had, the more she was sure that he was a good man. A very good man. That presented another problem. He was a good man who deserved a woman not saddled with so much baggage. He deserved a woman who wasn't a prisoner of her past, that he would be okay if she didn't contact him again. He would go on; do his work; find someone new. The thought of him giving someone else that special smile sent a sharp pain through her middle. It was so irrational. She thought he deserved better, but she really wanted to be the woman he chose.

It was hard discussing it with her friends without them knowing her past, so she skimmed the surface of her story, letting them know that Marc had been the FBI agent who was assigned to watch her.

"I understand your reservations, but I think him telling you now instead of later says a lot about his character," Rickie said, obviously wanting to encourage her to call Marc on Friday night when they'd bunked at Katrina's apartment that night. Her roommate was out of town for the weekend, and Katrina still wasn't fully comfortable being alone. It was one of Melanie's first overnight stays and she loved it.

"I know," Melanie countered, "But it's so embarrassing that he knows so much about my life."

"And?" Sophia asked. "I think it shows that he likes you more than you thought. He's known all along, and he still asked you out. Twice."

Melanie thought about that.

"I think it's better that he does know," Katrina chimed in. "It means that no matter what happens in your personal life, he's equipped to take care of you."

Melanie liked the thought of that. He'd done a great job so far.

Friday night was closed with her leaning toward calling him on Saturday, then Saturday morning met her with more doubts. What if she were not good for him? What if she and her past weren't good for his career? Now that she knew something more personal went on between her mother and Mr. Sable, Melanie was hesitant to involve Marc any deeper. Which, of course, didn't make any sense since Marc had disclosed the information about her mother and Mr. Sable to her, and not the other way around. He was in as deep as he could get but no deeper than he wanted.

He said he wanted her. It was a thought that made her feel cared for, but what if she couldn't give him what he needed? She had been so caught up in what she wanted, that she never thought to consider what his needs were. She thought back on their conversations and the fact that he handled himself pretty well in the grocery store.

Was she overanalyzing everything so she could talk herself out of being with him? What was so wrong with being happy? She could lose him. He could walk away with a piece of her like Brian did.

And there it was. She was afraid of loving and losing more of herself than what she began with. She barely recovered from the first time, but was that love or heightened emotional manipulation? Either way, it had done its job and kept her a prisoner of guilt for years.

By Saturday afternoon she'd made up her mind. She was done being a victim. Her conversation with her father had broken barriers she'd put up around her heart to keep people from seeing she was afraid and flawed. She wasn't flawed, and her father's words helped her to see that she was worth a great deal more than she gave herself credit for.

Melanie called Katrina and asked if her friend would want to come to church with her on Sunday morning. She'd told Katrina that Marc had invited them on Friday, but she wasn't sure if she wanted to go. Katrina jumped at the chance to thank Marc, and since she occasionally went to church with her roommate, she was looking forward to listening to some "spirit-filled" music. Melanie had no idea what Katrina was talking about but was hoping that was a good thing.

It turned out that it was a very good thing. After nervously accepting a hug, handshake and program from the man and woman at the door, she and Katrina were ushered to a half-full pew. She looked around at the nice-sized room filled with pews on both sides and what looked like a stage in the front with more pews.

"Ah, good. It looks like they have a good-sized choir," Katrina said.

"How do you know?" Melanie asked in a whisper, not sure if they were allowed to talk above a whisper.

Katrina pointed to the pews on the stage. "See the pews on the pulpit?"

"Pulpit? It looks like a stage," Melanie said.

"A stage is what performers use to entertain people. A pulpit is a sacred place that allows the participants to be seen only to help encourage the rest of the members to join in praise and worship. This church has the same feeling as my roommate's church. These people must sing or praise God and pray a lot. You might think it's just words and song, but it saturates the air and then the walls. It's hard to explain. I hope you will be able to feel it. The closest thing I can equate it to is a deep peace," Katrina finished.

"A deep peace," Melanie echoed. Peace was good.

Melanie scanned the sanctuary again, this time with another purpose. She didn't see anyone who looked like Marc on the left side of the sanctuary, but when the woman in front of her leaned over to speak in her pewmate's ear, Melanie saw him. Well, she saw the back of his head. He was looking straight ahead and she both looked forward to and dreaded the moment he saw her. The choir filed in at that point in blue-and-gray robes. She needed to remember to ask Katrina why they wore robes.

They stood facing Melanie and the people around her and remained standing when a gentleman in a really nice suit stepped up to the podium and asked everyone to stand for the exhortation. She had never heard that word before. She stood looking at her program but it read "Call to Worship." He began speaking of God and His goodness. He spoke of how mighty, loving, and alive He was. He was alive? What did that mean? She hoped she could keep up a little.

When the choir began to sing, she was blown away. Their voices weren't just beautiful, the sound seemed to be moving in and around her, if that made any sense. Some people joined in around her, and other's closed their eyes and raised their hands to the ceiling as if they were reaching, but for what? The only thing she'd seen like it was Paige lifting her hands when she wanted to be picked up. Oh, if people started levitating, she was out of there.

Katrina whispered again. "They're praising and worshipping God. Not for one thing, but many things. Close your eyes, and just listen to the music, otherwise you will be too distracted to feel it."

Katrina put her hand on the pew back in front of her and closed her eyes and Melanie followed suit.

At first there was nothing but the music, but then a feeling of freedom and hope pushed at her. Freedom from what? She didn't know. Hope for what? She didn't know that either, but both were beautiful. She followed some of the music and became familiar with the chorus and quietly sang along. By the end of the last song she felt energized. She wanted to jump up and down like the woman yelling "Thank ya! Thank ya, Lord!" at the end of her pew, but she was way too self-conscious to do anything but sit down when they were given permission. Her leg bounced, and she tried to stop it a few times before giving up. Katrina was right. The air was charged with a vibrancy or enthusiasm. It made sitting down hard.

She was still buzzing, for lack of a better word, when Pastor Edgar Roan stepped up to the podium. He started out saying he wasn't sure why he was given the message he had for the members, but he was sure it was for some who needed to hear it. She thought it odd that the leader of the church wouldn't make his own message. She wondered who he got it from.

He said his sermon was coming from the Book of Hosea. Katrina picked up one of the books shelved in front of them. It was a Bible. She'd seen one in their house, but she never really knew what to do with it. It was a book, and books were made to be read, but it seemed untouchable. That wasn't right. It was set apart, so she thought it was something not to be touched. Like the figurines in the china closet.

282

He started reading about God and how much He loved His children. The children of Israel. He took care of the children and made sure their needs were met but when He left—why, she didn't know—they were rebellious and disobedient. He used the situation they got themselves in to draw them back to Him. He chastised them because He loved them and wanted to keep them from getting themselves in danger and loved them again.

She sat there listening to this God who, over and over again, drew his disobedient children back to Him because He loved them. What a wonderful thought. A person who never gave up on loving their children, no matter what. This God sounded like someone she wanted to get to know.

All too soon, the sermon was over, but she remembered Hosea 2 and would look it up again in the Bible at home if she could find it. If not, she would buy one. She wondered how much they were.

"Are you going to go up to him?" Katrina asked after the service was over.

Melanie knew that was the plan, but her legs stopped obeying her. She looked at Katrina.

"I'm afraid."

"But you came all this way." Katrina frowned.

Melanie shrugged, feeling a profound sense of helplessness as she watched Marc finally get up and kiss and hug the older woman in his pew. He stepped out into the aisle and passed them on the way to the back. Katrina poked and nudged Melanie until she moved to stand. Marc turned around and looked like he was headed back to his pew when he caught sight of them and stopped.

He didn't do anything or say anything at first. She thought maybe he was surprised, but he blinked like he was seeing an aberration.

She got up, thankful her legs stayed under her, and walked slowly to him. She took him in and was thankful she'd come to her senses then wondered if she had done it in time. She greeted him, and he finally came out of his haze. He and Katrina exchanged greetings, and then he looked back at her. She blurted out the first thing on her mind, and it seemed to startle him, making her feel even more self-conscious. She went for it before she lost her nerve.

"I was wondering if we could talk." Melanie looked at him uncertainly.

He looked at her, his expression somewhere between wary and hopeful. It squeezed her heart. Besides the incident at the grocery store, he'd not looked uncertain about anything until now.

"Are you here to tell me to stay out of your life completely?" he asked.

It was so far from her intent, she was momentarily at a loss for words.

She shook her head in the negative.

"Are you here to tell me you can't see me again?" he asked.

She shook her head again.

He watched her for a moment, some of the wariness receding.

"Are you willing to give us a try?" he asked.

"Uh." *Wait. What was happening?*

Katrina nudged her back.

"Um. Yes. I do need to talk to you though," Melanie said. Was it really that easy? Where was the part where she asked him to forgive her for being stubborn, irrational, and angry at him, and he held out until she begged? Was he really going to let go of the edge he had so easily?

He glanced around Melanie at Katrina. "Did you drive?"

"Yes, and I know my way home," Katrina said.

"Nothing doing. I will follow you home then give Melanie a ride home from your house if that's all right with you."

"You don't have to follow me…" Katina started.

"That part isn't negotiable," Marc said.

"Okay. Then yes. That is perfectly fine with me."

Marc walked them outside and followed them as he had insisted.

Melanie couldn't stop smiling as Katrina drove to her apartment.

"Wow. You are way past lucky with that man."

"What do you mean?" Melanie asked, confused by her friend's words.

"My roommate said anyone can get lucky, but only a few are blessed, and you, my friend, are blessed."

"Why?"

"He is a special man, but I don't think you two being brought into each other's lives was a coincidence."

Melanie tensed at Katrina's words. Did her mom have something to do with this?

"Why do you look so scared?" Katrina asked when she glanced at Melanie before she turned back to the road.

"It's a good thing—a very good thing. What I am saying is that I believe God brought you two together as a way to show you how much He loves you," Katrina said.

Melanie didn't know she knew so much about God. She rarely spoke of Him.

"But I don't know Him. I mean at all. My parents aren't religious," Melanie said, a thread of hope pulling at her.

"He's bigger than your parent's religious beliefs. He's also bigger than your present ability to wrap your mind around the minutest part of Him. If He loves you, there is little you can do about it," Katrina said, seeming to know what she was talking about.

"Why?" Melanie said, trying to come to grips with their conversation.

"He thinks you're worthy," Katrina said with a finality that stopped Melanie in midthought.

He thought she was worthy of being loved unconditionally. The idea was so profound she said nothing else until she said goodbye to Katrina.

She hugged her friend and thanked her.

"If he tells you how he feels"—Katrina gestured to Marc waiting by the passenger door of his car—"believe him."

Melanie opened and closed her mouth then nodded and smiled.

Chapter 26

"Hi," Melanie said before slipping into the car, feeling shy all of a sudden.

"Hi," Marc said, his mouth tipping up on one side.

The tension between them was still thick, but if he were willing to work to get back to where they were before Wednesday night, so was she.

He closed her door and went around to get behind the wheel.

"I'd rather wait until we can speak face-to-face, and I don't have to divide my attention between you and the road. Do you mind if I take you somewhere for that?

Melanie looked down at her dress and shoes, wondering how much walking she might have to do.

"I promise you won't have to climb or hike anywhere," he said, seeming to read her mind.

"Okay."

He put the car in gear, and they pulled away from the curb. While he drove, Melanie organized her thoughts. It took a moment for her to realize where they were heading, but the closer they got to the university, the more curious she became.

"Are we going to campus?"

"Yes. I thought you would feel more comfortable in a familiar spot, and on Sunday mornings most of campus is quiet. There is a spot in front of the history building with oak trees, lots of grass and benches where we can talk."

Even when she was in the wrong and trying to make amends, he was taking care of her. She had never witnessed anything like it.

She kept her thoughts to herself. Women talked about a good man and wanting to be treated well, and she wanted the same, but she wasn't sure she knew how to accept it. She was momentarily afraid she wouldn't be able to accept it.

Marc parked and came around to assist her out. She wondered if it would be like getting used to sitting and waiting for him to open the door for her. It had taken a few tries, but he had patiently continued to show her that he thought she was worth him coming around to help her out of the car. It was probably a little thing in the big picture, but her life was made of little moments, and this was one she cherished.

He went to his trunk and took out a blanket before guiding her to a bench looking out over the west side of the campus. The grass was lush and green with patches of flowers circling some of the trees. She took a deep breath of the crisp air and watched as he covered the bench with the blanket. She shook her head before she sat down.

"What?" he asked as they faced each other.

"It's a little embarrassing, but I've never been fussed over like this," she said, gesturing to the blanket.

"No fuss. It's a nice dress and I didn't want you to ruin it if there was something on the bench."

She nodded. "And you open doors for me, guide me around cracks in the ground, pull out my chairs and continually ask if the temperature is comfortable in the car. Fuss."

He shrugged. "It's kind of second nature to me. It's the way my dad treats my mom."

She smiled at him sadly. "It's not how my dad treats my mom. They are rarely in the same room anymore. I actually don't think they will stay together long. I just hope for Paige's sake that they don't split up anytime soon," she said, getting lost in thought and veering off the subject.

"Would you want to take her with you?" he asked.

"I would, but my mom would probably try to sue for custody, and that would bring up too many questions that I can't answer yet." Marc merely nodded.

"Is it really that important to keep things quiet?" he asked sounding sincere.

She looked him square in the eye. "It is a matter of life and death."

"Okay. I will take you at your word," he responded.

She blinked. "Just like that?" she asked.

"My concern is your welfare. If you tell me this will have an impact on that, then yes, just like that," he said.

She watched him for a moment, Katrina's words echoing in her mind. "If he tells you how he feels, believe him." She would try.

She took a deep breath. "I'm not sure where to start," she said, her palms growing wet.

"How about the beginning," Marc said, leaning back as if he had all the time in the world.

Melanie stared at him for a moment. She hadn't considered going that far, but it might help him understand her better.

"Okay," she said before taking another deep breath.

"My earliest memories of my mom was of a woman who didn't necessarily wrap me in love but didn't abuse me either. I was more like a piece of furniture that she took good care of. I was mostly homeschooled. I didn't develop too many social skills because I wasn't around kids my own age much. I found speaking to other children awkward and uncomfortable. I rarely knew what to say and usually just observed kids playing whenever we went to the park. I wasn't interested in sports. I had a condition. Or, at least, I thought I had a condition. I became anxious easily, and my mom started giving me these vitamins to help ease me."

"Did they work?" Marc asked.

"I guess so, but I didn't really feel much to begin with," Melanie said, thinking of the nasty orange pills.

"I went through puberty a few months after I started taking them. I thought nothing of it. I had nothing to compare the timing to. I wasn't around other girls."

She saw him rubbing his hands on his pants but when he noticed her watching he stopped.

"You okay?" she asked.

He nodded, and she continued.

"So anyway, my mom started adding books in biology to my curriculum. I figured it had to do with the fact that I was maturing.

I began going to school at the base when I was nine years old. I remember being so scared the kids wouldn't like me, or worse yet, make fun of me. I'm not sure if I could have borne that." She gave him a sheepish smile. It was funny how huge that was in her life at the time.

"My mother was very protective. I thought it was because my dad was on tour for two years, but I saw later she was just being controlling. It was maybe three weeks before she let me take the school bus. I would have been fine without the experience. I was one of the last stops for the school bus. I was afraid no one would make room for me on their bench seat but Brian did." She went quiet for a brief moment remembering that life-changing moment.

She focused back on Marc and worked to stay in the present.

"I asked Brian why he made room for me. He told me he had been in the same position only a few months before. I felt a kinship with him right away. Sometimes I wonder if things had been different, and we were allowed to grow up slowly, if we might still be friends. I see now that what I felt for him was gratefulness, friendship and shared loneliness. Everything else was a reaction to whatever drugs we were ingesting with our foods."

She could tell that Marc was trying hard not to physically react to what she was saying, but she saw the tension grow in his jaw and hands. From the look of it, he definitely didn't like the thought of her having any type of emotional attachment to Brian, but you couldn't have children with someone and not have some emotional tie, even if it had to cross time and space.

"Brian and I spent a lot of time together. My mother and his parents became friends so we were always thrown together. Brian wasn't very sociable either. He collected comic books and *Star Wars* figures. I remember thinking he had some great hobbies. He was always willing to talk about them, and since I wasn't easily accepted by the other girls in school, I was starved for attention and his friendship."

"Do you have any hobbies?" Marc asked, and she was grateful for the brief reprieve.

"I write. Nothing that I would share with anyone. Just journaling and getting my feelings out on paper," she said, feeling self-conscious about bringing it up.

"Do you write about me?" he asked

"Sometimes," she hedged. Her current journal was almost all about him.

He nodded slowly, looking down at his hand, then gave her an even slower smile before asking her to continue.

"We were thrown together overnight many times telling each other scary stories trying to see who could scare who the most. He taught me how to jump the back fence, since we were backyard neighbors.

"A few months after we met, my mother started asking me questions about Brian. It was like she suddenly became my girlfriend. She would ask me if I liked Brian. I told her he was a great friend. She asked me if I thought he was good looking, and honestly, I had noticed he had nice eyes. They were as dark as mine were light, and they were kind."

293

A squirrel passed them at a dead run then scampered up a tree. It held her attention for a few more seconds, then she turned back to Marc who watched her with fascination.

"What?" she asked.

"I love the way you look at everyday things," he said. "It's like you're savoring it."

"Isn't life supposed to be savored?" she asked.

"Yes, but not many people do," he replied.

She glanced at the tree then back at Marc. "I'm not most people."

"No. You are not," he said.

She paused to take in his words and expression. It encouraged her to keep going.

"My mom told me Brian said I was cute and he liked me. I didn't know what to think, so I asked him even though my mom told me not to. He said that his parents told him that I liked him. We laughed about it and let it go.

"Then two weeks later, Brian asked me if he could kiss me. He was my friend. I thought nothing of it and it was nice. My body was doing weird things. I mean I was feeling things that didn't seem completely natural." She shook off the thought. She wasn't willing to venture there again even for Marc. She skimmed over the rest.

"Well, needless to say, things progressed over the next few months, and I ended up pregnant with twins. We weren't allowed to see each other much after that, which was excruciating. Brian had become so much of my world. I was so alone. We had set up an emergency code early on in our friendship. It was more for fun than anything else, since we were both nerds. We liked having a secret language.

"It came in handy though. I was at the end of my seventh month when I overheard my mom talking to someone about the plans she had for my babies." She watched Marc's jaw tighten again.

"We secretly met, and it was then that I found out he was in contact with Mr. Luca Sable. My mom was going out of town for a few days, and since she'd pulled me out of school, and Brian's parents wouldn't let us see each other, let alone talk to one another, she wasn't worried about me doing anything on my own.

"Brian's grandfather planned everything. A few hours after my mom left, a midwife came and examined me and the babies and deemed it safe enough to induce me. I waited until I was deep in labor before I called the ambulance. I gave them Brian's parents' information and told them my dad was deployed, and my mom was away on business.

"I'm pretty sure my mom paid off Brian's adopted parents, but the joke was on her.

"Brian told me Mr. Sable threatened them as only he could. I was taken to the hospital and delivered a boy. Paige was the holdout. I almost died having her. I lost consciousness before I delivered her and woke up a few days later. My mom told me that my baby boy died before she arrived, and I was in intensive care. Paige, on the other hand, was healthy and hungry.

295

"I cried because after everything, I was still left with only one child," she said, barely able to voice the words.

"Do you know what your mom was planning?" he asked.

"Paige wasn't supposed to make it." The words were like bile in her mouth.

"It's pretty obvious my mom didn't get what she wanted. Soon after that there was an attempt on Brian's life, and we were taken out of WITSEC. You saw me four years later."

"Are you still in contact with Brian?" Marc asked, looking like he didn't really want to know the answer.

"No. My last communication with him was three months after I gave birth," she said, remembering that day so long ago, and relieved to find that the pain once associated with it was almost gone.

"How"—Marc cleared his throat—"how did you get through that?"

She shrugged. "In the beginning I was afraid for Paige's life. I was constantly on guard. I was so afraid my mom would do something to her. I don't think I got a full night's rest until my dad came home."

Marc sat there for a moment seeming to take in her story. "I could have done something four years ago. I could have stepped in and removed you and Paige from that house," Marc said.

Melanie reached forward and placed her hand on his. "It was meant to be this way." He looked at her hand for a few seconds then up at her. He swallowed and nodded his agreement even though his eyes were bleak.

"Is that why you were so upset? I can understand why you don't trust easily."

"You think I have trust issues?" she asked

"You have more reason than most," Marc responded.

"With you, it wasn't a matter of trust." She bit her lip in consternation. "It was more about me wanting a relationship untouched by my mother's scheming."

She paused then plowed ahead. "And I was embarrassed. I wasn't ready for you to know all of that about me."

"It wasn't your fault," he said earnestly.

"But it's still baggage."

"You would rather me like you without knowing your past than me like you in spite of your past?" he asked, looking perplexed.

"It sounded a little more logical in my head. Not much, but just not as dumb as that." She quirked a smile then continued.

"You were right," Melanie said, squeezing his hand. She leaned forward so she was looking him square in the eyes.

"I'm sorry. I was wrong to cut you off and not call you."

Marc looked at her oddly.

"What?" she asked, wondering if she needed to say more to convince him that she was sorry.

"Could you say that again and let me record it? I have some friends who don't believe that women apologize," he said, looking serious until his lips twitched.

She smiled in relief. "Uh, no. I'm not sure how it works, but if I let you record me I might lose my woman card."

He shrugged and smirked. "It was a good try."

She wanted to giggle but nodded instead. "I missed you."

His gaze warmed, and he gave her that smile he seemed to hold just for her.

"I forgive you, Melanie."

"Thank you," she said unable to say anything else.

He pulled her against him and hugged her tight. He smelled good like cedar and musk, and the strength of his embrace warmed her all the way to her soul. She held on, hoping he wouldn't let her go anytime soon.

"Oh, Melanie, please don't break my heart," he said as he breathed out.

Her breath caught at his plea. Feeling warmth at the back her eyes she closed them tightly to keep her emotions from spilling over. She'd hurt him more than she realized. He seemed invincible at times, but with those words he revealed his vulnerability.

She squeezed him a little tighter.

"I'll try not to," she said, meaning if from the bottom of her heart.

Chapter 27

"Are you hungry? Want to go to lunch?" Marc asked as he pulled away from Melanie. He needed to lighten the mood, otherwise he might start crying like a baby. He already revealed more than he meant to, but the fact that she didn't throw it back in his face gave him hope.

Her eyes were suspiciously wet. "I could eat. What do you have in mind?"

"Well, we could go to this restaurant I know that has decent soul food, or we could go to my parent's house and eat my mother's really good food," he said.

She couldn't help but smile. "The restaurant, please."

He looked at her in surprise and a little hurt. "You don't want to meet my mom?"

"Not today. Not just after we made up and whatever pain I caused you is still fresh in her mind. I might not make it out of the house," she said, half serious.

"My mom wouldn't hurt you," he said.

Melanie just raised an eyebrow at him.

"Really. She was hoping you'd come to church today," he said, trying to convince her.

"As much as you love your mother, she loves you more. If anyone hurt my daughter, I wouldn't be too jazzed about sitting across from them at the dinner table," she said.

He considered what she said and conceded, though he knew his mother would have welcomed her with open arms. He didn't want Melanie to feel awkward though.

"Okay. What are you in the mood for?"

He watched her consider his question then a light came into her eyes.

"Popcorn."

"Popcorn," he repeated.

"Yes. Could we see a movie?" she asked, almost sounding like a child.

He checked his watch. "Sure. Do you have anything in mind?"

She shook her head, frowning a little. "Can we find out what's playing when we get there?"

"Of course," he said, feeling indulgent.

"When was the last time you went to the movies?" he asked, not knowing what he expected, but her answer made him happy he was still sitting down.

"Um, *The Champ*," she said. "It was the last movie I went to see with my dad."

"That was like eleven years ago," he stated, indignant on her behalf.

She shrugged.

"Aw, baby." He pulled her up from the bench. "I'm going to buy you the biggest tub of popcorn they have…with extra butter. Then we will get nachos and hot dogs and candy."

"How many movies are we going to see?" she asked, starting to look concerned.

"Just one," he said, pulling her toward the car.

"That's a lot of food for just a two-hour movie," she said, sounding reluctant.

"We will find the longest movie playing, and I'll share your popcorn," he offered.

"Okay, but you'll have to get your own hot dog, because there is no way I am putting ketchup on mine."

He laughed, feeling joy well up in his heart. "Deal."

***

They ended up seeing two movies that day: an epic romance and an action adventure. He liked both of them, but he really liked spending time with Melanie. He watched her reactions to the concession stand and some of the scenes in the movies. Her face was so full of expression. Everything she felt flowed across her face like the movie screen.

He drove her home slowly, reluctant for their day to end.

"Will you be okay with your mom and all?" he asked, a little concerned.

"Yep. I didn't tell you. Wednesday night my dad and I had a long overdue talk. It was..." She seemed to struggle for the word for a moment. "Healing."

"That's good," he said with sincerity.

"That's great!" she responded with a huge smile.

"So something good came out of Wednesday," he said.

She stopped to stare at him. "A lot of good came out of Wednesday. I just see now that it could have happened without causing you so much pain." Her eyes grew sad, and he wanted to reassure her it was okay, but all he could do was shrug. It hadn't been okay.

She blinked rapidly and whispered, "Sorry."

He took her hand and kissed her knuckles. "No need to apologize again. It brought us to this moment."

"Will you tell me what you were thinking this week?"

He shook his head. "No."

She closed her eyes briefly but when she opened them, they glistened. "Okay."

He wished he could find the words to soothe her, but the pain was still too close to the surface.

She leaned in and kissed his cheek softly as if to sooth the hurt. She lingered for a breath before pulling away.

His throat muscles convulsed at the tender gesture.

"Thank you," he said once he could get air through his windpipe again.

She gave him a watery smile then waited.

He sat there watching her working hard not to get too far ahead of herself.

"I have to go now," she said, and he was surprised to find that she had been waiting for him to come around and let her out.

"Oh sorry," he said and chuckled to himself as he got out and walked around the car to help her out.

"You don't have to walk me to the door," she said, suddenly looking nervous.

He watched her worry at her bottom lip and guessed at what was causing her agitation.

"It's going to have to happen sometime," he said, placing his hand at her elbow.

He accompanied her up the short path and stairs. Her key had just entered the lock when the door opened. Instead of Melanie's mom, there stood Paige with a much less enthusiastic greeting.

"Hi, Mel." Paige gave Mel a smile before turning her cold gaze on Marc. She put her hands on her nonexistent hips and glared up at him.

He would have thought it was cute if it weren't directed at him.

"My sister wasn't very happy when she came home Wednesday," Paige said.

Melanie looked like she was going to push beyond Paige, but he stayed her with his hand. He wanted to have a chance to get this cleared up, so he was willing to listen to what Paige had to say.

"I don't care how fine you are. If my sister ever comes home upset again after going out with you, I will find you, and if I can't find you, I'll get my dad to find you."

"I'm sorry for the distress my date with your sister caused you. It was unfortunate, but I think we have everything settled now." He looked over at Melanie as he finished his statement, and she nodded her head in agreement.

Paige let go a deep breath. "Good, because I really didn't want to have you thrown in the brig."

Marc figured she would find out soon enough that civilians weren't thrown in brigs, so he went along with it to humor her.

"Yes. That is really good. Now that you know that all is good with your sister can we shake?"

He held out his hand, and Paige took it, gripping his hand and yanking it down a few times.

"I'm glad I can like you again," Paige said after stepping back and letting go of his hand.

"Me too, Paige," Marc said before the girl turned and walked upstairs.

He glanced over at Melanie. "See, I'm back in her good graces."

"Well, I might not be so easy to win over."

Marc turned back to the doorway to see an older version of Melanie. She was slightly fuller and shorter and very, very beautiful. There was another difference he noted as she stared at him. Her eyes were cold where Melanie's eyes were warm.

"Marc, is it?" she said, offering her hand.

"Yes, ma'am. Marc Miller," Marc said, defaulting to his manners.

"Call me Grace," she said, turning her lips up, though her eyes never thawed.

It was actually a disturbing sight, and he downright refused to call her by one of Melanie's names.

304

"Well, Mrs. Morganson, I was just showing Melanie to the door. It's getting late, and I don't want to keep her from her studies."

"About that. Did I hear Paige correctly? Have you been dating my daughter?" she asked, though they all knew she already knew.

"Yes, Mrs. Morganson," Marc said politely.

"Why is it I haven't heard of this before?" Melanie's mother asked, turning to Melanie.

He watched Melanie take a deep breath. "I figured I would let you know when it was relevant."

"Relevant?" her mother repeated.

"Well, I wasn't sure if we would have more than a few dates since I've never done this before." Melanie sent him a look that made him feel ten feet tall before she looked back at her mother.

"I'm sure now," she said.

"Really?" her mother said, assessing him thoroughly. "What do you do for a living?"

Marc saw it coming from a mile away. She already knew. He saw it in her eyes. "I work for the FBI, the Atlanta branch."

"Hmm. Special Agent Miller." She said his name like she'd heard it somewhere.

"Are you the same special agent that had us under surveillance four years ago?"

"Well, the *bureau* had your family under surveillance for a week, four years ago. I was just one of the agents assigned to that task in that instance," he corrected but went on to sugarcoat his

305

comment. "You must have a memory like a steel trap and be pretty observant."

Mrs. Morganson glanced between him and Melanie, and he couldn't be more sure that his decision to tell Melanie right away about how their pasts intersected was the right thing to do.

"You know my daughter is on a full scholarship, and she is carrying a very heavy load this semester? I'm not sure she will have a lot of time to date," Mrs. Morganson stated.

"Melanie and I have talked about that," came yet another voice, this time from Melanie's father.

He stepped into the doorway behind his wife and held out his hand to Marc who shook it gratefully.

"Colonel Morganson. How are you doing this beautiful Sunday afternoon?" Marc asked in greeting.

"Good. Very good, and you?" he volleyed, a faint gleam in his eyes.

"Very good myself. After I ran into Melanie at church, I talked her into catching a movie with me," Marc answered.

"Church?" Mrs. Morganson said, surprised. "I thought you were going out with Katrina?"

"Yes, to church. It just so happens Marc goes to the same church," Melanie answered without hesitation.

Colonel Morganson glanced at his daughter and sadness crept into his eyes, but his smile remained brilliant.

"That sounds like fun. It's been a long time since I've gone to the movies. Maybe we should all go sometime," her father said before checking his watch.

"Have you two eaten?" Melanie's dad asked.

"Too much," Melanie said, rubbing her stomach.

"I'm afraid I couldn't help indulging her. It was too much fun witnessing her excitement," Marc said somewhat apologetically.

"You should never apologize for making my daughter happy," Melanie's dad said.

"Thank you, I had such a great day," Melanie said, turning to him.

"So did I," Marc returned, wishing he could hug her goodbye. He settled for taking and squeezing her hand.

"It was nice to meet you Mrs. Morganson, and nice to see you again, Colonel Morganson," Marc said before turning and walking back down the path to his car. He didn't look back even though he could feel three sets of eyes on him.

Once in the car he took a few surreptitious breaths and looked back at the house and the now-closed front door.

He worked his jaw as he started his car. For how badly he wanted to have Melanie's mother flogged for what she'd done to her young daughter, he thought he'd handled himself pretty well.

He shivered at the thought that Grace Melanie could have grown into a bitter, vengeful woman like her mother, but he couldn't let go of the feeling that Melanie had an innate will to love instead of hate.

Marc checked his watch. He had an overwhelming desire to visit his parents. He'd called his mother to let her know he wasn't going to make it before the first movie started. She was disappointed but understood Melanie's reluctance.

Marc wanted to believe the hardest part was over—and some ways it was—but from the way Melanie's mom had reacted to finding out they were dating, he knew she would be ongoing trouble.

   ***

Marc thought about Mrs. Morganson for most of the evening until thoughts of Melanie took over. He knew she wasn't happy about him dating her daughter. It didn't take a rocket scientist to figure that out. He considered a few different scenarios and put preparations in place to counteract them, including telling his superior that he was dating the daughter of Brenda Lattimore aka Grace Morganson.

He picked up Melanie from her classes each day that week since she was getting close to midterms and couldn't spare the time for a traditional date. The twenty-minute drive went by too quickly, but it was better than not seeing her at all.

Friday night he asked if she wanted to come to church and Sunday dinner with him, but she'd already made plans to ride with Katrina and study afterward. He was disappointed but glad they were both going to attend.

Sunday morning he got to church early and waited for them to arrive but was surprised to see Sophia and Rickie in tow. He greeted them wondering if it were a last-minute decision or a ploy on Melanie's part to keep from coming to his parents' home. She

308

and her friends met the part of his family who were in attendance after church, but her usual vibrancy had dimmed a little.

At dinner, his mother didn't mention noticing anything amiss. She just told those who hadn't been at the service of Grace Melanie's beauty, manners and kind nature. She smiled happily at Marc and he smiled back.

When he told her what his mother said about her when he picked Melanie up on Monday evening, she looked pleased, but the expression dimmed way too quickly.

He turned into a restaurant parking lot and turned the car off.

He turned to her. "I know you have to study, so I will not keep you any longer than it would normally take for you to ride the transit," he stated first. She looked uncomfortable, and he wanted to know why.

"I don't think I am a needy man. I don't need to have you around me all times of the day, though it would be nice," he said with a smile. She returned his briefly.

"I do, however, believe in communicating. Since we spend more time away from one another than with one another I want to make sure there are no crossed wires, and at this moment I am feeling like we are on the verge of doing just that." He watched as she continued to stare down at her hands, and he got a dark feeling in the pit of his stomach.

"Am I assuming things? Am I being oversensitive?" he asked.

She looked up at him and back down at her hands before replying, "No."

He swallowed back the retort and thanked God that she was being honest.

"Did you change your mind about us?" he asked.

She looked up and into his eyes. "No."

"Is your mother giving you a hard time about us?" he asked, and saw her eyes widen before she tried to mask her surprise. He saw her struggle with the truth before her shoulders fell, and she nodded before looking back down at her hands.

"I'm all that's left between her and Paige. My dad has been better at being a buffer lately, but he's going back on tour. I can't keep her safe," Melanie said, not looking up from her lap, a tear splashing on her thumb.

A fierce protectiveness rose up in Marc, and he turned her around, wrapping her up in his embrace as best he could in the confines of the car.

She shook but didn't utter a sound, which in some ways was worse than if she sobbed out loud. The intensity was somehow deeper. He squeezed a little harder and prayed.

"Dear Heavenly Father, the creator of heaven and earth and everything we see, touch, hear, smell and even what we cannot see. I give you thanks for giving me the desire to know you more every day and the desire to acknowledge you. You hold each and every concern in your hands and know what is going to happen before we do.

"Lord, I pray to you, asking that you direct me on what to do where Melanie is concerned. I ask for guidance on how to move on her behalf, what to do to keep her and those she loves safe. I ask for patience and your wisdom in dealing with those who wish her harm or wish for only their gain.

"I pray you will give both of us understanding of what to do first, second, third and so on. Show me how to calm some of her fears. Show me how to be the man that she needs. Continue to show me when I am wrong and when I am right. Please give me an understanding of what I can help with and what is truly only for You to deal with.

"I ask that you keep a hedge of protection around Melanie's father. Your hand is far-reaching, so please cover him at home and wherever he is deployed. Keep your hand upon Paige, Lord. Keep her safe, Father; keep her strong and give her a dream that is greater than she is.

"Touch her mother's heart, Lord. Heal her of her pain. Give her something to live for instead of die for. All of these things I pray in the matchless name of Jesus Christ. Amen."

"Amen," he heard Melanie repeat.

Her breathing evened out. He thought she had gone to sleep until she had repeated certain words in his prayer.

"You pray so beautifully. It's like you are speaking to Him right here," she said with a little bit of wonder in her voice.

He smiled. "I was speaking to Him. I was asking Him for help."

"I know. It was just…personal," she said, still in his embrace.

"It is personal," Marc answered, needing the closeness for a little longer.

"Does He hear you?" she asked. "When you pray like that?"

"Yes, but he also hears me when I call His name and just need to talk. He's my confidant, my friend," he said.

"Thank you," she whispered.

"Please don't thank me. It's my honor to pray for you," he said, finally pulling back from her.

"I feel better," she said. "It's not so huge."

He breathed a sigh of relief and felt contentment for three seconds before she spoke again.

"I wasn't completely truthful when I said I hadn't changed my mind about us being together. I changed my mind a few times, but I only counted my final decision. I was going to break up with you," she said, looking at him. He thought her tears were going to return.

He knew exactly how she felt.

"And now?" he asked, needing the answer but not wanting it at the same time.

"She's not so big. My mom. She seems more ordinary somehow. Your God seems bigger, stronger, but also more loving. I like that," she finished with a sheepish smile.

"He could be your God too," he said softly.

She smiled, but he could tell she didn't believe him.

"You know when the pastor asks if anyone wants to come to the altar after his sermon. He asks if there is anyone who wants to accept Jesus Christ in their heart. He is asking if there is anyone who wants the one and only living God to be their God."

312

"You know I thought that was what it was, but it's so embarrassing to walk up in front of all of those people," she said looking ashamed.

"Do you want to do it now?" he asked.

Her eyes widened to saucers. "Now, but I thought I had to wait until Sunday."

"God is Lord all the time. He is listening all the time. He is waiting with his arms open all the time," Marc said, his heart hammering against his breastbone.

Melanie bit her lip as she considered his words. Then she looked up with a tremulous smile. "Yes, please."

Her request was so hopeful and open it humbled him. He, who was supposed to know more about God, but had also in some ways taken Him for granted. He blinked back the water distorting his sight and prayed the sinner's prayer with her—wanting to shout and laugh when they were done—but simply smiled because he didn't want to scare her.

She had given her life to Christ. She received the gift of salvation. She would spend eternity with God. Death had no claim over her spirit or soul. She was freer on this day more than she knew…for now.

"Do you have a couple of extra minutes? I want to take you somewhere. I promise it won't be long," he said, afraid she would tell him she had no more time.

"Sure," she said, snuggling into the passenger seat. She looked serene.

He couldn't help the laugh. He was so happy.

313

"Where are we going?" she asked, putting her seat belt back on but turning toward him.

"To the bookstore. I'm getting you your own Bible," he said, looking at her before he put the car in gear.

"Can we have Bible study together?" she asked.

"Definitely," he said about to reverse when he felt her hand on his forearm.

"I'm sorry for thinking of breaking up with you. I didn't want to, but I was afraid."

"And now?" he asked.

"My God is bigger than what I fear," she said, lighting up the cab with her smile.

"I would like to stay with you," she said.

He could help it, but he didn't want to. He put the car back in park, reached out to cup her jaw with his palm and pulled her face to his. He kissed her like it would be the first of many. He caressed her lips with his, learning the feel of them then pressed his lips against hers more firmly and breathed in the scent of her. He could get lost here and never want to find his way out. He pulled back, giving himself enough room to give her shorter kisses, feeling her kiss him back in return. He was euphoric and a little woozy and finally able to pull back far enough so that their lips were no longer touching.

"If you'd led with that a few weeks ago, I never would have even considered letting you go," she said.

He laughed out loud before kissing her again briefly.

314

"Sassy mouth," he whispered, and watched her lips widen into a huge smile.

Chapter 28

The next few weeks went by with a blur for Melanie. She was either in class, studying, home or at church. She saw Marc every day though. He drove her from school slowly, they talked on the phone just before she was ready to go to bed, and he took her to church on Sunday. If her friends wanted to come, he would meet her there since Katrina's vehicle was bigger.

The week after Marc led her to Christ and laid that amazing kiss on her, Melanie sat down to eat with Marc's family and fell in love. They were so welcoming and loving. There wasn't a moment's hesitation on her end or theirs when they hugged her at the door. They didn't fuss around her. They simply accepted her like she was one of theirs. They asked her likes and dislikes then told her to make herself at home, and meant it.

Next to church it was the most peaceful place she'd been in. She wanted a home like this. A home where people liked to come to relax because it was warm and welcoming.

They were in the middle of dinner when Marc shared the news of her giving her life to Jesus Christ. He didn't go into detail for which she was grateful, but you would have thought she won the Nobel Peace Prize the way they cheered and congratulated her. They asked if she had her Bible so they could sign it and leave her a few words of encouragement. She had never heard of such a thing but was excited about the prospect and had Marc go and retrieve it from the car.

The visit was unforgettable, but when his mother asked her to come sit with her while everyone else washed dishes as she decreed, Melanie became nervous.

"Child, there is no cause to be nervous though if you weren't, I would wonder how much you value Marc." She smiled at Melanie, and it eased some of the tension.

"I didn't bring you in here to warn you, berate you, threaten you, or make you cower in front of me. I know some of the things you have gone through. My son tries not to keep the big things from me. You, my child, are a big thing."

Melanie didn't think Marc's mom knew how much her words touched her. It felt like a piercing warmth had finally broken through some of the coldest parts of her heart.

"I know it is early days, but if you choose to marry my son, you will become family as if I birthed you myself. You will know I love you and never have to doubt I will be there for you. Your joy will be like my joy, your pain will be like my pain, your children— whether they come from your womb or not—will become my children."

Marc's mother got up from her chair and stood in front of Melanie. "Today on, though, I will be your mother figure. You can ask me what you like unless it is something you should ask Marc. Got it?"

Melanie understood why Marc loved this woman so much. She had spent all of five minutes with her and just wanted to stay.

Melanie nodded.

"Good. Now I want to thank you for what you did for my son when you two went to the grocery store." She waved her hand when Melanie was about to protest.

"I know you didn't know what he was dealing with, but that didn't matter. What you did do was ease the last vestiges of his pain from a day that shouldn't have happened. I think sometimes people's pain isn't fully healed by God directly so He can use others, if they are willing, to help heal and create bonds. Those bonds create different types of relationships. Some last a lifetime and some last for a season." She peered into Melanie's eyes.

"Understand?"

Melanie nodded.

"Come, get up, child. I want to give you a hug."

The tears pressed at the back of her eyes before she could straighten. Her throat tightened and as Marc's mother embraced her, the rest of the ice around her heart began to melt and turn into tears that ran down her cheeks.

She was home.

Epilogue

Eight months later

He was acting so weird, she thought as Marc came around and helped bring her chair closer to the table.

He placed a hand on her shoulder briefly and she nodded. He'd been doing that lately: touching her instead of talking. It was like a language all their own. It felt…intimate.

There'd been eight months of long talks on the phone, in his car when he took her home the first six months, and Sundays after church, before they had dinner with his family which was gradually becoming her family. With all of the time they had managed to spend with one another, she felt like she had only scratched the surface.

She'd even invited Paige knowing she needed more interaction with a family like his. Paige seemed excited, and Melanie knew she had a wonderful time with little Katherine, but one Sunday Grace told Melanie that Paige wouldn't be going anymore.

When Melanie approached Paige, her daughter looked reluctant but said she didn't want to go anymore. Melanie knew it was Grace's doing, but her hands were tied. She could push only so much before her mother shut her out and hurt her by punishing Paige.

Melanie watched Marc go around to his side of the table. He had asked her two weeks ago if he could cook for her tonight. She hadn't known why he asked. He had cooked for her before. He made her homemade lasagna to celebrate the end of her first successful year. She had taken fewer units her second semester of school since trying to keep her 4.0 GPA, and twenty units had made her brain hurt.

Marc smiled at her, but it wobbled at the edges. What was that about?

"I know I keep asking you this, but are you sure you're okay?" she said, watching him intently.

"Yeah, sweetie," he said not quite meeting her eyes, and it dawned on her that he was lying. Her stomach roiled at the thought that he would lie to her about something that seemed so small…unless it wasn't. Was he sick? Was he unhappy? Was this a goodbye dinner? She thought they were happy…

He must have seen her expression change because he sucked his teeth and put his napkin down.

"I love you," he blurted, and a little of her tension eased.

Since it wasn't the first time he'd said those words she wasn't shocked, but the way he told her was suspicious.

"I love you too, Marcus." She had started using his full name when she wanted to tell him something really important. It always drew his attention immediately.

His gaze softened, and some of the agitation left his hands. He got up from the table, which confused her since he had just sat down.

"It is part of my job to categorize my feelings, set some thoughts or emotions aside while I work and bring the logic to the

321

forefront. I could do it better than most. I would focus on a task and get it done. It didn't matter if the assignment was large or small, I would take it piece by piece." He came to stand next to her then knelt in front of her.

"But not with you. You came into my life and took over like gangbusters. There was no category to put you in. You took over every piece of my heart that wasn't already occupied. I don't really have a choice, and if I did, I wouldn't choose any differently.

"I want you in my life. I want you as my wife. They are pretty much the same since my mom has already adopted you." He chuckled, but she had sobered.

He was proposing, and he was doing such a great job. Bravo, Marcus Miller!

"So," he said and exhaled while he reached in his pocket and pulled out a black velvet ring box.

"I have been waiting to do this for a while." He smiled sheepishly, rubbing the box with his thumb, but I wanted to give you time to concentrate on school, your relationship with God, and know for yourself if you loved me enough to trust me with your heart."

She gave him a half smile. She'd known somewhere around month four that she loved and wanted to marry him, but there were some issues she was working through with God, including being convinced that Marc would be fine with however big or small their family was.

The Lord was constantly showing her how much He valued her, and the realization finally took root in her heart and spread. It

322

allowed her to see another way she was different than her mother and she began to work at forgiving her mother.

Marc's words brought her to the present.

"I was hoping." His eyes glowed with emotion and he swallowed. "I mean really hoping that you would do me the honor of becoming my wife because though I can survive without you, I want to live with you."

She wouldn't have been able to hold back the tears if she tried.

"Marcus, you don't need hope. You have my heart. If you promise to keep loving me as you already do, my answer is 'yes.'"

Marc's face went blank for a second, but then an expression of joy so profound took over his features it had Melanie crying in earnest.

"Yes?" he asked.

"Yes!" she answered through her laughter. He drew her up and into his embrace. He hugged her to him then kissed her nearly senseless. Nearly, because nothing could fully overwhelm the joy in her heart.

Three years later

"Mel?" The voice over the phone pulled her the rest of the way out of the deep sleep.

"Paige?" Mel half croaked. What time was it? She glanced at the red light illuminating 3:45 a.m. on her bedside nightstand.

"I need you," Paige said, her tear-filled voice had sent a jolt of alarm through Melanie, and she threw back the covers.

"Where are you?" she half whispered, aware of Marc's sleeping form on the other side of the bed.

"The hospital. Mom wants me to kill them. I can't kill them. I can't. I'm sorry I said I would. I'm sorry. I was so angry. I just can't." Paige broke down crying almost hysterically.

The alarm racing though Melanie's veins turned to stark terror. "Sh-sh-sh. Honey, I can't understand you when you're crying so hard. Please, I want to help you. Just slow down, and I will be wherever you need me," Melanie said, surprised her voice was so calm.

Melanie felt movement on Marc's side of the bed.

"I'm at the hospital," Paige said haltingly.

"I'm pregnant." It was all Melanie got before Paige started crying again. "I didn't want you to know. Mommy said Marc would kill him."

Melanie's heart bottomed out. Not again. Oh, Jesus please, not again. She ran a shaky hand through her hair to keep from screaming the words. Sharp anger rose up in her, tinting her vision red.

If it was what Melanie thought happened, Marc might still kill the man who dared touch her baby.

"It's not fair. It isn't even my fault. I hate him. I hate him," Paige said, but her words were cut off by a groan.

She felt Marc get out of the bed, but she couldn't concentrate on anything except trying to understand Paige through the sound of her own heartbeat.

"Mom wants me to abort the babies, and I said, 'yes,' but I can't do it. I can't kill them. No matter what," Paige said once she'd caught her breath.

Babies. Did she say babies?

"Which hospital, Paige?" Melanie needed to be there next to her girl even if it was as a sister.

"St. Mary's Hospital," Paige responded.

"Listen to me, Paige. Don't sign anything," Melanie said more forcefully than she'd meant to.

"Um, okay, but I'm a minor." Paige started whimpering. It sounded somewhere between a sob and a groan.

"Listen. I will be there as soon as I can. Are you in labor?"

"Yes," Paige hissed through her teeth. "Mel, please come get me. I don't want to do this. It's not fair." Paige started whimpering again, and Melanie wanted to go ballistic.

Every protective instinct in Melanie rose up like a tidal wave. She was going to go protect her child.

"I'm coming, honey. You are going to be all right. Do you hear me?" Mel said, her voice shaking with both anger and pain.

"I gotta go. She's coming. I gotta go," Paige said between pants then the line went dead.

"Paige. Paige!" Melanie said into dead air. She looked at the phone then brought it to her chest and rocked a couple of times, her vision going blurry with tears.

My baby. My baby.

"Melanie?"

She looked up to see Marc standing in front of her with her clothing in his hand. She took a deep breath and thanked God for him again.

"Paige is at Parker General Hospital. She is in labor with babies. I don't know how many? Grace was trying to talk her into aborting them. Paige doesn't want to." She stood up, taking the clothes from him and allowing herself one brief hug to gather her strength. This was not the time to break down. It was time to rescue her daughter from the tentacles of hate, which Grace had wrapped around Paige.

"I think Paige was raped," she said, feeling the tension roll over Marc. She stepped out of his embrace but kept her hands on his arms. Paige said my mom took her to the hospital to get an abortion, but Paige has changed her mind." Melanie's voice caught on a sob, and she closed her eyes to gain some composure.

"I need you to call Mr. Sable. I will need him to pull strings, call in favors, do whatever he can to keep those babies out of Grace's hands."

Marc's eyes became unfocused, and Melanie shook him lightly knowing the look meant he was plotting. It was the same look he'd had when he'd rescued her and her friends from the house party.

"Later," she said before moving away.

Melanie got ready as quickly as she could. She met Marc at the door to the bedroom as she pulled on a jacket and picked up her purse.

"Mr. Sable is on it," Marc said.

"He's on it. He's on it?"

That surprised her.

"Was he on it before you asked or because you asked?" she said, stopping in her tracks. Marc blinked at her as if he were trying to put her words together.

Did he know?" That surprised her. She stopped in her tracks.

Marc shrugged. "I don't know."

She continued through the door and the house to the garage. She didn't even consider driving. She walked around and waited the two seconds it took for Marc to open the door for her.

Then he opened the garage door and got in the driver's seat.

"Will you call Mom, please?" he said, starting the car.

She nodded as she clicked her seat belt in place. She pulled out her mobile phone and started dialing.

The next few minutes were full of prayer. It was what Mama Katherine did anytime she got a call in the middle of the night.

As they drove, Melanie thought back to all of the times she'd tried to get Paige to come and stay with her and Marc. She worked to keep from blaming herself for not doing more to stay in Paige's life.

Marc's mobile phone rang, and he put the receiver to his ear instead of putting on the speaker. Melanie thought it was a work call until he hung up and told her what Mr. Sable had just disclosed to him.

Her heart broke at what she learned from Marc regarding the twin's conception. For a moment she thought she would be ill at hearing what her own cousin had done to her daughter.

Two weeks after her wedding to Marc her parents moved closer to her mother's sister, almost two hours away. Melanie thought it was a ploy by her mother to keep her and her new extended family away from Paige, but her father told her it was something he instigated so Paige could be surrounded by more children and family.

A few months after that, her parents separated then divorced. He'd asked Paige to come with him to Los Angeles, but she decided to stay with Grace.

By the time Marc pulled up to the hospital he had the room number for Paige, from Mr. Sable, and Melanie was just a little calmer.

She got out at the curb and ran through the hospital doors and up to the room number Marc gave her. He would join her after he parked the car.

She stepped out of the elevator and scanned the signs on the walls in order to be directed to Paige's room. She took a half a dozen deep breaths before she turned the corner and came face-to-face with her mother.

The woman's eyes momentarily showed her surprise before she covered it with a frown.

"I knew she would call you. Evidently, she hasn't learned from the last time you abandoned her."

Melanie opened her mouth to give the woman a scathing retort, which more than likely would have led to an all-out shouting match, but the peace she'd been praying and reaching for during the last hour and a half came over her, and she closed her mouth. It was disconcerting that she would give up the chance to tell Grace what she thought of her But it wasn't like anything she said would change Grace's rocky heart.

Melanie straightened her shoulders and moved to walk past Grace, but her mother grabbed her arm to stop her.

"I am not going to take care of those babies, and Paige certainly isn't in any place to do it," Grace almost hissed at her.

Melanie meant to pry Grace's hand off her arm, but instead her hand lay on top of her mom's. It seemed her body also chose to obey God over her.

"It's not the babies' fault for how they were conceived. Though the act may have been derived from hate, the children need to be loved. If you won't do it, I will. Love may be the one thing that keeps them from turning into the same violator as their sire," Melanie said as she watched Grace's complexion drain of color. The gray pallor startled Melanie, and she moved to get her mother help, but Grace shoved her away and stumbled to the women's restroom just behind Melanie.

Melanie took a step to see if her mother was going to be all right but remembered Paige and turned back around toward Paige's room. She would ask one of the nurses to look in on her mother.

She reached the designated door and opened it to the sound of her daughter screaming as she bore down. The sight almost brought her to her knees. She clutched at the door latch making eye contact with the doctor coaching Paige. She gathered her strength then asked God for more before releasing the door and walking over to her child.

She was ushered back out and taken down the hall so she could don scrubs and shoe covers. It assuaged more than irritated Melanie. It was good to know they were taking every precaution with her daughter.

"Her mother walked out when she went into labor. Are you going to be able to hang in there?" the nurse asked.

"As her sister I do not intend to leave this hospital until she does," Melanie said, looking the woman squarely in the eye.

The nurse nodded after a moment, and Melanie followed her back into the delivery room, walked to Paige, kissed her cheek and took her hand.

"I'm here now. Everything will be just fine," she said, giving Paige a small smile even as her heart wept at her child's struggle.

She stood by Paige's side all the way until her daughter began hemorrhaging during her last push while delivering the first of her set of twin girls. The doctors swarmed the room, and Melanie was guided out and walked into Marc's arms where she cried. Mama Katherine wrapped her arms around them both.

When she'd been able to regain her composure she noticed that the waiting area was full with her extended family. It reminded her of her mother.

"Have you seen my mom?" she asked Marc.

He looked reluctant to respond. "She said you could take care of this," he said, but she could see he was holding something back.

"It's okay. She can't hurt me anymore," Melanie said, realizing that she really believed it.

"She just made some crack about hospitals being your territory," Marc said.

Melanie shook her head. So much hate. So much pain.

Melanie didn't have anything to say. She just joined Marc and Mama Katherine in the waiting area and prayed until a nurse called for her.

When she walked back in the room, one baby was being covered and taken away, the form too still for a delivery room, the other was being weighed and examined on another table. Melanie placed her hand over her mouth to keep the sob in.

Paige was unconscious, and the past came up and smacked Melanie in the face. She was back in her delivery room for a few seconds, then back in the present. She would be there for Paige as much as she could be.

The nurse placed the squirming bundle in her arms, and her heart dipped then righted itself. She looked at her sleeping daughter and back at the baby. A hope planted itself in her heart, which she was too afraid to even think of.

She held the little girl as they carted Paige to intensive care. She held her as, one by one, her family came in to peer at the baby. She mourned one child even as she celebrated the health of the one in her arms.

Melanie rubbed her cheek against the downy curls on the child's head and took in her baby scent. She watched as the little girl yawned and opened her oddly colored eyes. She wondered if they would change from the smoky gray to something lighter or darker. She stayed when everyone else went home.

She whispered "what if's" to her husband because saying them out loud felt like a betrayal. They made extremely tentative plans and prayed a lot. He called in to work and they remained, holding hands as they held vigil.

She was there when Paige woke up, and as promised she didn't leave the hospital until Paige did.

She and Marc stayed in a hotel near the house for the first week since Grace wouldn't allow her to stay at the house. She sat down at the end of the week when it was still clear that Paige was in no shape, mentally or physically, to take care of her child.

She made a pact with Paige to take care of the child until Paige was able to do so. Paige wanted to give over her rights, but Melanie refused to accept the offer, hoping one day Paige would heal enough to claim her child again.

Meanwhile, Melanie was over-the-moon happy to have received such a beautiful gift, no matter how long she would have her.

Melanie and Marc named the beautiful baby girl with the silver-gray eyes, Gladys, after Marc's maternal grandmother, and Melanie thanked God for placing a promise back in her hands that had been stolen from her so many years before.

~The End~

Dear Reader,

I was so excited to get a closer look into Melanie and Marc's lives. I didn't know they had so much in them.

Even though this timeline came before My Beauty For Your Ashes I realized that there were pieces that would give people a better understanding of the Morganson family dynamic. It would also give a few clues to the big secret that started to unravel when Paige met Mason and Vivian.

Marc was such the Knight in Shining Armor, but I was happy to see that every now and then he would allow himself to be rescued as well.

My very first thoughts of Melanie were of a very strong motherly type in My Beauty For Your Ashes. As her character developed I wondered if she was the master puppeteer, but I'm glad she is exactly who she is.

I hope you enjoyed this breakaway novel and will continue this journey with me on to *Promises Fulfilled.*

Thank you for reading and I hope you share your thoughts with me on this series or my others.

Please send your questions or thoughts to me at tawcarlisle@gmail.com

You can also visit my website at www.tawcarlisle.com and follow me at www.twitter.com/traciwcarlisle and www.facebook.com/traciwoodencarlisle

Until next time,
Keep reading and expand your dreams
Traci Wooden-Carlisle

My Books

Promises of Zion series

My Beauty For Your Ashes

My Oil of Joy For Your Mourning

My Garment of Praise for Your Spirit of Heaviness

Stolen Promises

Next in the series:

Promises Fulfilled

Chances Series

Chances Are…

Chandler County Series

Missing Destiny

Missing Us

Missing the Gift

If you enjoyed this book please join Christian Indie Author Readers Group on Facebook. You will find Christian Books in Multiple Genres with opportunities to find other Christian Authors and learn about new releases, sales, and free books. Here is the link: https://www.facebook.com/groups/291215317668431/

About the Author

Traci Wooden-Carlisle lives in San Diego with her husband. She designs jewelry, writes as much as she can and freelances as a graphic artist. She loves her coffee in the morning and fuzzy slippers at night. She loves to read anything romantic – the more inspirational the better. For fun she dances and teaches the occasional fitness class.

Acknowledgments

Thank you to the Fabulous Five who help make my world go around.

Thank you for your inspiration, strength, encouragement and love Cathy, Aziza, BriAnna Nicole, LaNeisha, Llara, Jackie, Montrice, Sylvia, Barbara, LaVern and Cheryl.

I will come out to play soon.

Thank you

Dana whose creative talents make me want to turn my book covers into banners.

A.I.R.R.E. Firm who helped smooth out the edges in my timeline.

Paula who edited this book into something legible.

Made in the USA
Las Vegas, NV
30 March 2024

88032854R00193